SKELETON JUSTICE

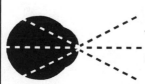

This Large Print Book carries the
Seal of Approval of N.A.V.H.

SKELETON JUSTICE

DR. MICHAEL BADEN AND LINDA KENNEY BADEN

THORNDIKE PRESS
A part of Gale, Cengage Learning

GALE
CENGAGE Learning

Detroit • New York • San Francisco • New Haven, Conn • Waterville, Maine • London

GALE
CENGAGE Learning

Thorndike Press® Large Print Crime Scene.
The text of this Large Print edition is unabridged.
Other aspects of the book may vary from the original edition.
Set in 16 pt. Plantin.
Printed on permanent paper.

LIBRARY OF CONGRESS CATALOGING-IN-PUBLICATION DATA

Baden, Michael M.
  Skeleton justice / by Michael Baden and Linda Kenney Baden.
    p. cm. — (Thorndike Press large print crime scene)
  ISBN-13: 978-1-4104-1862-3 (alk. paper)
  ISBN-10: 1-4104-1862-6 (alk. paper)
  1. Forensic pathologists—Fiction. 2. Women lawyers—Fiction.
3. New York (State)—Fiction. 4. Large type books. I. Kenney,
Linda, 1953– II. Title.
PS3602.A358S56 2009b
813'.6—dc22   2009017238

Published in 2009 by arrangement with Alfred A. Knopf, Inc, a division of Random House, Inc.

Printed in the United States of America
1 2 3 4 5 6 7 13 12 11 10 09

For our siblings
Robert "Unc" Baden
and
Joan Benincasa

There is no such thing as justice — in or out of court.

— Clarence Darrow

CHAPTER ONE

The harsh buzz of the doorbell shocked the knife out of Annabelle Fiore's hand.

She jumped back to avoid being nicked by the blade as it clattered to the floor. *Just what I need right now . . . chop off my own toe.*

As Annabelle put the knife safely on the counter, the microwave clock rolled to 7:00. The Linggs were unfashionably punctual. She had been counting on their tardiness to give her time to finish making the salad.

But Rosemarie and David weren't expecting to be entertained. Her friends were here to distract her from pre-opening-night jitters, relax her — they'd be happy to sit in the kitchen while she cooked. Annabelle crossed the foyer and opened the door of her Greenwich Village brownstone. The final aria from *Tosca,* piped through her high-end sound system, tumbled into the rain-darkened street.

"Welco—"

A person dressed in black — not Rose-marie, not David — pushed Annabelle backward. A hand, gloved despite the balmy night, grasped her forearm. A steel-toed boot kicked the door closed.

Annabelle opened her mouth. The quick intake of breath needed to scream accelerated her downfall. A cloying, harsh scent burned her nose and mouth as a thick square of damp cloth pressed into her face. The bold tones of the Roger Selden abstract paintings on the foyer wall faded into the distance. Annabelle's knees buckled, and the gloved hand released its grip.

Falling, she glimpsed a flash of metal.

Her attacker's fist opened, revealing a small glass vial. Annabelle's last coherent thought formed. *Why me, dear God, why me?*

CHAPTER TWO

Get back where you belong.

Dr. Jake Rosen could hear his boss saying it as he looked down at Annabelle Fiore. The opera singer's olive skin had blanched to white; her arms lay stiffly at her sides. Jake reached out to touch her wrist. Her eyelids fluttered.

The living are not your concern.

That's what Pederson would say if he knew his leading forensic pathologist was at St. Vincent's Hospital conducting a physical exam of a living victim. As deputy chief medical examiner of the City of New York, Jake spent most of his working hours at crime scenes or in the autopsy suite of the morgue. The chief ME, Charles Pederson, frowned on unauthorized field trips.

Gently, Jake turned Fiore's right arm to examine the inner side. There, in the crook of her elbow, was a tiny puncture where a needle had been inserted to draw blood. He studied it closely. No multiple attempts, not even much bruising around the site.

The emergency room physicians and residents who had treated Fiore the night before wouldn't have noticed this. They had saved the opera singer's life by evaluating her injuries from a medical standpoint. To them, the lack of trauma at the blood-extraction site was good news: no treatment required, so they could focus all their attention on her compromised central nervous system. To Jake, that tiny, perfect puncture was significant.

Whoever had attacked Fiore knew how to extract blood from a vein. This was not the work of an amateur. Not a random act of violence.

His gaze traveled down the length of her arm. There, near the wrist, were three distinct bruises. Her assailant had gripped her arm tightly and held her until she stopped struggling. Just as with the first four victims.

Jake hadn't examined them, but he'd been briefed by Vito Pasquarelli, lead detective on the case. The first attack had occurred over a month ago. A young mother on the Upper West Side had responded to a knock on her door in the middle of the day. The next thing she remembered was waking up groggy from ether-induced unconsciousness. She, and the police, had assumed the attacker had come to rob her. Except nothing was missing from her home.

It wasn't until hours later that she noticed the tiny needle mark in the crook of her arm. The police shrugged it off. She hadn't been harmed. It was weird, but weird was status quo in New York. File a report and move on.

Then it happened again. A teacher in the Bronx, an investment banker in Battery Park City, a foreign tourist attending a pharmaceutical conference in midtown. None of them seriously hurt, all of them thoroughly freaked-out. It didn't help that somewhere along the line the tabloids started calling the stalker "the Vampire."

Although Jake didn't subscribe to the media melodrama, he did understand the public's fear. New Yorkers, blasé about drive-by shootings and shoves onto subway tracks, were terrified by a guy with a needle. He'd seen it often enough in his medical training — hulking football players who stoically endured compound fractures, then passed out when the nurse arrived to give them a tetanus shot; gang members who survived knife fights, only to whimper when it was time to be sewn up. Needles were scary.

And now the Vampire had nearly killed someone, a famous someone, not with his needle, but with an overdose of ether. Jake pulled a stethoscope from his pocket. He'd had to search to find one; it wasn't an instrument he had much use for in the normal course of his day. Fiore stirred slightly as he listened to her heart. The beat was steady, but the rate was slow, consistent with having been drugged into unconsciousness. This is where the Vampire analogy fell apart. Vampires, the kind who lived in Transylvania and flapped around in black capes, didn't anesthetize their victims. And apparently, New York's vampire wasn't too adept at it.

Of course, even a trained anesthesiologist could easily make a mistake with ether. That's why it wasn't used much anymore. And if you were administering the drug via a soaked rag, getting the dosage right became even more problematic. Perhaps the biggest surprise was that an overdose hadn't happened until Fiore, the fifth victim.

Annabelle Fiore's central nervous system had been seriously depressed. She would have died had her friends not arrived shortly after the attack. The effects still hadn't worn off. Jake would have liked to ask her some questions, but although she stirred slightly as he examined her, she was only semiconscious. An interview would have to wait.

Jake turned away from the hospital bed just as a short, rumpled man entered the room.

"Hey, you made it!" Detective Vito Pasquarelli shook Jake's hand enthusiastically. "Thanks for coming. Have you looked at her?"

"Yes. It's hard to draw much of a conclusion, given that I didn't get to examine the others. But if their blood-draw sites were as perfect as Ms. Fiore's, I'd say you're dealing with someone with some medical training."

Pasquarelli nodded. "What about the ether?"

"Hard to know if the overdose was accidental or intentional. He seems to have given her quite a bit more than the others." Jake ran his hand through his hair, moving his style further along the scale from casually wild to unkempt. "But here's a thought that occurred to me. I know you said none of the victims is acquainted with any of the others. But you might want to ask them if they have any ties to a person who works around laboratory animals."

15

"You mean like rats and mice? Why?"

"When researchers conduct experiments on animals and then have to autopsy them, they often kill them with an overdose of ether. That's the most common use for the drug these days."

Vito perked up as they walked toward the elevator. "And a medical researcher would know how to draw blood, right?"

Jake nodded. "And how to test it. Which is what I'd like to do."

"Our CSI guys already did that. No trace of drugs in any of them. Nothing hinky."

Jake grinned. "Funkiness is in the eye of the beholder. Send the samples over to me. I'd like to run my own tests."

"You got it." The packed elevator arrived and the men descended in silence.

"What do you think *he* does with it?" Vito asked as the impatient crowd pushed past them into the lobby.

"I think he tests it, just like I'm going to do with it," Jake said.

The detective looked relieved.

Jake raised his hand in a mock toast. "Unless he drinks it."

Chapter Three

Manny studied herself in the full-length mirror and heard her mother's voice echoing in her head. *Philomena Manfreda, you are not leaving the house like that.*

Sighing, she pulled off yet another outfit and tossed it onto the growing pile on her bed. As a solo practitioner with her own civil rights practice, Manny had a closet that was stuffed with suits for every lawyering occasion: suits to help convey her erudition to judges, suits to charm juries, suits to woo new clients. Plenty of cocktail dresses, too — opera, theater, five-hundred-dollar-a-plate charity bashes — all pressed and ready to go. But ask her to come up with the perfect outfit to wear to share a plate of antipasto with a man who dissected bodies all day, and she was utterly at a loss.

Manny reached for one more hanger in her overstuffed closet. *Vogue* had devoted three pages to gushing about this dress. If it didn't work, she was giving up. Slipping on the purported miracle garment, she turned to face the bed.

"Well, what do you think?"

The mound of clothing quivered slightly. A small spot of auburn emerged, followed by two big brown eyes: her toy red poodle, Mycroft. The dog surveyed her latest attempt, then laid his head between his paws and whined.

"You're absolutely right." She studied her reflection in the mirror. "Too . . . contrived."

She returned to the closet and yanked out her favorite black slacks. Why make such a big production about getting dressed to meet Jake anyway? The man was oblivious. She could appear in a muumuu from Wal-Mart or any couture outfit and he wouldn't notice because his eye would be plastered up against a microscope.

They had met in the line of duty, the last time working together to bring justice to the long-dead victims of a killer who had preyed on defenseless patients in an upstate psychiatric hospital. They'd flirted over dead bodies in the morgue and bonded by escaping attempts on their lives. The Lyons case was solved and now they were . . . what? Having a rendezvous? That implied romantic getaways to inns in the Berkshires or beach houses in the Hamptons. Dating? No, that would require regular phone calls and invitations to movies or concerts.

Instead, Manny spent hours in Jake's laboratory looking at gruesome crime-scene photos, peering at slides of poisoned-tissue samples, comparing exit-wound patterns. Then, for a nightcap, they would discuss the autopsies he had performed that day, before falling into bed under the watchful eye of a taxidermied raven — his honorarium for speaking about murder to the local Edgar Allan Poe club.

But whatever she had going with Jake Rosen, it sure beat the hell out of attending the annual Bar Association dinner dance with Evan Pennington III or going to Knicks games with that yahoo bond trader, Troy what's his name.

So why was she agonizing over what to wear? Maybe because, for once, Jake had actually called her up and invited her to have dinner in a charming little Italian trattoria. No sharing pepperoni pizza on a stainless steel morgue gurney tonight — this was a real dinner date. The place had great food, but it wasn't pretentious-fancy. She didn't want to arrive overdressed, showing how thrilled she was to be out with him.

Why is my confidence so undercut? This

guy spends his days dissecting people's brains, and now he's messing with my head.

Manny zipped the pants, pulled on a pink silk knit sweater, slipped her feet into fuchsia snakeskin Manolo slingbacks, and checked her reflection. The look was chic, classy, but casual. Not bad. Not bad at all.

When she reached for Mycroft's Goyard carrier, monogrammed with the initials MM, the little dog shot off the bed and jumped in.

"That's right, Mikey, we're going on a date. And you're the chaperone."

CHAPTER FOUR

Jake looked up from the case folder he'd brought with him to Il Postino in time to see Manny crossing the street toward his sidewalk table. Red hair flying, hips swaying, high heels tapping, Manny made quite a few heads turn as she strode through the early-evening crowd. It pleased him that she didn't seem to notice the effect she had.

Now she caught sight of him and waved. He rose to greet her and she kissed him lightly before settling Mycroft under the table.

"Where are your groupies?" Manny asked.

"Huh?"

"You're quite a celebrity — front page of the *New York Post*." Manny grinned as she took the newspaper from her bag and read the headline aloud, " 'ME Enters Vampire Investigation.' That must've really pissed Pederson off."

Jake stared at her.

"Your jaw's dropping. You want to be careful of that, eating outside in New York. Flies, you know."

Jake started to laugh. Why did it surprise him that Manny had immediately grasped the trouble that trip to St. Vincent's had brought him? No sooner had he exited the hospital than he'd been besieged by a horde of TV and print reporters. His natural reaction was to answer their questions briefly but honestly. Stupid — when would he ever learn? Somehow, they had managed to spin his responses into lead stories, and their flashing cameras had splashed his startled face across all three New York dailies and the evening news.

"I wish you'd've been with me yesterday," Jake said. "You would've known to throw a jacket over my head and 'No comment' me out of there."

"How did Pederson react?"

"Let's just say I thought I was going to have an opportunity to brush up on my CPR."

The post-Fiore lecture had gone on and on: "violating jurisdictional boundaries"; "no regard for chain of command"; "no understanding of limited resources. . . ." For Pederson, work was all about protecting his turf, hoarding his budget, and ramping up his media coverage. With one unauthorized trip, Jake had managed to score a trifecta of violations.

"You know he thinks you're angling for his job." Manny tapped the newspaper. "He sees this as grandstanding."

"I didn't know they'd be lying in wait for me," Jake protested. "And I don't want to be chief ME. Balancing budgets and sitting through endless meetings — no thanks."

"I know you like nothing better than being elbow-deep in an abdominal cavity, looking for signs of unnatural death." Manny reached for his hand resting on the table. "You have to remember that not everyone understands the appeal."

The soft touch of Manny's fingers took the sting out of her words. Her ability to go straight to the crux of a problem had caught his attention the moment he'd met her; her beauty had dawned on him a little later.

"Yeah, this little escapade of mine has had unintended consequences. Pederson has explicitly warned me off the Vampire case."

"So you're dropping it?" Manny's eyes opened wide, then, as she caught sight of the blue case folder beside his plate, crinkled into a smile. "You scared me there for a minute — thought you were going soft."

The waiter approached the table, introduced himself as Luigi, and rattled off the specials.

"I'll have the wild prawns," Manny said without hesitation.

Jake continued to scan the menu. "Do you know that shrimp are scavengers? I once autopsied a pilot whose plane crashed into the ocean. Had to take half a dozen off his body. Funny, too, because the poor guy had shrimp in his stomach — his last meal. Gave new meaning to the word *payback*."

The waiter looked pale. Manny's stomach grumbled loudly. "You know, I may just go vegan tonight. I'll start with a large salad. . . ."

"Careful, *E. coli* gives leafy greens serial-killer potential," Jake whispered.

Manny shuddered. "If I had your job, I wouldn't be able to stomach anything more than applesauce and dry toast."

"I'll get you a position as a morgue assistant." He slipped his arm around her and squeezed her shoulder. "The Diener Diet! The newest way to lose weight. I bet you could get on *Oprah* with that."

Her flimsy shoe, which had been tracing a delicate pattern up and down his calf, crashed down on his instep like a guillotine. He grinned. The pain was worth it.

After the waiter finally left with an uncontroversial order of salad, appetizer, pasta, and steak, Jake set about making amends.

"I was hoping you'd help me brainstorm." Jake edged the case folder toward Manny, and caught her glancing at the label. "Will you take a look for me?"

Manny twisted around to face him and flipped the folder open. "Other men seduce women by telling them they're beautiful and sexy. You do it by whispering pathology reports in my ear."

Jake grinned. "I admire you too much to take such a hackneyed approach. Look at this."

Manny and Jake began to sort through the paperwork, focusing on the test results from Vampire victims that he had brought with him. Jake stared at the jumble of numbers and medical terminology. What was it the Vampire was looking for in this blood? None of the toxicology reports showed substances normally associated with drug abuse, so the victims weren't linked through a shared drug habit. Another door closed.

By the time the appetizer arrived, the waiter had to struggle to find a paper-free spot on the table to set Jake's calamari.

Manny stared at the reports. "No motive?"

"None. Pasquarelli thinks he's a nut. But there's more here. These are organized blood draws. They don't have the character-istics of a disorganized mind. The victims didn't know what happened to them until they woke up and saw the holes in their skin or the blood droplets on their clothes, the swelling, the beginnings of black-and-blue marks. Hallmarks of neat, precise, and care-fully plotted attacks."

"The Devil Bat," Manny muttered.

Jake gulped from his glass of ice water and waited. Manny was usually very analytical, yet totally open to every possibility, able to see connections a more cautious mind would overlook. That passion, that lightning response, had attracted him in the first place. But sometimes her sudden reversals, the wild leaps in her thought process, left his relentlessly logical mind floundering.

"A forties horror movie with Bela Lugosi," she explained. "Used to watch the reruns with my father when I was growing up."

Signs of a misspent youth, he thought, but he didn't say it aloud, or else the spike of her heel would be in his calf, rather than massaging it.

"The movie's villain was a beloved town doctor who killed to seek revenge for wrongs he perceived had been committed against him."

"You have something against doctors?"

26

"I'm a lawyer, remember. A mixed marriage between the two professions would never work. Like the Hatfields and McCoys."

"Or Romeo and Juliet."

"They committed suicide. I rest my case."

Jake shuffled his papers to bring Manny back to the here and now.

"Blood is what the guy is after, so somehow these people must be linked by their blood," she said. "Do they share a common disease?"

"None of them is HIV-positive. Two are diabetic. One must be an alcoholic — terrible liver function." Jake rattled off the facts, tapping the pertinent data with the tip of his pencil. "But those are the results of running standard blood work. We can't test for every obscure disease in the book — it would take forever. We have to have some idea of what to look for, then run the test to prove or disprove the theory. Otherwise, you're searching for a needle in a haystack."

"So they could all be linked by having some rare disease, but you just don't know which one?"

"Possible, but unlikely. The police CSI team interviewed them all. No one has any unusual symptoms or medical history."

"What about the DNA profile?"

"The results have come back on only the first three. We're still waiting on the two latest. But these people are not related. And no genetic anomalies."

Manny chewed a zucchini flower and thought for a long moment before speaking. "Do you know how much blood he draws?"

"It's impossible to know the precise amount, but the victims were all checked out after the attacks and they had normal blood volume, so he's probably taking a vial at most."

"All right." Manny gestured with a forkful of draped arugula. "My knowledge of bizarre satanic rituals is admittedly small, but it seems to me if he were taking the blood for some kinky reason, he'd want more of it, yes?"

"I agree," Jake said. "I think he's doing what we're doing — testing it."

"Himself, or sending it to a lab?"

"Certain basic tests he could do himself with the right materials, or he could send the blood out to a lab. There are hundreds on the East Coast alone. We'd never be able to check them all."

"But not for DNA testing," Manny prompted. "You can't do that on your kitchen table. And because of the backlog, it usually takes months to get DNA results back. Believe me, my innocent clients know how behind those labs are."

"Those are the labs accredited to do forensic DNA testing. There are private labs, too, like the ones you see ads for on the subway — places that do paternity testing for civil cases."

"I wouldn't know. I haven't been underground in New York City since the St. James class trip to the Museum of Natural History."

Jake let her comment pass. Every once in a while, Manny's Jersey girl bridge and tunnel gene reared its head. He preferred not to dwell on the fact that when she had been puzzling over Dick and Jane in her green plaid Catholic school uniform, he had been a senior at City College. He waggled his pen at her. "But why go to all the trouble of collecting blood if all you want is a DNA match? He could get that much more easily by collecting a few hairs or picking up a cigarette butt from his targets. What he's looking for has to be something you can find only in blood."

"So tell Pasquarelli to start subpoenaing every blood lab in the metro area till he finds the one that worked on these samples."

Jake massaged his temples at the thought of the massive paperwork this would entail.

"Pasquarelli's already thought of that. He was hoping I could come up with something a little less labor-intensive. But I guess the Vampire will stay on the front page of the papers for another week. The mayor won't be happy."

"Pasquarelli may be in luck there," Manny replied. "I was listening to the evening news while I was getting dressed tonight. The Vampire's been pushed aside by the Preppy Terrorists."

"And who, pray tell, are the Preppy Terrorists?" Jake dug into his steak, trying to ignore the sensation of Manny's gaze boring into him. It was like eating while Mycroft watched every bite travel from plate to mouth. "Did you want to try some of this?"

"Certainly not! This hand-rolled fettucine is just delicious." Manny slowly sucked a strand between her lips to prove her point, then continued. "The Preppy Terrorists are a couple of kids from the Monet Academy who got it in their heads that it would be a fun science experiment to put a small incendiary device under a U.S. mailbox in Hoboken."

"That's pushing the Vampire off the front page? We used to put firecrackers in old man Isbrantsen's mailbox whenever he'd confiscate our kickball."

"Was a federal judge ever strolling by when you did it? Because that's what happened in Hoboken. Judge Patrick Brueninger took a piece of twisted metal in the throat."

"Brueninger. That name sounds familiar. Wait — wasn't he the federal judge who presided over the Iqbar case?"

"You got it."

Jake drained the last of his Chianti. "These kids tried to take him down? Why?"

"Too soon to know," Manny said. "There are certainly quite a few Muslims who don't think the mullah got a fair trial. They swear that Iqbar really was just running a nice friendly mosque in Jersey City."

Jake snorted. "Right. Not laundering millions to finance the Taliban in Afghanistan. But these prep school boys aren't Muslims, right? Why would they want to off the judge?"

"Exactly — no motive whatsoever. My guess is it's just a prank gone terribly wrong. But with 9/11 and anthrax and the shoe bomber, the FBI's talking about prosecuting these kids to the fullest extent of the law, just to prove that they don't go after only dark-haired guys in turbans. These kids are toast. They're going to be —"

Manny was interrupted by a tinny rendition of the opening strains of George Thorogood's "Bad to the Bone" emanating from somewhere under the table. She dived down, resurfaced with her Fendi bag from the designer's newest collection, and answered her cell phone before George could utter another note of his trademark tune.

Sorry, she mouthed silently at Jake. "Hi, Kenneth," she trilled into the phone. "What's up?"

Jake's eyebrows lowered. He still was a tad suspect of Manny's paralegal assistant, Kenneth, a former client whose knowledge of the law stemmed from the two times he'd been arrested. Kenneth consulted with Manny at least twenty times a day on items ranging from the latest gossip on the Web page of the New York Social Diary to the advantages of arguing stare decisis in a brief submitted to the federal second circuit court of appeals.

"Of course you were right to call. This is very important. Hang on just a minute." Manny rose from her chair and moved to the edge of the canopy, out of earshot. Jake stabbed at his peas.

In less than ten minutes, Manny returned to the table, but Jake kept his eyes focused on his plate.

"Guess why Kenneth was calling?"

"Special three-hour sale at Saks."

"Very funny. Actually, it was a sale at T.J. Maxx. I can restrain myself sometimes."

"Manny, I know your relationship is diff — well, special, that he honors you as his savior and you view him as your Eliza Doolittle, but. . . ."

"But what? He's a talented kid who was born poor. Just because he's a diva doesn't mean he can't appreciate honest, hard work."

Manny had been assigned by the local court to represent Kenneth Medianos Boyd pro bono on charges of conspiracy to destroy evidence — drugs — by flushing it away. Then there was the time when he was nabbed for a wardrobe malfunction during the annual Greenwich Village Halloween parade. His alter ego, formerly a waitress and now the chantcuse Princess Calypso, lost some strategically placed plumage taken from turkeys dispatched the Thanksgiving before.

Manny immediately appreciated Kenneth's worth: a keenly dramatic fashion sense coupled with a paralegal certification obtained while behind bars before his drag reincarnation. Kenneth adored Manny because she treated him as a person with skill and brains. They cemented the bond while shopping at the TSE cashmere outlet; she offered him a job as her legal assistant.

"I know, I know, and he watches out for your backside. But does he have to call you so many times a day? What's the point of having an assistant if he's always ringing you? Kind of defeats the purpose of easing your workload."

"You're just jealous of the other men in my life." She glanced down at Mycroft to hide both her annoyance and her smile.

" 'Men'? Last week, Kenneth wore heat-sensitive nail polish when he delivered those documents to my home. Started talking to me with pink nails, which became royal blue by the time he handed me the manila envelope. And let's not forget he was in a full-length evening dress."

"He's just a *girl* making an honest living as a chanteuse in downtown clubs, when he's not running my law office, writing my motions, collecting my bills, and keeping my clients happy on the phone so I can go off gallivanting to help with *your* cases."

Manny paused for breath, then continued. "Kenneth was calling because the mother of one of the Preppy Terrorists just phoned to say she wants to retain me as his defense attorney."

"I thought you said those kids were toast?

Why would you want the case?"

"First, these kids are being railroaded to make them examples so that the government can say 'Look what we're doing to protect you from terrorism.' "

"Railroaded!" Jake pointed his fork at her. "You can't say that. All you know about this case is what you heard on the news. And we both know how inaccurate that is."

Manny pushed the accusatory fork away. "I know from experience how prosecutors work. Besides, this case is huge. When I show the government this kid is not guilty, I'll have more credibility in the future on other cases."

"Manny, so far you've dealt mainly with civil rights cases and nonviolent offenders," Jake said. "Are you prepared to tangle with terrorists and the federal government? This case is awfully risky."

"I'm prepared for anything. Gotta run. Sorry." Manny pushed away from the table, sloshing water out of the glasses on the table.

She paused to deliver a parting jab. "What about when *you* nearly got blown up trying to find Pete Harrigan's killer? It's okay for you to take risks but not me. Showing your age, aren't you?"

Jake winced. All he wanted was to shield

her from harm. He struggled to keep the protective edge out of his voice. "Just be careful."

His calm words were like a gust of wind on a brush fire. Manny pivoted. "Don't talk to me like you're my keeper, Jake. We don't have any commitments to each other, remember? I'll call you tomorrow after I meet with the client." She was halfway across the street with Mycroft in tow before Jake could flag down the waiter for the check.

Tossing some crumpled twenties on the table, Jake set off in pursuit. With her cascade of red hair and electric pink sweater, Manny was as easy to track as a microburst. What he would do when he caught up with her, Jake wasn't sure. Vulcan mind meld maybe.

That might be the only way to make her see how irrational she was being. It was one thing to be a champion of the oppressed, quite another to be a sucker for some crackpot sob story. And how would she handle all the work this case would entail? The big-time criminal lawyers had a whole team to back them up; Manny had a drag queen paralegal.

Jake felt a sensation over his heart not caused by Manny's behavior. His cell phone vibrated. The display indicated it was his office. What timing.

"Rosen," snapped Pederson. "Get over to Fourteen West Fifty-third. Looks like the Vampire has struck again. And this time, he's left you a body."

CHAPTER FIVE

Jake began working the moment his cab pulled up to the curb. As deputy chief medical examiner, his duties were coldly delineated by the chief medical examiner: Confirm the identity of the victim, what happened, where it happened, when it happened, and how it happened.

But he saw the scope of his work as larger than that. To him, every victim told a far more complex story than the blood spatter surrounding the body or the fibers and hairs clinging to it. The why and whodunit were often intricately woven into the historical fabric of the victim's life. Life merged with death.

Amanda Hogaarth's story began here on the spotless sidewalk outside the very expensive building where she had lived. Jake noted the shaken expression of the doorman who admitted him, and the rigid bearing of the concierge standing behind his desk. Somehow, these two had let a killer into what was supposed to be an enclave of safety.

Jake glanced around the marble-floored lobby with its plush but impersonal furnishings. Co-op, condo, or high-end rental? Co-ops, even large ones like this building, tended to be clubbier. The neighbors knew one another, at least in passing, from all the endless wrangling of the board of directors. In a condo or rental, Amanda Hogaarth would more likely have lived in anonymity.

Jake took the elevator of this pre–World War I relic to the thirteenth floor, where the door slid open on a maelstrom of activity. The police were conducting a door-to-door inquiry, interviewing the immediate neighbors. The crime scene techs had arrived with all their equipment. As he walked toward the open door of 13C, repeated flashes of light told him the police photographer was at work.

Jake met Detective Pasquarelli in the hall. "Can I look around the apartment?"

The detective nodded. "Give it another few minutes and the techs will be done."

Jake glanced at the front door. "Any sign of forced entry?"

"No. He pushed his way in, or she let him in. The doorman claims he didn't send anyone up to her apartment, so our guy must've gotten in the building by requesting someone else, or he came in through the service entrance. Luckily, this place is guarded like Fort Knox. There are security cameras trained on all doors, and in the elevators. We'll need a few hours tomorrow to review the tapes."

"Maybe we'll get lucky."

Pasquarelli grinned. "Don't count on it, Doc. I never do."

"Who found her?" Jake asked.

"Maintenance man came up here just before five p.m. Last call of the day. Bet he wishes he'd knocked off early." Pasquarelli tugged on his already-crooked tie. "Apparently, Ms. Hogaarth called yesterday to say her air-conditioning unit was making a rattling noise. Since it wasn't an emergency, the guy didn't make it up here till today. Opened the door with a passkey when she didn't answer. Called nine-one-one at four-forty-eight p.m."

Jake glanced at his watch: 9:35 p.m. "What took you so long to call me?"

"The responding officers thought it was a natural death," Pasquarelli explained. "The tour doc from the ME's office came. He's the one who noticed the needle mark in her arm, and a few other suspicious things. Said if this was related to the Vampire, we'd better bring you in."

Jake's expression flickered between a smile and a scowl. His subordinates knew how interested he was in the Vampire case; he was surprised Pederson had been willing to let him have it after that display of authority in his office yesterday.

Stepping past Pasquarelli directly into the living room of the apartment, Jake recognized it instantly — the faint but distinctive smell of ether. That's why he never followed OSHA guidelines by wearing a face mask — the possibility of missing such transient evidence was too great. And once overlooked, it was gone forever. Now he could be certain he was dealing with the Vampire.

Ms. Hogaarth appeared to have preserved her dignity, dying a tidy death in what had been a very tidy home. Jake glanced around. The overwhelming impression was beigeness. Off-white walls, thick cream carpeting, matching light tan sofa and love seat. The only contrast came from mournful streaks of black fingerprint powder as the crime scene investigators went about their work, which destroyed the cleanliness Ms. Hogaarth had obviously held dear.

The body was stretched out on the middle of the living room floor. Jake nodded at his colleague from the office, Todd Galvin, who jumped from a crouch beside the body and rushed over to him.

Only two years out of his pathology residency, Todd was the youngest member of the ME's staff, and eager to show what he had learned. "I found a needle mark," he began, gesturing Jake toward the body. But Jake turned away.

"Remember what I've been teaching you, Todd. Let's look through the crime scene first to see what that tells us about the victim, before we get distracted by her body. She's not going anywhere."

Jake headed straight for the bathroom. The medicine cabinet revealed the usual lineup of over-the-counter remedies, but just one prescription: Lasix for high blood pressure. Other than that, Ms. Hogaarth had been quite healthy. He opened a drawer and found a shabby stethoscope and a blood pressure cuff. "Interesting — maybe she had been a nurse and used her old gear to monitor her own blood pressure."

Todd nodded. "Possibly. A layman would be more likely to use one of those new blood pressure monitoring kits they sell at the drugstore."

The young man peeped behind the shower curtain. "Sure is clean in here. This lady wouldn't have liked to see my bathroom."

They moved on to the bedroom, a room of almost monastic simplicity. Jake looked at the tautly drawn bedspread and lifted up the bottom. Just as he suspected — hospital corners on the sheets. In the closet, the shoes stood in military rows; the clothes all were hanging in the same direction. Nightstand: lamp, clock, one issue of *Reader's Digest.* Dresser: comb, brush, lavender talcum powder. Bedspread, curtains, carpet — all beige. Jake made a 360-degree rotation — not a single photograph, picture, or knickknack. "What kind of woman makes it into her sixth decade of life without acquiring a single tchotchke, a photo of grandchildren, nieces, or old friends?"

"Yeah, it's like a hotel room," Todd agreed. "Kinda creepy."

Jake led the way to the kitchen and looked into the refrigerator. "The contents of the refrigerator can also help you establish the time of death." Jake smiled at Todd and shook a carton. "The milk expiration date is your friend."

Todd peered over Jake's shoulder. "Jeez, there's even less food in her fridge than in mine. English muffins, low-fat margarine, juice, and milk. She must've eaten out a lot."

Jake glanced into the garbage can —

43

empty. Dishwasher — cleaner than a showroom model. "The killer didn't leave anything behind in here."

The living room revealed nothing more than it had on first glance — no clutter, no photos, no soul. Looking down at the coffee table, Jake's eye was drawn to a single round clean spot, where no fingerprint powder had fallen. The CSIs must've removed something from here, he thought, a mug or a glass. In the average home, he wouldn't have thought anything of it, but in Amanda Hogaarth's home, it seemed extraordinary.

Now Jake moved toward the body. Amanda Hogaarth lay on her back, her knees slightly bent to the right, her arms splayed to either side. A brown tweed skirt covered her stocky legs to mid-calf; a beige sweater met the skirt demurely, leaving no flesh exposed. She had the stiff Margaret Thatcher–like hairstyle typical of a woman in her late sixties, and not a hair had been disturbed as she fell.

Todd crouched down beside the body. "Look at this," he said as Jake joined him. He pointed to a tiny needle mark and a speck of dried blood inside the elbow joint of the victim where blood had obviously been drawn.

That alone was not suspicious. The

woman might simply have been to the doctor's and had blood drawn for tests the day she died.

"And," Todd continued with rising excitement, "look at her mouth."

Ms. Hogaarth's perfect white top teeth were false, and the denture had been knocked askew in her mouth, giving her a slightly grotesque expression. Around the corners of her lips were tiny abrasions.

"She was gagged," Jake observed. He glanced down. Her legs were bare, and her feet, contorted with the bunions and calluses of old age, lay uncovered on the rug. He had been in her home for only ten minutes, but Jake felt strongly that this was not a woman who would have padded around barefoot. "Have you found her panty hose?" he asked Todd.

"I told the criminalists to look for it, but I doubt they'll find it. The killer probably took that with him.

"Rigor is receding," Todd continued. "She's been dead about twenty-four hours."

"Maybe more, Todd. The algor mortis will provide more information. Check her core body temperature, and take the ambient air temperature, too. That may have prevented some decomposition."

"The air conditioner has been running on

high. It's sixty-five degrees in here," Todd reported.

"Yes, her body temperature would have dropped more rapidly in this cool room," Jake explained, "making it seem that she's been dead longer than she really has been."

"Her livor mortis is fixed." Todd pressed his thumb against the maroon pooling of blood on her back and could not produce a white pallor. "There's no doubt she's been dead for more than eight or nine hours at least, and she hasn't been moved at all since she died."

"Good work, Todd." Jake rose and signaled to the two morgue workers lounging by the door. "Go ahead and take the body to the morgue. And keep her in this same position, or you'll destroy any trace evidence on her back. I'll do the autopsy first thing tomorrow morning. If you want to assist, Todd, be there by eight a.m."

Jake watched as they transferred the body, the extremities still partially stiffened with rigor, onto a gurney. If this was truly the work of the Vampire, why had his methods changed? Why had he found it necessary to kill this victim, when he hadn't seriously harmed the others? The case had morphed. What had been a fascinating academic puzzle for him to decode had escalated to murder. He'd gotten what he wanted — the chance to work on the Vampire case — but it had come at the cost of Amanda Hogaarth's life.

"Have you contacted the next of kin?" Jake asked the detective.

"Doesn't seem to be anybody. Her apartment application lists a lawyer as the person to contact in an emergency. Least I don't have to break the news to some heartbroken daughter or sister." Pasquarelli grunted thanks to a passing stream of CSIs.

"We didn't get much," the oldest one said. "Cleanest apartment I ever saw."

Jake thrust his hands deep into his pockets. "Something's here, Vito. We have to look with our eyes wide open. I'm going to nose around again."

"Be my guest."

Jake did the roundabout again, but if anything, the apartment seemed even more nondescript than before. Then in the kitchen, amid the spotless cabinets and appliances, Jake found it. There, pushed back behind the gleaming pots, was one clue that Amanda Hogaarth had lived a real life and knew someone else on the planet — a battered book with a faded cover and spidery hand-written notations in the margins: *Recetas Favoritas*.

Jake cradled it in his hands. A cookbook, a Spanish-language cookbook, not placed on a shelf for easy reference, but hidden away. Like love letters, Jake thought. Or pornography. He gently put it down.

CHAPTER SIX

Manny stormed up the steps of the federal building in Newark, New Jersey, her heels rapping out a battle cry. Tossing her red leather tote on the conveyor belt to be x-rayed, Manny charged through the metal detector, which immediately began hooting out a warning.

"Step back out, ma'am," the marshal instructed. "Any keys or change in your pockets?"

"Of course not," she snapped. Her sea green Donatella Versace suit didn't even have pockets, and if it did, she certainly wouldn't destroy its sleek lines by carrying around lumps of keys.

"Unbutton your jacket."

Manny did as she was told. "Whoops! I forgot I was wearing that." She undid the vintage double-link chain belt from her waist, dropped it in the guard's basket, and stepped through the metal detector without incident.

On the other side, the guard was holding the belt, calling for a tape measure.

"C'mon, give that back," Manny commanded. "I'm in a hurry. I've got an urgent meeting with a client."

"I'm sorry, ma'am, but security regulations prohibit lengths of chain longer than four feet. Can't let metal belts longer than forty-eight inches into the building. Same regulations as on a plane."

"That accessory set me back a few hundred dollars. Do you honestly think I'd use it to chain a federal prosecutor to his desk?"

"I need to measure it first," the guard insisted. "I gotta find a tape."

Manny opened her mouth to howl in protest at the absurd delay. But before a word escaped, she stopped, grinned, and held open her suit jacket. "Look, Xavier," she said, reading the guard's name tag, "you're insulting me here. I know I'm not a size two, but does it look like I need four feet of chain to go around this waist?"

Xavier flushed as he studied her hourglass figure. "Um, I guess not. Sorry, ma'am. Here you go."

"This terrorism stuff is getting ridiculous," Manny fumed to the man riding the elevator with her. "They spend all their resources hassling average citizens, and there are probably Al Qaeda operatives camped out a mile from the Pentagon."

The man said nothing, but he took a step away from her as she pounded the button for the seventh floor yet again. When the elevator finally delivered her, Manny was in a fine state, and woe be unto the federal prosecutor who crossed her.

"Philomena Manfreda here to see Brian Lisnek," she told the receptionist ensconced behind the bulletproof glass window.

The young woman started to gesture toward a chair in the waiting area, but one look at the set of Manny's jaw changed her mind and she buzzed Lisnek immediately. "You'll have to sign in. And wear this tag at all times." She spoke as if she carried a gun.

Lisnek, a stocky sandy-haired man in a rumpled gray suit, opened the secured door. Manny soon found herself seated with him in a typical government office — windowless, crammed with unfiled papers, furnished with a metal desk and old scarred wood chairs, and equipped with a computer whose screen dissolved into the American bald eagle.

"Where is my client, Travis Heaton? I want to talk to him before I talk to you."

"He's in a holding cell downstairs with

51

one of our agents. I'll have the guard take him to a lawyer's window. His mother is in the waiting area down there, in case she's needed."

"You mean in case she's needed to sign a statement giving her son permission to confess to a crime he didn't commit. Well, there will be no statement. Tell your homeboy not to question him any longer. My client is exercising his Fifth Amendment rights."

Lisnek seemed unperturbed, as if this was just another day in his life dealing with a run-of-the-mill defense attorney. Manny didn't care for the look of smug self-confidence on the prosecutor's round face. "What are the charges against him?"

"Terrorist attack on U.S. government property. There will be a number of charges of violation of Title 18, then double that for violations of the U.S. postal code. And, of course, attempted murder. Assume twenty, thirty main charges, a few related subsidiary charges, a number of conspiracy charges, and maybe a racketeering charge, give or take a few."

"Oh, come on. Whoever did this, you know it was just a prank with a regrettable unintended injury."

"Ms. Manfreda, the attempted assassination of a federal judge is not a 'regrettable unintended injury.' And there are no pranks in the metropolitan area these days."

"Thank God you're here!"

Manny would not have pegged the woman who greeted her in the visitors' area as the mother of a Monet Academy student. Slightly overweight, with deeply etched worry lines in her forehead, she wore a plain gold band on her right ring finger, indicating she was a widow, and jeans and a sweatshirt that she must've thrown on when she got the call that her son was in jail. No diamonds, no Cartier, no tightly Botoxed skin. Mrs. Maureen Heaton looked too normal, and too hardworking, to be the kind of mother who could produce the money and the connections necessary to get her son into the city's most exclusive prep school.

Manny extended her hand. "Philomena Manfreda, Mrs. Heaton. I'd like to sit down with your son and find out exactly what's going on. But it's hard here. We have to talk through a wired-glass window by phone. And now, under the Patriot Act, even my conversations can be monitored if they think I am passing messages on to his accomplices."

"But that's only if he's guilty," Mrs. Heaton protested. "My Travis is a good boy. You've got to get him out of this place. They can't keep him here. And you can't let them take him to a prison. He's only a child. Please."

"How old is Travis, ma'am?"

"He just turned eighteen, in his senior year at Monet. He's always been small for his age, and a little immature, but very bright."

Inwardly, Manny winced. Eighteen was bad — the kid would be charged as an adult, and if she didn't manage to get him off, he'd face a prison term and a criminal record that would follow him all his life. A really bad trade-off for the momentary thrill of watching a mailbox explode.

Manny checked her watch. "They'll be bringing Travis in any minute, Mrs. Heaton. You'd better step out into the hall."

"What? I want to see my son. I need to be with him when you talk to him."

"That's not possible, Mrs. Heaton. It would violate attorney-client privilege."

"But I'm his mother," Maureen Heaton wailed.

"Even so, now that Travis has turned eighteen, he's considered an adult. The government could call you as a witness

54

against your son."

"I've been working my hospital job during the day and doing private-duty nursing at night to keep him in school. Do you understand? He's my *child*."

Manny felt her own eyes well with tears, but she blinked them back furiously. Getting emotionally involved with a client and his family did no one any good. Travis would be best served if she kept her emotions in check. "I'll make sure he's okay. I promise." Manny turned her impulse to hug into a brief pat on the shoulder and gently urged Travis's mother toward the dispassionate uniformed guard waiting to escort her out.

Another guard led Manny to a folding chair outside one of the confessional-like booths lining the wall of the narrow room. The door behind the Plexiglas partition opened and Manny watched a guard escort a thin, hunched young man with the makings of a scraggly beard up to the window.

He stared at Manny, managing to convey both belligerence and sullenness. From the dark rings under his eyes, he must have been awake all night.

This was one of the Preppy Terrorist?

Even if you replaced the orange prison jumpsuit with a navy blazer and club tie, this kid was not going to be appearing in a Brooks Brothers ad anytime soon. Where was the air of nonchalant entitlement? Where was the cocksure self-confidence? That's what parents sent their sons to places like the Monet Academy to acquire. Algebra and biology you could get at lesser institutions; Monet prepared boys to be masters of the universe. Travis might have been a straight-A student academically, but he hadn't acquired that Monet panache.

Manny picked up the telephone receiver, which would allow them to talk with limited privacy, while keeping her eye on the glowering guard by the door. She gestured for Travis to pick up his receiver.

He held it gingerly an inch or two from his ear, as if he suspected her of being able to transmit poison through the line.

"Travis, I'm a lawyer. My name is Manny Manfreda and your mom has asked me to represent you."

At the mention of his mother, Travis's shoulders slumped even more and he looked down at the floor.

"You need to answer my questions truthfully, or I won't be any help to you at all," Manny said. "Do you understand?"

Travis nodded, but he still wouldn't make eye contact.

The first thing Manny wanted to know was how much damage her new client had done to himself. "Have you been talking to the police and the FBI since you were brought in? Did they advise you of your rights?"

Travis nodded. "A police car came around the corner right after the explosion. They must've been patrolling right around there. The cops stopped us and said they just wanted to get some information from us down at the station. We went because we didn't want them calling our parents. We weren't even supposed to be out that night."

"So they didn't arrest you at the scene, but you agreed to go with them to the police station." Manny leaned forward. "This is important, Travis. Did they threaten you?"

The boy shrugged. "No, but they're cops, ya know. You do what they tell you to do. Besides, I didn't do anything wrong, so I figured I didn't have anything to worry about."

Manny tried not to think about how many wrongfully convicted people had spoken those words before being hauled off for long prison terms. Before she could ask her next question, Travis asked her one.

"When the cops were driving away with us, I saw an ambulance pull up. Did someone get hurt when the mailbox exploded? Later, the cops kept asking me about some man with a dog."

Manny studied her client. For the first time since they had started talking, he met her eye. Was he being sincere? Was he really not aware that the explosion had nearly killed a federal judge? The subtle cues you got when you spoke to a client face-to-face were hard to read when his face was obscured by scratched Plexiglas, his voice distorted by a primitive sound system.

"The man walking the dog was Judge Patrick Brueninger. He was seriously injured by a flying piece of metal."

Manny watched as Travis absorbed this news. His face didn't register any of the emotions she would have expected: shock and fear if he were innocent, or if he really had intended to kill the judge, elation at having hit his target, disappointment at not having killed him. Instead, Travis seemed just mildly concerned.

"What about the dog?" he asked.

"Huh?"

"The dog — did it get hurt in the explosion?"

"Uh, not that I'm aware." Manny looked down and made some notes on her pad to give herself a moment to think. Her new client seemed utterly unfazed by being involved in an incident that had nearly killed a judge, but he was worried about the victim's dog. She had no experience representing juveniles — would a jury believe he was screwy or that he merely had his priorities straight?

She resumed the interview. "Do you know who Patrick Brueninger is?"

Travis shrugged. "No. Why would I?"

The truth or a lie? Manny couldn't be sure. That bored teenage demeanor was so hard to read. For a newshound like her, Brueninger's name was instantly recognizable. But teenagers, even smart ones, were famously self-absorbed. Maybe Travis really didn't have a clue about the prominence of the man who'd been injured by this stunt. She moved on. "How many kids in your group?"

"It was just Paco and me from Monet. We met these four other guys at the club. They were a little older. They bought us some beers." Travis's voice got softer and Manny had to strain to hear. "After the music was over, we all went to the deli for some food. We passed the mailbox, and one of the guys bent down, like he'd dropped something. The next thing you know, everyone was running, so Paco and I ran, too. And then the mailbox exploded, the cops came, and here I am."

"And you never saw these guys before you met them at the club?"

Travis shook his head.

"What were their names?"

Travis shrugged. "One was named Jack, and there was one they all called Boo. And Gordie and Zeke, or Deke or Freak or something. It was so loud in there, I couldn't hear what they were saying."

"And they came down to the police station, too?"

"Paco and I got into one police car." Travis twisted the edge of his cuff as he spoke. "The other guys were standing out on the sidewalk, talking to the cops. We couldn't hear what they were saying, except they kept shaking their heads. And finally they all showed the cops their driver's licenses and the cops wrote stuff down, and then they let them go."

Manny rubbed her temples. Clearly, "Freak" and "Boo" knew a bit more about dealing with law enforcement than this little rabbit. The older guys had simply declined to make the trip to the station, and the cops, not having enough to arrest them, had let them go after checking their IDs. God only knew if the IDs were real.

"And what about Paco?"

"They put us in separate rooms when we got here, and I haven't seen him since."

"How much did you tell the cops once you got here?"

"Just what I told you. That Paco and I were supposed to be sleeping over at his house but came over to Hoboken to check out this club and met those guys. One of the guys dropped something by the mailbox; then we all ran. That's it."

"Which guy dropped something?"

"The guy whose name I didn't catch. Zeke . . . whatever."

Travis sounded impatient. Manny guessed he was tired of telling his story. Well, too damn bad. He'd tell it until she understood every detail. No wonder the cops were holding on to him. This was the oldest cover-up in the book — a version of the old "The drugs aren't mine; I was holding them for a friend" routine.

"There's nothing else? You stuck to this story?"

Travis bristled. "It's not a story; it's the truth!" Then he glanced over his shoulder at the guard. "I thought they were going to let me go, until they opened my backpack and found the book."

"What book?"

"A book on Islam that I'm reading for my comparative religion class. That's when they really started coming down on me. How did I know how to build a bomb? Was this the first one I'd ever set off? They wouldn't let up. That's when they read me that Miranda thing, just like on TV. That's when I knew I had to call my mom. Those cops think I'm some kind of terrorist, don't they?"

Manny didn't want to tell Travis what the newspapers were calling him. She honed in on something Travis had said earlier. This could be her salvation. "You said they searched your backpack. Did they do that without your consent?"

"No. They asked permission and I said okay. I figured they were looking for drugs and I knew I was clean. I forgot all about the book being in there."

Shit! So far the cops had done everything by the book. This case was looking worse and worse. But she plastered a smile on her face for her client's sake. "Okay, Travis. That's all for now. In a little while, I should have you out of here."

"You'll explain to them that this is all a mistake?"

"I'm afraid it's a little more complicated than that. But we'll try to get you out on bail." Manny watched Travis shuffle forlornly to the door. He turned once to look at her; then he was gone.

Maureen Heaton sat in the waiting room, her back pressed against the pea green plastic chair, her fingers picking at a frayed thread on her canvas purse. Manny greeted her, careful to banish all signs of worry from her face. "All right, ma'am, first things first. He was with a group of boys who may have done something. But he says he is innocent, and I believe him. Let's arrange to get Travis out of here. Then we'll work on our strategy for his defense."

Mrs. Heaton twisted her dulled wedding band on her right ring finger continuously, as if trying to conjure up some genie who would make this nightmare go away. "Defense! But he's innocent. It's obvious those other boys set the bomb."

"Yes, but the police don't have those other boys; they have Travis. And a suspect in custody is worth four on the streets. We may have to hire our own investigator to track them down."

"Investigator? I'm a widow; I work two jobs. Where do you think I'm going to get all this money?" Mrs. Heaton groped in her purse for a tissue. Manny could see billable hours evaporating before her eyes. She patted Mrs. Heaton on the shoulder. "Don't worry. I know someone with some time on his hands who may be able to help us." This was the perfect chore for Sam, Jake's perpetually unemployed brother.

Mrs. Heaton gazed at her with brown eyes full of pathetic hope and Manny could feel the burden of worry shift from the mother's shoulders to her own. She hoped she was strong enough to carry the load.

CHAPTER SEVEN

"We're opposing bail." Lisnek leaned back in his desk chair, straining the blue oxford cloth of his shirt over his belly. "We want him in custody until his trial."

Manny was thunderstruck. "The kid's never been in trouble before. He's from a hardworking family with limited financial resources. He poses no flight risk. Why would you oppose bail?"

"We suspect he's part of a larger conspiracy. We found this in his backpack." Lisnek held up a dog-eared paperback book — *Understanding the Koran* by Imam Abu Rezi.

"Required reading for the comparative religion class he's taking at Monet," Manny explained.

Lisnek shrugged. "Students have been known to be unduly influenced by their subject matter. The police just called with the results of their search of Travis's home. They found a whole shelf of books on

Muslim theology, Islamic fundamentalism, jihad, et cetera. I rather doubt that prep schools delve into the topic that deeply."

Manny jumped up. "That's absurd. Even in these crazy times, no judge in the District of New Jersey is going to deny bail based solely on the suspect's reading material." But even as she said those words aloud, she felt a worm of doubt wiggling within. Why would a Christian teenager possess so many books on Islam? Did Travis have some political agenda he wasn't revealing to her or to his mother?

"Don't jump to conclusions, Ms. Manfreda. I never said that's all we had. Mr. Heaton has been linked to the crime with a piece of solid forensic evidence. A bite mark in an apple."

"A bite mark in an apple proves my client is a terrorist? Was it a McIntosh or a Red Delicious? Am I missing something here?"

"We have an eyewitness, Mr. Park Sung Ho, counterman at the Happy Garden all-night market on Washington Street. Mr. Heaton and his friends went in and bought sodas and snacks. They gave Mr. Park a hard time, tossing money back and forth, trying to confuse him with the change. He watched them carefully as they left and saw Mr. Heaton take an apple from a display by the door. By the time Mr. Park got out from behind the counter to chase them, the boys were down at the corner by the mailbox. He saw the one with the apple take a bite out of it and toss it in the gutter. Then the kid crouched down, placed something under the mailbox, and they all ran. A few seconds later, the mailbox blew up."

Manny kept her face impassive, but inside she was seething. Travis had conveniently forgotten to mention this forbidden fruit. "And you recovered the apple."

"We did. And we intend to prove it has Mr. Heaton's bite mark in it."

Manny was puzzled. Why would they be focusing on the bite pattern? Anything that a person had bitten into would retain traces of his saliva, which could be tested for DNA. A DNA match was infallible, while the forensics of bite comparisons was wildly speculative. She began to feel a flicker of hope.

"You're testing the apple for my client's DNA, of course?"

Lisnek looked down at his scuffed penny loafers. "Uh . . . it's been sent out."

Manny detected something squirrelly in his response. They'd probably mishandled the evidence. She didn't let the smile she felt inside touch her lips. This chump had nothing, and he knew it.

Manny forced Lisnek to meet her gaze and held it for a long moment. Lisnek was the first to look away.

As she left the U.S. attorney's office, Manny turned to ask one more question. "So where is the other kid you brought in? Who's representing him?"

"Paco Sandoval has been released."

"Released? How come he gets out and my client's still here?"

"Because Paco Sandoval is the son of Enrique Sandoval, ambassador to the UN for Argentina. He has diplomatic immunity."

Chapter Eight

"Shall we begin?"

Jake Rosen; Todd Galvin; their *diener,* a Croatian émigré named Dragon; and Detective Pasquarelli stood around the autopsy table at 8:01 a.m. Before them lay the fully clothed body of Amanda Hogaarth.

Todd and Jake performed the first routine tasks: Using an alternate light source, they searched for traces of microscopic evidence on Amanda Hogaarth's clothing. Finding nothing, they photographed her in her clothing, front and back. Jake then carefully removed each of the garments and photographed them completely, even inside out.

Even without her tweed skirt and sensible undergarments, Ms. Hogaarth managed to project an air of quiet dignity. Jake was sure this woman would have been very surprised to know she had ended up here. The other seven autopsy tables held drunks and drug addicts and street punks. They had led hard, violent lives, so it was no surprise that they had met hard, violent ends. Amanda Hogaarth seemed to have led a blameless, soft, rather dull life. Yet she, too, had wound up under the probing tools of the medical examiner.

Then Jake stepped up to examine the victim's skin closely. Her body was covered with the fine wrinkles, freckles, and age spots that plagued the fair-skinned, but there were no wounds. On her left wrist, Jake noted four evenly spaced bruises. He pointed them out to Todd and Pasquarelli. "The attacker grabbed her here and held her arm steady while he drew the blood." Jake's gaze traveled up the woman's arm until he found the tiny hole left by the assailant's needle. He instructed Dragon to photograph both areas, then turned the victim's hands over and looked at the palms. On each palm were four half-moon impressions. Amanda Hogaarth had clenched her hands so tightly that her own fingernails had pierced her skin.

Gently, Jake opened the victim's mouth. Dragon photographed the abrasions he and Todd had noted the night before at the corners of her mouth. Using a magnifying glass, Jake searched for fibers there, but he found none, supporting his hypothesis that nylon stockings had been used for the gag. Sometimes, gagged victims choked on their own vomit, but that was not the cause of death here. Amanda Hogaarth's throat and windpipe were clear.

After removing her top denture, Jake looked at the fillings in her bottom teeth. "You don't see that type of dental work here. I don't think this work was done by an American dentist."

The neck and torso revealed nothing unusual, but the thighs, large, cushioned with a thick layer of adipose tissue, showed two distinct bruises above the knees. "Looks like he knelt on her to hold her down," Todd commented.

"Correct." Jake directed a light to shine on Ms. Hogaarth's vulva area. "Let's look for signs of sexual attack."

"Why do that, Doc? She was dressed when the detective here found her." Todd was quizzical.

"Because many times crime scenes are staged. Plus, if you look at her panties under a light source, there appears to be a slight stain . . . maybe blood.

"As I thought, there are definite signs of violent penetration. Tears in the vagina but no semen present."

"He wore a condom?" Todd asked.

"No, he didn't rape her. She was violated by a hard object shoved into her vagina. Look at this." Jake stepped aside so that Todd and the detective could get a closer look.

The younger doctor's brow furrowed. "What . . ."

"See the labia? That tissue is burned. The margins of the burned area look like electrical burns. Do a frozen section," Jake told Todd. "We'll verify it under the microscope."

Pasquarelli recoiled. Dragon muttered something. It wasn't necessary to speak Croatian to catch his meaning.

"Would that be enough to kill her?" the detective asked. "Did she die of electrocution?"

"No, if she'd been electrocuted, we'd see an exit burn somewhere else on her body. It's time to look inside." They worked with quiet efficiency, making a Y-shaped incision from each shoulder to the lower part of the breastbone, then down to the pubic bones. In one smooth movement that produced a faint zipping sound, Jake pulled the skin back from the rib cage, exposing the ribs and the abdominal organs.

Pasquarelli winced and looked away.

"Come on, Detective." Jake elbowed the

cop. "You must've seen that procedure scores of times."

"Seen it. Doesn't mean I have to like it. Some cops barf every time they have to do this. Me, I got a cast-iron stomach. What bothers me more than the blood and the smell are the sounds, especially when you guys fire up that saw." The detective reached into his pocket and pulled out two tiny earplugs. "Okay, I'm ready."

Jake used the saw to cut through the ribs near the breastbone and removed the breastplate, exposing the heart and lungs. "The heart weighs five hundred and fifty grams, twice as big as it should be," Jake commented as he worked. "There's narrowing of the arteries, and an enlarged left ventricle, indicative of high blood pressure. Both lungs are filled with frothy fluid."

Jake straightened. "Cause of death: hypertensive and arteriosclerotic heart disease with congestive heart failure, along with a fatal cardiac arrhythmia, while being held down."

"English, please," Pasquarelli requested.

"Heart failure induced by torture."

Chapter Nine

Jake stepped through the door of his town house and slid on a pile of mail that had been shoved through the slot onto the parquet floor hours earlier. Scooping it up, he tossed it on a table so full of unopened bills and unanswered invitations that its fine Empire lines were utterly obscured.

When he had bought this dilapidated brownstone in the mid-eighties, the bus ride from his office at Thirtieth Street to his home north of Ninety-sixth Street had been an exercise in urban survival. He had needed to stay constantly alert to sidestep roving packs of teenagers who hopped on the bus looking for pockets to pick, staggering panhandlers shaking their paper cups of change under the noses of riders, and assorted drunks and crazies. Reading, or even daydreaming, was done at your peril. These days, the ride on the clean air-conditioned bus was so uneventful, you could go into a

Zen-induced trance and still emerge unscathed at your stop. And his neighborhood, once populated by dealers and pimps, had sprouted a Starbucks and a Gap — not necessarily improvements, in his view.

All in all, coming home was less stressful but also less exciting than it used to be. And, since his divorce nearly two years ago, less organized. Still, the five-story house, packed with forensic specimens, haphazardly furnished, partially remodeled, was his personal sanctuary. The place where he could go to lick his wounds and gather strength for another round of battle. And today, after the disturbing evidence gathered at the Hogaarth autopsy, and the strain of explaining to Pederson why it still hadn't brought them any closer to catching the Vampire, Jake deeply craved the restorative peace of his home.

"Your girlfriend called me today."

The voice — deep, amused, irreverent — emerged from somewhere in the shadowy front parlor.

"Why are you sitting there in the dark? And she's not my girlfriend."

"Companion, lover, significant other — what's the politically correct term you prefer?"

What was Manny to him? At the moment,

pain in the ass or thorn in the side seemed the most fitting description. Jake walked toward the sound of his brother Sam's voice, only to crash into a randomly placed display case.

"Ow! Would you turn on the damn lights!"

Sam reached out a long arm and flicked on a lamp, revealing himself, prematurely gray ponytail and all, sprawled on a wing chair and ottoman, and the astonishing clutter of Jake's living room.

"I find this room more habitable when it's only illuminated by that neon sign across the street," Sam said.

"No one asked you to inhabit it." Jake found his brother's tendency of popping in unannounced for extended stays both infuriating and entertaining, especially since he had his own rent-stabilized apartment in Greenwich Village. Today, infuriating had the upper hand.

"Come, come, big brother. No need to snap at me just because you're in the doghouse with Manny."

Heading for the chair across from Sam, Jake moved a box of disarticulated bear bones that some less experienced ME had sent him, thinking they were human, and sat down. "She called you to complain about me?" He could feel his heart rate rising. How juvenile!

"No, she called to offer me a job, and in the course of describing said job, she — quite inadvertently, I'm sure — revealed her frustration with you."

Jake looked at his younger brother's teasing grin and felt the same overwhelming need to jump on top of him and twist his arm that he had felt when they were twelve and five, respectively. "A job? What kind of job — bag carrier for one of her shoe-shopping swings through Bloomies?"

"You underestimate me, bro. I'm temporarily employed by her as a trial-prep resource — doing a little investigation work on a case. Tracking down four kids who were in the company of the Preppy Terrorists and who have since vanished."

"Last time I checked, you weren't licensed for that."

Sam brushed off this concern as if it were one of the cobwebs hanging off the replica of the Maltese falcon in the corner. "Anyone can ask a few discreet questions. I'm just assisting Manny with her inquiries, so to speak." Sam sat up straight, took his feet off the ottoman, and leaned forward to look his brother in the eye. "I hear you think she's not up to handling this case."

Jake kicked the box he'd just moved. "I

never said that! I just cautioned her not to eagerly accept what may turn out to be an unwinnable case for *anyone.*"

"Ah, caution. You're good at that, aren't you, Jake? As I recall, you cautioned me against traveling cross-country on my motorcycle, climbing Mount McKinley, and touring the world with the Pacifists for Peace Rugby Club."

"I didn't want you to get hurt. And I hoped you would focus."

"OMmmmmmmmm." Sam started to chant, drowning out Jake's paternal explanations before launching into his response. "I didn't get hurt. I succeeded, and I had a hell of a good time along the way. And I learned. So will Manny. Trust me. Trust *her.*"

Jake opened his mouth, then clamped it shut again. Sam had never been married, had never even had a serious relationship, at least not with anyone he'd ever bothered to introduce to his family, but he felt free to dispense love advice like a regular Dr. Phil. And yet his brother, as feckless and carefree as he seemed to be, had a core of common sense, a rock-solid emotional stability that Jake envied. It seemed he'd always been that way, maybe because Sam had been too young to remember when their father abandoned them, while seven-year-old Jake had reacted so uncontrollably that their mother had finally sought help from a Jewish charity. Jake had been sent to a reform school for troubled kids, until he learned that the surest way out was to repress his emotions and pour all the energy required for anger into the study of science.

Jake extracted a Thai take-out menu from the clutter on an end table and tossed it to Sam. "Order us some dinner. I'll go call Manny."

Half an hour later, the pork with basil sauce and the lemongrass chicken had arrived, and Jake, Sam, Manny, and Mycroft sat around (and under) the dining room table, dissecting the case between fiery bites. Jake had been unable to bring himself to actually apologize for warning Manny off the Preppy Terrorist case, so he had simply issued the invitation to dinner as if nothing had happened. Manny had accepted readily enough, but it wasn't lost on Jake that she had breezed right past him when he opened the front door, heading straight for Sam and the food.

"Apparently, Travis Heaton is a brainiac kid with no street smarts whatsoever and an inconvenient interest in Islamic culture."

Manny waved her fork for emphasis, sending a piece of chicken sailing off the tines. Mycroft leaped and caught it in midair. "Did you see that? Good dog, Mikey!"

"Have you ever heard of teaching your dog manners?"

"Have you ever heard of Rin Tin Tin, Lassie, Clifford the Big Red Dog? That was a trick Mycroft learned after hours of study."

"Is he earning a graduate degree at that doggy day-care place you send him to every day?" Jake asked.

As soon as the words were out of his mouth, Jake wished he could have reeled them back in. A few days ago, he'd been teasing Manny about enrolling Mycroft in some goofy place called Little Paws, but that was before the blowup in the restaurant. He saw her smile replaced by a scowl and knew he'd just dug himself deeper into a hole.

"Actually, Mycroft is no longer attending Little Paws. He was" — she paused for a breath — "expelled."

Even Jake knew better than to laugh, and he kicked Sam sharply to head off any hilarity from that side of the table. "Expelled?"

Manny dismissed his inquiry with a wave. "It's too complicated to get into now. I want to tell you about Travis. Where was I?"

"Smart but no street smarts, studying

Islam," Sam prompted.

"Right. He's at Monet on a scholarship," Manny continued. "His mom is a widow who works as a nurse at New York–Presbyterian. She knocked herself out getting him into private school because she thought the public schools were too dangerous for him. Now she's finding out kids can fall into bad company no matter how much tuition you pay."

Sam nodded. "Yeah, at Boys High School, where Jake and I went, all we had to worry about was pot and the occasional knife fight. Prep school exposes you to designer drugs and international terrorism. A much better class of criminal."

Jake refilled all the wineglasses. "So, do you think your client's telling you the complete truth about what happened that night?"

"No. Criminal clients always lie to you about something. Travis already lied about the apple by not telling me the whole story. And he said the book in his backpack was for a class, conveniently forgetting about the shelfful of books on Islam he had at home. Maybe he thinks leaving things out is not really lying, but I think it shows a certain amount of cunning."

"So you *do* think he tried to kill the

81

judge?" Sam asked.

Manny shook her head. "My gut feeling is that he's telling me the truth about his lack of involvement in blowing up the mailbox. When I went back to ask him about the apple, he claimed that he and this Zeke character both swiped apples on the way out of the deli, and that it was Zeke the deli man saw take a bite and toss the rest. But Travis can't remember what happened to his apple."

"What about the books?" Sam asked.

"His mother claims it's just a phase he's going through. Apparently, he's always had a compulsive streak. When he was four, it was trains; seven, dinosaurs; ten, medieval weaponry. He's just that kind of —"

"Dweeb," Sam said, completing the sentence as he handed his brother a beer. "Jake was like that when he was a kid. Remember your obsession with asteroids and meteors?"

Jake laughed. "I had our great-aunt Flo so worried about rocks falling out of the sky, she carried an umbrella everywhere she went."

"Yeah, and he wouldn't shut up on the subject," Sam said. "As I recall, we got excluded from the Passover seder that year because no one in the family wanted to listen to you."

Manny picked up Mycroft and held him on her lap. "That's a small price to pay for pursuing your passions. I'm afraid Travis is truly being persecuted for having this interest. We have to prove he wasn't involved in a conspiracy with those other guys."

She turned to Sam. "That's why it's vital that we find them. They definitely have something to do with this, but I can't tell if Travis knew them before or not."

"What about Paco, the diplomat's kid?" Jake asked.

"I'm trying to get hold of him, but the school and his family and the embassy have closed ranks around him. I can't wait for Paco; I'm requesting a reconsideration of bail, so I can tear apart the forensic evidence on this apple."

Jake paused with a forkful of food halfway to his mouth. "But I thought you just said you weren't sure whether or not your client was telling you the truth about the apple?"

Manny shook her head pityingly. "You're such a scientist, always worrying about what's 'true,' so sure that true and false can always be quantified. I worry about what's just. And an eighteen-year-old kid with no criminal record being held without bail for a crime in which the state can't prove a link between the suspect and the victim is not just. An eighteen-year-old kid who, at the very worst, pulled a stupid stunt on a dare being held as a terrorist so the Department of Homeland Security can hold a press conference announcing how effectively they're protecting us is not just. And the fact that the government is using a freakin' apple to make its case is even more unjust." Manny raked her slender fingers through her hair as she talked, ruining all the effort she put into keeping her wild red mane under control. "So, yes, Jake, I'm going to go into court and argue against that apple even if my client *did* bite into it. You got a problem with that?"

Jake's eyes hadn't left Manny since she started talking. When he saw her like this — eyes shining, hands waving, hair flying — his heart started pounding, and he sincerely wished his brother wasn't sitting at the same table. He got up, put his hands on her shoulders, and buried his face in the hair next to her ear, breathing in the scent of very expensive shampoo. "No, I don't have a problem with that."

Manny twisted around to look him in the eye. "Oh, fine. You're forgiven. You'd think a man with such an exalted vocabulary would be familiar with the words *I'm sorry,* but apparently not."

"He didn't know them when he was a kid, either, Manny," Sam chimed in. "I don't know how he managed to get such a high score on his SATs."

"I hope you two are enjoying yourselves." Jake massaged Manny's shoulders.

"I am." She leaned back and smiled. "Now, tell us what's happening with your case. Is this woman who was murdered in midtown really a victim of the Vampire?"

Jake's elation at being back in Manny's good graces evaporated as soon as she mentioned the Vampire. He dropped his hands from her shoulders and rubbed his eyes. "I don't know. The MO is totally different. No sign that he pushed into the apartment — she appears to have let him in. And then the torture — why has he suddenly turned so violent? I don't think it's a copycat. The only link is the puncture on her arm, where blood was obviously drawn, and the use of ether."

"What was the time of death?"

"Sometime between noon and five yesterday."

"Middle of the afternoon and no one saw or heard anything?"

"The police spent all day reviewing the security tapes. There's only one person who entered the building during that time frame who can't be accounted for. A woman wearing oversize sunglasses and a baseball cap, carrying a big purse. The concierge remembers that she spoke with an accent of some kind. He said he announced her to apartment 50E. The lady in 50E says she approved the visitor because she was expecting her masseuse. But then no one showed at her door. She was just getting ready to call down when the concierge buzzed her again, and the masseuse arrived. She thought it was a little screwy at the time, but she didn't complain."

"So this mystery woman is obviously your Vampire! Can they get a good description of her by studying the tape?"

Jake shook his head. "Hat, glasses, and coat cover every identifiable feature. She could be any medium-height woman — or man, for that matter — in the city. This is not a woman's crime. A woman doesn't sexually torture an old lady. It just doesn't add up."

"So what's your next step?"

Sam and Manny were looking at him expectantly, waiting for him to pull a rabbit out of a hat. He knew they wouldn't be impressed with what he had to offer.

"Research. I plan to spend tomorrow calling colleagues here and abroad and trolling through databases and medical journal articles until I figure out just what caused that unique burn pattern. If I know what the Vampire used, maybe I can figure out why he — or she — used it."

CHAPTER TEN

Sam parked Manny's Porsche Cabriolet at the curb, pulling in between a jacked-up Trans Am and an ancient Honda Accord. His drive down Wilkens Street, on the west side of Kearny, New Jersey, had been monitored by two slavering pit bulls behind a chain-link fence and several gimlet-eyed statues of the Virgin Mary in front-yard shrines. Glancing at the small yellow house fortified with wrought-iron window grates overlooking his parking spot, he noticed a curtain flick back into place. Alert, alert! Stranger spotted on the street!

As Manny had predicted, the IDs produced by the remaining young men who had been with Travis and Paco on the night of the bombing bore the addresses of nonexistent buildings or unknown streets in the metropolitan area. The fact that these guys had been carrying fake IDs raised no suspicions among the police. No sir, they had their bomber, Travis Andrew Heaton, and damned if they were going to let suspicious behavior by the other people present that night get in the way of their case. So, no need to track them down, uh-uh.

That was Sam's job. The previous night, after Jake and Manny had slunk off to the bedroom to kiss and make up, he had headed across the river to hang out at Club Epoch. Despite being fifteen years older than most of the people on the dance floor, Sam had managed to insinuate himself in a group of regulars. It had taken him until nearly four o'clock in the morning to tease out the identity and possible location of one Benjamin "Boo" Hravek, thought to reside in Kearny, known to hang out at Big Mike's Gateway Inn in that fair city.

After returning to Jake's brownstone and encountering Manny and Jake at the breakfast table, both dressed in business suits and sporting disapproving stares, Sam had crawled into bed for a few hours' sleep, and then pulled into Kearny in time to have a late lunch at the Gateway Inn.

He strolled down the block, heading for a windowless building covered in gray asphalt shingles. Nowhere did the name Big Mike's or Gateway Inn appear. If you had to ask, you weren't welcome. But his search of liquor licenses held in Kearny had revealed that the license granted for 440 Wilkens Street was held by Lawrence M. Egli, DBA the Gateway Inn.

As he drew closer, Sam revised his approach. "Lookin' for Boo Hravek, an old buddy of mine" would never fly here. In Kearny, everyone knew one another from the moment of conception — old friends didn't appear out of the woodwork.

He thought about the girl who had told him last night, after five Cosmos, where to find Boo. Today, if she was able to remember their conversation, she would be regretting it. Telling strangers about the neighborhood boys was not the done thing, not even when the stranger was nicer than you were used to.

Sam took a second to get the appropriate expression fixed on his face, then opened the door to the Gateway Inn. Momentarily blinded by the sudden switch from the bright sunshine of the sidewalk to the dim interior illuminated only by the glow of the TV above the bar, Sam paused on the threshold.

"Shut the fuckin' door," a disembodied voice rang out.

Fresh air was clearly not a welcome commodity here; it diluted the rarefied scent of stale beer and cigarette smoke. Smoking in New Jersey bars was now illegal, but Sam figured the law must be routinely flouted at the Gateway. Either that or so many cigarettes had been smoked here that it was going to take decades for the place to air out. Sam made his way toward the bar, feeling the soles of his shoes sticking to the residue of last night's spilled beer.

The bartender, a guy in his fifties in a short-sleeved white shirt, made fleeting eye contact. Sam interpreted that as the Kearny equivalent of "Hi, what can I get you?"

"Give me a beer and the fried fish plate." He didn't need a menu to know that the deep-fat fryer was the only method of cooking available in the Gateway kitchen. But Sam had eaten stewed monkey in Bangkok and grilled locusts in Ghana — he enjoyed going native.

The bartender plonked Sam's beer down and returned to polishing glasses at the far end of the bar. The only other customer, the guy who had shouted for the door to be closed, sat a few stools away, resolutely studying the pattern of foam in his glass. Sam also sat in silence. Eventually, the bartender approached with silverware and the steaming plate of fish and fries.

"Lookin' for someone to do a little work

for me." Sam directed his comments to the food, not the man carrying it. "Guy in the city said Boo Hravek might be right for the job. Know where I can find him?"

The bartender stared at him for a long moment without responding. Then he moved away, methodically wiping the already-clean bar as he went. When he got halfway down its length, he said, "What kind of work?"

"The kind of work he's good at."

"Who'd you say sent you?"

"I didn't."

The man nursing his beer suddenly roused himself. "Boo don't work for just anyone."

"I know." Sam dunked his french fry in catsup and held it suspended over his plate. "That's why I want him." He watched the two men exchange a glance. Apparently, he'd given a good response. He pressed his luck a little further. "There's good money in it." He didn't want to name a price, since he didn't know what Boo customarily received for doing whatever dirty deeds he specialized in.

"Boo'll be here in a little while. Sit tight." The bartender disappeared into the kitchen.

Sam returned to the mound of food before him. Not too bad, really — the cod was flaky and fresh, and that carefully aged grease gave it a nice tang. He ate and drank and watched drag racing on ESPN, waiting for Boo. There were worse ways to spend an afternoon. This working for Manny wasn't too bad.

Ten minutes later, the door of the bar flew open and crashed against the wall. Two men — very big men — stood outlined by the bright sunlight at their backs. The bartender and the other patron vaporized.

Boo had arrived.

CHAPTER ELEVEN

Carefully, Sam wiped his hands and his mouth and placed the napkin on the bar. He did not like to meet new people with grease on his fingers or catsup on his lip. Standing down from the bar stool, he nodded to the punks who had entered. "Sam Rosen."

The larger of the two men, early twenties but already toting a big beer belly, stepped forward and shoved Sam against the bar. "Last night, you were messin' with Deanie. What the fuck's up with that? What kinda bullshit you tryin' to pull?"

Deanie? Had that been the name of his informant at Club Epoch? Sam thought she'd been referring to herself as Teeny, which, given the size of her boobs, he'd assumed was a nickname bestowed upon her ironically. Good to have that clarified.

Ignoring the man who had pushed him, Sam stepped away from the bar and faced his companion. From the description of Boo Hravek provided by Travis via Manny, he was pretty sure that the quieter guy was the man himself and the other one was just along for some fun — fun that Sam hoped could be avoided.

Unlike the blockhead bodyguard, Boo Hravek had a gleam of intelligence in his eye as well as a set of pectorals that any man would envy. He was Sam's height, but a good fifty pounds of solid muscle heavier. Sam extended his hand. "Nice to meet you, Boo. Deanie speaks very highly of you."

"The bitch should learn to keep her mouth shut," the bodyguard said. Boo remained silent but took Sam's hand and crushed it in his grip.

Sam smiled, ignoring the pain shooting up his right arm. He watched as Boo relaxed, having established his alpha male status. It was important to Sam that his opponents not feel threatened by him. He wanted them cocksure and careless.

If he'd thought he and Boo could have their conversation in a civilized manner, Sam certainly would have pursued that route. But Boo had seen fit to bring the goon with him, and Sam could tell that rational discussion was out of the question in that quarter. So the only alternative was to neutralize the bodyguard and bring Boo into a position where he valued the opportunity to talk. It was doable — not easy, but doable.

"Have a seat." Sam gestured Boo toward the bar's empty tables and chairs as if he owned the place. When he saw Boo start to lower himself, Sam turned toward the goon and, without a blink of warning, rammed his head directly into the big man's soft gut. The bodyguard staggered, and Sam used that unbalanced moment to hook his foot around his opponent's ankles. The huge kid crashed down so quickly, he had no chance to put out his hands to break his fall. He landed flat on his prominent nose, which cracked with an audible snap. A blossom of red unfurled — dripping from his white polo shirt onto the floor next to his shoulder.

His bodyguard's collapse had come so suddenly that Boo was just beginning to rise from his chair when Sam pivoted and upended the heavy table, pinning the young man momentarily. The goon still lay on the floor, stunned that the blood pooling around him was his own.

"Broken nose makes a hell of a mess, doesn't it?" Sam reached down and compressed the carotid arteries on both sides of the goon's neck. Within eight seconds, he had passed out.

Sam returned his attention to Boo, who was now standing, warily keeping the table between them. When Boo spoke, his voice emerged incongruously high-pitched for a man with a steroid-thickened eighteen-inch-round neck. "You killed him. Why did you have to kill him?"

"Nah, that's just the Mr. Spock trick from *Star Trek*. Except I do it correctly — both sides of the neck. I *could* have killed him, but I chose not to." Sam straightened his shirt, which had come partially untucked in all the commotion. "Choice is a good thing, wouldn't you agree, Boo?"

Boo said nothing, his eyes darting from the main entrance to the kitchen door, neither of which promised any help or easy escape.

"Now *you* have a choice," Sam continued. "You can sit and have a little talk with me, or you can join your friend there."

Boo sat.

"Good. Deanie said you were a smart guy, and I see she was right." Sam remained standing and smiled down at his companion.

"Who are you?" Boo asked.

"Uh, uh, uh — I'm the one asking the

questions here. Tell me about the other night at Club Epoch."

Boo's eyes narrowed. "You're a cop. Why don't you just arrest me, then?"

"You insult me, Boo." Sam extended one long, skinny foot. "You ever see a cop in Bruno Magli loafers and a Hugo Boss blazer?"

Boo, a brand-sensitive thug, looked even more puzzled and uneasy. "Why you wanna know about Club Epoch?"

"Because a friend of mine is taking the fall for that bomb. I want to know who set him up."

"It wasn't me. I swear to God I didn't know what was going to go down. When that mailbox blew, I nearly shit myself."

"Boo, I'm losing respect for your intelligence. That's not even close to being a convincing lie."

Boo sat forward in his chair. "No, man, seriously — I didn't know about the bomb. All I was supposed to do was get this rich kid into Club E, buy him some drinks, then invite him to go to this after-hours club. We were on our way there when the whole mailbox thing went down."

"Boo, you're forgetting one little detail. It was one of your friends who put the bomb under the box. A guy named Zeke, or Freak or something. Maybe you have a reason for wanting to get rid of a federal judge."

"No, Freak wasn't one of our guys. He showed up at the club. Was hangin' around, talkin' to the boys. Knew a lot about music. When we all left, he came, too. I coulda run him off, but what did it matter? I was just supposed to take the kid to the after-hours place. If he wanted to come along, so what?"

"Did you see him put the bomb under the mailbox?"

Boo shook his head. "We were walking in a big group. I was in the lead with Paco. Suddenly, someone shouted 'Run' and everyone raced past us, so we started running, too. When the bomb blew, we were at the corner and we stopped to look back. Right away, the police showed up and started askin' questions. That's when I noticed Freak wasn't with us anymore."

"Did you tell the cops about him?"

Boo nodded. "They didn't seem all that interested. They talked to the Korean guy in the market, came back and talked to us some more, then said we could go. That's all I cared about. We split."

Sam studied Boo. A fine sheen of sweat clung to the punk's forehead. Systematically, he cracked all the knuckles on one big paw, then went to work on the other hand.

Sam had the sinking feeling that this yahoo was telling the truth. And that meant Manny's case was even more complicated than they'd suspected. "So, who asked you to get Paco into the club?"

Boo squirmed in his seat like a kid in the principal's office. "See, that's the part you're going to have a hard time believing."

"Try me."

"I got this call and a guy with a funny accent offered me five hundred bucks to get Paco into the club, get him some drinks, and take him out after closing. He was actin' all mysterious, said he'd leave the money in a paper bag at the playground." Boo shook his head. "It was like he watched too many movies, yanno?

"I thought someone was messin' with me. I went to the playground expecting some kind of scam. But the bag was there with the money, just like he said. So I figured, what the hell. It's no skin off my nose. We go to Club E all the time anyway."

"You didn't ask who he was, why he contacted you for this job?"

"He had my cell number. He had to have been referred by a friend."

Sam raised his eyebrows. "Some friend. Let's see your cell phone. Is this guy's number still in the calls received?"

"I already tried that. After the bomb went off and the cops came, I was pissed. We talked our way outta there, but I coulda been in big trouble. So I called the number back to ask what the fuck was going on, and the phone just rang and rang. Finally, some guy who sounded like a drunk answered and said it was a pay phone at Penn Station. I heard a train announcement in the background, so I knew he was telling the truth."

"All right, give me your cell number. We may need to talk again." Sam looked down at the congealing blood on the floor. "And I don't think we're going to be welcome here."

Boo rattled off a number and Sam stored it in his own phone, then pressed the call button just to make sure he hadn't been given the number for the Monmouth Park Racetrack. A shriek that passed for music emanated from Boo's pocket.

"Answer that and save the number," Sam directed. "Your mysterious friend calls again, let me know."

CHAPTER TWELVE

Manny raced from the parking lot toward federal court, feeling like she'd just been presented with a white-ribboned robin's egg blue box from Tiffany's. God bless Sam — he'd uncovered just the information she needed to clinch this bail hearing. And just in case, she had her usual small piece of red cloth pinned to the inside of her suit jacket to ward off the evil eye, just like her mother and her mother's mother had taught her. Can never be too careful, after all. Manny was a third-generation Scorpio, her generational DNA included an allele for the belief in the supernatural.

"By the time I'm done with Brian Lisnek, that prosecutor is going to be so covered with egg, you could make an omelette out of him," Manny crowed to Kenneth, who matched her stride for stride past the cement barriers protecting the massive new building across from the old post office.

"The last omelette you made for me was dry and rubbery," Kenneth complained. "Don't get overconfident."

Manny waved his warning off with a laugh, realizing as she did that if Jake had said the same thing to her, she would've been highly insulted. But Kenneth could get away with a lot of things that Jake wouldn't dare try, including, but not limited to, singing "Over the Rainbow" or anything Cher while wearing a vintage Dior sheath.

Jake had been impressed when she told him the judge had granted her the opportunity to examine the government's so-called forensic expert as well as their eyewitness at the bail hearing. That was highly unusual, but the Preppy Terrorist case was generating so much publicity that the judge had reluctantly agreed.

Now with the information Sam had provided and the research she had done on the shaky science of identifying bite marks through forensic odontology, Manny felt sure that she'd have Travis Heaton out on bail by the end of the day.

Sailing through the security check without setting off any alarms, Manny entered Judge Freeman's courtroom and took her place at the defense table. Lisnek was already at the prosecutor's table with a whole phalanx of assistants. "How many federal prosecutors does it take to change a lightbulb?" she muttered to Kenneth.

"You mean, to screw in a lightbulb. And the answer is none. Prosecutors only screw defendants."

Manny paused from unloading her briefcase. "Did you just make that up, or have you been reading joke e-mails when you're supposed to be working?"

"Keeping you amused is part of my job description, remember?"

Manny grinned. It was true that with Kenneth by her side she felt much more relaxed than she would have if she were assisted by some navy blue pinstriped-clad minion with an Ivy League law degree. Today, Kenneth had dressed to match the dark green marble that heralded the floors and walls of the imposing house of justice. He wore a slightly used Oscar de la Renta suit he had purchased on eBay, and two-toned green-and-ivory shoes with matching green horned-rimmed glasses. She slid some files across the table to him. "Here. Organize this for me. I don't want to be fumbling for notes when I have their so-called expert on the stand."

She sat down and watched Lisnek for a while. He was so busy conferring with his assistants, he didn't even notice her. Her client was escorted in by a muscular federal marshal and seated next to her. He wore the clothes he had been arrested in — big baggy pants and a black cotton shirt. The bailiff entered the courtroom and Lisnek snapped to attention, finally glancing her way. She smiled sweetly. The assistant U.S. attorney looked away.

"All rise," the bailiff intoned.

Showtime.

Manny and Lisnek danced through the opening procedures like Fred and Ginger, so familiar with the steps that they didn't even have to think about what they were doing. Then Lisnek rose to make his argument for why Travis should remain in jail without bail. "An act of terrorism against the federal government . . . possible coconspirators, so the accused must be kept in isolation . . . a matter of national security . . ." On and on he went.

Manny could feel her adrenaline surge and her stomach churn. This is what being a trial lawyer was all about — face-to-face combat with the enemy. Honestly, how could Lisnek say all this with a straight face? The man was shameless in his pursuit of publicity. She'd defended clients against bogus, trumped-up charges before, but this case beat all.

The judge was also tiring of Lisnek. With a slight elevation of the hand, he cut the prosecutor off in mid-speech. "Very eloquent, Mr. Lisnek, but this isn't a dress rehearsal for the opening argument of the trial. I believe Ms. Manfreda has some issues with the quality of your supporting evidence, so let's move directly to the expert testimony."

The witness, Dr. Eugene Olivo, forensic odontologist, was called and sworn in. In a jury trial, Manny would spend considerable time establishing the expert's qualifications or lack thereof, because juries tended to believe every word coming from the mouth of anyone who called himself a doctor or scientist. Judge Freeman, thankfully, was not so gullible. He had been a federal judge for more than four decades, handling all the hard cases: Mafia killings, an Aryan gang prison trial, massive drug cartel trials. Freeman was now on senior status, a form of hardworking retirement that allowed him to pick and choose his cases. Not impressed with the pretentiousness of office or enamored with the trappings of power, he no longer wore a robe on the bench. But make no mistake: He was a highly respected jurist, one you weren't late for unless you were dead, who mandated preparedness and honesty.

"So in other words, Doctor," the judge said, addressing the expert witness, "for the laypeople in the audience, what you are saying is that a forensic odontologist is a fancy word for . . . dentist?"

"Well, it's from the Greek, Your Honor."

"I see." A cross between a snort and a chuckle emanated from the bench. "Do you get to charge the government more in Greek?"

Touché. Old, retired, on senior status, Freeman took the words right out of her mouth.

Satisfied that Judge Freeman was going to give her fair latitude in cross-examination, Manny sat back and let Lisnek walk the witness through his evidence. "The average set of permanent teeth in an adult numbers thirty-two, including the four wisdom teeth," Olivo informed them.

Yada yada yada. She forced herself to listen to every word and make careful notes, only daydreaming for a split second about the Carramia case, where she had cross-examined Jake. Jake had been a charismatic expert witness in a geeky, scientific kind of way. Almost sexy, talking about vomit and death. His brown hair, interspersed with gray strands, complemented his big frame and professorial tone. Olivo was no Jake. Thank God for that.

"In short," Olivo finally opined, "the gap between the upper right lateral incisor and the adjoining canine tooth, also called a cuspid, along with the snagglelike characteristics of that canine tooth, establishes within a reasonable degree of medical scientific certainty that the impression in the apple is consistent with the bite dentition of Travis Heaton." He demonstrated his testimony with digital pictures of the subject apple.

Olivo sat back in the witness chair and folded his hands over his paunch. Manny smiled. How nice to see a witness so confident and comfortable.

She rose and walked toward the witness stand. Today's hairstyle, red mane caught back in a tortoiseshell clip, left the strand of pearls at her neck and the simple pearl studs in her ears exposed. She looked younger than her nearly thirty years, and too demure to cause trouble for a respected scientist.

Pompous old fart.

"Good morning, Dr. Olivo." She beamed at him. "Thank you for that fascinating information."

He nodded. "I've been at this a long

time." He left the "Not like you, girlie," unsaid.

"Tell me: Were you present at the crime scene after the explosion?"

"No, of course not." *I'm too important for that, you stupid twit.*

Manny smiled. Maybe the government's witness was so well rehearsed he would know the chain of custody of the oh-so-important piece of forensic evidence he wanted to use to damn her client to hell.

"So, who collected the apple?" she continued. "Was it the FBI's crime scene technicians?"

"No."

"Perhaps it was the CSI team from the Hoboken Police Department?"

"No."

"Then it must have been a tristate terrorist response unit?"

"Uh, no."

"So, who did pick up the apple, Dr. Olivo?"

"Uhm, I believe it was a police detective who returned to the scene later to look for it."

"And what did he do with it? Did he put it in a brown paper bag so that moisture wouldn't collect and bacteria wouldn't grow on it?"

Olivo shifted in his seat and straightened his triclub tie. "No, it was in a plastic Baggie when I got it."

"I see. Do you know what the temperature was on the night in question, Doctor?"

"I don't know the exact temperature," he snapped.

Manny walked back to the defense table and accepted a sheet of paper from Kenneth. "National Weather Service records show that at one a.m. on May seventeenth, the temperature at the monitoring station in Hoboken, New Jersey, was seventy-five degrees. Pretty warm for May, huh?"

"Yes." Olivo stared straight ahead.

"Did you examine the evidence that night, sir?"

"No."

"When did you get the evidence?"

"Let me look at my notes." As the page flipped, the doctor grabbed for the small plastic cup of water nearby.

Manny pretended not to notice how he gulped it down. She was making him squirm.

"The day after the bombing. I received the specimen at my office in Manhattan at one-forty-three in the afternoon."

"The apple had been refrigerated during the period of time since its collection, had it, Doctor?" Manny asked.

He hesitated.

Come on, give it up, Mr. Know-It-All expert witness. I already know the answer, or I wouldn't have asked the question.

"No."

Manny could tell he thought he knew where she was headed, but Lisnek looked impatient. She smiled at him in passing and returned to stand in front of the witness. "You know, Dr. Olivo, my Italian immigrant grandma grew up during the Depression and she hated to waste food. When I was a little girl, it would drive her crazy when I took a few bites out of an apple and then couldn't finish it. You know what she'd do? She'd wrap it up in plastic and put it on the counter and try to get me to eat it the next day. I never would. You know why?"

Lisnek jumped up. "Objection. We'll be here all day if we have to listen to Ms. Manfreda's reminiscences about her family heritage, Your Honor."

But Judge Freeman was grinning. "Tell us why you wouldn't eat it, counselor."

"Because by the next day, a bitten apple wrapped in plastic in a warm kitchen was all brown and mushy. Decay had set in. Yes, decay had completely broken down the exposed surface of the apple." Manny whipped around to take possession of something from Kenneth, keeping her back to everyone in the well of the courtroom. Murmurs began to rumble from the spectator pews. Manny turned to Olivo with the flare of a Miss Universe contestant whipping around a bathing-suit pareu on the turn toward the judges to show off her wares.

She held up an apple — a discolored, drying, decayed, smelly brownish red apple. "Let me represent to you that this is a Delicious apple, sir."

"Objection! Objection," bellowed Lisnek.

She ignored him. Judge Freeman was laughing too hard to rule on the objection.

"How can you say with scientific certainty that the bite marks in that apple were those of my client when the apple had been rotting away for over twelve hours under improper storage conditions?"

"Overruled," came the belated decision from the bench, allowing Manny to officially proceed. She looked over at Lisnek. He really needed to get shirts with collars that weren't so tight. His head looked like it was about to pop off his neck.

Olivo sputtered and offered some qualified justification, buttressed with technical jargon. "Scientific certainty only means it is more likely than not."

Ah, the dirty little secret of experts reared its head. Their opinion was nothing more than a game of chance.

"Are you telling this courtroom that your opinion, one that would incarcerate my eighteen-year-old client without bail, disrupt his schooling, prevent his graduation, and —"

"Objection," Lisnek again bellowed, his voice echoing through the courtroom doors and reverberating into the hall.

The recovered Judge Freeman turned to her. "Okay, enough with the sob story, Ms. Manfreda. Get on with the question."

"— is based on a mere possibility about a degraded apple?"

Manny continued to hammer him, rebutting his claims about the reliability of bite-mark evidence with quotes from articles on forensic odontology, and the language in recent court decisions where bite-mark testimony had wrongfully imprisoned innocent people.

Before she concluded her inquisition, she made a few final thrusts.

"Did you bring the apple with you today?"
"No."

"Did the prosecutor tell you to leave it in the city?"

"No."

Manny smelled something wrong, and it wasn't just her one piece of forbidden fruit. This ordinarily talkative expert had become a one-word-answer witness.

"Where is your apple now?"

"It's been discarded. Once we documented the impressions with photographs, there was no reason to keep it any longer."

A hush came over the journalists listening to the proceeding. She thought she heard Mrs. Heaton gasp. Her client reached out and grabbed Manny's hand.

"Your Honor, I move the whole case be thrown out also. The assistant U.S. attorney has specifically withheld this material fact from the court. Spoliation of evidence, Your Honor, is cause for dismissal."

Lisnek tried to respond. Judge Freeman interrupted the proceedings. "There is no need to deal with that issue today."

Lisnek preened. His smugness was short-lived.

Judge Freeman had listened to it all attentively, but it was clear that in the end he was most impressed with the unintended scientific study of Granny Manfreda. "Your rotten apple is out as evidence, Mr. Lisnek. I'll issue my written opinion next week. What else do you have?"

"We have an eyewitness who saw Mr. Heaton place the bomb, sir." Lisnek spoke in a firm, steady voice, but Manny noticed him gripping his government-issued pen until his knuckles turned white.

CHAPTER THIRTEEN

Manny took a deep breath as Mr. Park Sung Ho was sworn in. The cross-examination of Dr. Olivo had gone very well, but she wasn't out of the woods yet.

Mr. Park was a delicate man with the bright, watchful eyes of a songbird. He took his duty seriously, both as an employee of the Happy Garden deli and as a witness in federal court. Juries automatically liked earnest, hardworking people like him. Even though there was no jury present today, Manny felt she had to be careful. It had been okay to make that pompous ass Olivo look like a fool; it wouldn't do to humiliate Mr. Park.

Manny tuned in as Lisnek took the witness through the preliminaries. No, he didn't own the deli; his cousin did. Yes, he had been working alone there on the night of May 17. He worked every night. "Cousin only trust me to work overnight shift," Mr.

Park said.

Six young men had come in together that night; Mr. Park's eyebrows drew down as he recalled what had happened. "They try trick me. They give twenty-dollar bill. They take back, give ten. They add candy bar, take away chips, switching, switching. Try confusc so not have to pay for everything."

Manny glanced over at Travis, who had slid down in his seat. So far, Mr. Park's memory was accurate. This man had the power to send her client to prison for a long timc, but Manny found herself sympathizing with him. An immigrant, struggling to make it in a tough town, protecting his family's assets — who couldn't feel for the little man as he was hassled by a group of kids?

"On way out the door, that boy" — Mr. Park pointed at Travis with assurance — "take apple from bin. No pay."

With ever-increasing confidence, Lisnek led Mr. Park through his testimony about the explosion. Did Mr. Park get to the door of the store in time to see the boys reach the mailbox? Yes. Did Mr. Park see the boy who had stolen the apple take a bite and then throw the apple in the gutter? Yes. Did that same boy then bend down and place a package under the mailbox? Yes, most emphatically. Did the mailbox then explode? Yes, yes, yes.

"No further questions." Lisnek turned his back on the Korean store clerk and strode back to his seat.

Manny rose and smiled at the witness. "Good morning, Mr. Park. Thank you for that account. You're obviously a very observant person."

Mr. Park nodded, pleased that Manny recognized his good qualities.

"Mr. Park, did you see one of the other boys also take an apple from the bin?"

"No, just that boy."

"Were all six boys at the cash register at the same time?"

"No. Come and go."

"So one of the other boys could have taken an apple while you were busy with the ones who were paying."

"I watch all customer. Make sure no one steal."

"I'm sure you do, Mr. Park. But while some of the boys were trying to trick you as they paid, maybe another also took an apple. Is that possible?"

He shrugged reluctantly. "Maybe."

"When you followed the boys out onto the sidewalk, did you see the face of the one who put the package under the mailbox?"

"No. See boy who took apple bite it, then throw down. He one who put package."

"What was the boy wearing?"

"Blue jean. T-shirt."

"What color T-shirt?"

Mr. Park hesitated. "Dark."

"What were the other boys wearing?"

"Same. Blue jean, dark T-shirt," the witness replied promptly.

Poor Mr. Park. He was so eager to be honest and do a good job that he didn't even realize how he had undermined his own evidence. This was why eyewitness testimony was so unreliable, especially cross-racial identification. Most people didn't lie intentionally. They said what they were sure they saw. But there were so many variables, so many subtle differences that could create the same reality.

Manny looked Mr. Park in the eye and spoke without any hint of accusation. "So, if all the boys were dressed similarly, and you couldn't see their faces from where you were standing, and it's possible one of the other boys also took an apple, isn't it possible that the person you saw eating the apple and placing the bomb was *not* my client, Travis Heaton, but one of the others?"

Mr. Park's eyes darted from Lisnek to the judge and back to Manny, searching for some guidance. The courtroom was silent.

"Mr. Park, please answer the question," Judge Freeman said. "Is it possible that the person you saw placing the bomb was not Travis Heaton?"

Mr. Park seemed to have shrunk inside the cheap black suit he'd put on for this important occasion.

"Possible," he whispered.

"Mr. Park, after the explosion, when all the boys ran, did you notice if one of them ran in a different direction?"

"Yes. One run down Washington Street, turn up Eleventh. Go toward hill, Sinatra Drive. Others stop on corner. Then police come."

"Did you see if the one you thought placed the bomb ran straight or turned down Eleventh Street?"

Mr. Park bit his lower lip and lowered his eyes, concentrating. Then he looked up at Manny. "Cannot say for sure. Explosion big bright light, everyone running. Then one boy turn, others go straight. Not sure which." Mr. Park was the soul of honesty. Yes, you had to like this man.

"Thank you, Mr. Park."

Mr. Park looked around the courtroom, expecting praise from every corner. Judge Freeman smiled benevolently. Manny beamed. Brian Lisnek's lips were compressed in a thin line, his eyes focused resolutely on the yellow pad before him. He never looked up as the Korean grocer exited the courtroom.

"Well, you've certainly established reasonable doubt, Ms. Manfreda." The glance Judge Freeman cast at Lisnek implied he thought the prosecutor better get busy improving his case. And that was the risk of this bail hearing — it gave Lisnek an advance look at her defense, allowing him to prepare for her best shots. The information Sam had provided was her ace in the hole. Would she have to use it?

"I'm inclined to grant Ms. Manfreda's request for bail," the judge continued. "My only concern is the implication that this bombing is part of some larger conspiracy. What evidence do you have to support that, Mr. Lisnek?"

Lisnek turned to the other lawyers on his team. A lot of low murmuring and head shaking ensued. Finally, the assistant U.S. attorney rose.

"We would prefer not to reveal that information at this time, Your Honor."

Manny's eyes narrowed. Did that mean he had nothing to back up his claim, or did he really have information that she should know but didn't?

"We will agree to the bail of five hundred thousand dollars, cosigned by his mother," Lisnek continued.

"Five hundred thousand!" Manny protested. "It might as well be ten million. My client can't make that!"

"We're not releasing a terrorist on his own recognizance." Now Lisnek was up and shouting, too.

Manny turned to Judge Freeman, trying to tap into the sympathy she'd felt coming from him. "Your Honor, what is accomplished by holding this young man in prison with truly violent rapists and murderers? It's like a death sentence before he's even convicted of any crime."

"No need for melodrama, Ms. Manfreda. We'll hold him in protective custody," the judge said.

Manny's heart rate kicked up a notch. Protective custody was just another word for solitary confinement — more punishment, not less. The government could drag its feet for months on this case. By the time they got to trial, Travis would be a total head case from spending twenty-three hours a day alone in an eight-by-ten cell. But Judge Freeman wouldn't be moved by that argument. Manny aimed below the belt.

"Protective custody didn't help Roberto Vallardo."

Manny saw the judge flinch. Vallardo, awaiting trial for molesting his young stepdaughter, had been killed by other inmates while supposedly being kept in protective custody. Two days later, DNA evidence proved that someone else had raped the child.

Judge Freeman tapped his pen and studied Travis. Manny kept her mouth shut, letting her client's scrawny arms and hunched shoulders do the talking.

When the judge spoke again, his tone was softer. "I can't just let him go. He has to realize there are ramifications to his actions."

"Absolutely, Your Honor," Manny said. "I suggest that my client be confined to his home, permitted to leave only to go to school, and monitored by means of an electronic ankle bracelet."

More conferring at the enemy table. "Fine," Lisnek said. "But one transgression with that bracelet and he's behind bars."

CHAPTER FOURTEEN

Cold beer, greasy food, sassy waitresses —
Ian's Pub was the kind of neighborhood
joint you used to be able to find every
couple of blocks in New York. Now, with
sushi and tapas and pinot noir encroaching
from every side, the place was an isolated
fortress of grit. Jake entered and dodged
around some dithering women who apparently thought a maître d' was going to
materialize from somewhere and escort
them to a table. They'd be waiting till next
Sunday. He strode over to the very last table
without guilt — and kept an eye on the door
for Pasquarelli.

While he waited, Jake mulled over the
information he had gathered on the kind of
implement that might have been used to
cause the electrical burns on Amanda Hogaarth. He had spoken to several other
forensic pathologists, both in the United
States and abroad, who specialized in cases

of torture. Electrical shocks were a common form of torture, yet the photos of the Hogaarth autopsy that he had sent them by e-mail had not produced any exact matches to the kind of burning experienced by recent victims of repressive regimes in Africa and the Mideast. Most of these people had obvious external burns caused by a cattle prod or similar large instrument. Amanda Hogaarth's burns had been more subtle.

The Vampire's other victims had all reported the assaults committed on them, outraged at their violation. Would Ms. Hogaarth have done the same had she lived? Had the Vampire intended to kill her, or had the torture just gone too far, given her already-weakened heart?

Vito Pasquarelli appeared shortly after the waitress interrupted Jake's reverie by slamming two beer mugs on the table and vanishing for parts unknown. The detective's polyester tie and brown sports coat looked like they were dragging down a drowning man. If clothes could surrender, Vito's would have marched themselves off to Goodwill.

Jake pushed a beer toward Pasquarelli as he collapsed into the booth. "Here. I took the liberty of ordering for you while I had the chance."

"The usual?" Pasquarelli inquired hope-fully.

"Is there anything else?"

"Good. This may be the last meal I get today. This case gets weirder by the minute, and the commissioner is all over us to get it solved."

"What have you found out about Amanda Hogaarth?"

Pasquarelli took a long swig from his beer and started to talk. "The woman lived in that apartment for eight years. It seems she just popped up in New York one day. We can't find any trace of where she lived before. No relatives. The emergency contact she listed on her apartment-rental applica-tion is her lawyer. Guy says he met her once, eight years ago, to draw up her will. She left all her money — a cool two million — to a place called Family Builders."

"Which is . . ."

"A nonprofit agency specializing in find-ing homes for hard-to-adopt kids. Older, disabilities, emotional problems. Folks over there can't believe their luck."

"Let me guess: They've never heard of Amanda Hogaarth."

Pasquarelli nodded. "Not on their mailing list, never applied to adopt a kid, never even sent them ten bucks at Christmas."

"Neighbors, building staff — what do they know?"

"Jackshit. Neighbors say she'd say hello only if you greeted her first; otherwise, she'd walk right by you. Both the doorman and the concierge say they can't ever remember her having a visitor, and the doorman's been there eight years. Went out almost every day around ten a.m., came back around two."

"And she went . . ."

"Shopping in the neighborhood, lunch every day at a coffee shop on Madison near Sixtieth. Left a good tip, never chatted to the waiters. It's positively creepy the way she never talked to anyone. I mean, how is it possible to live eight years in New York and never say more than 'I'll have the tuna on toast'?"

"She had to have left some financial trail," Jake said.

"No credit cards. Paid cash for everything. Kept about five hundred grand in CDs at Citibank, the rest in a blue-chip stock portfolio. Every few months, she'd cash in a CD, put the money in her checking account, and draw it down. She doesn't show up in the IRS system until eight years ago, when she started paying income tax on the interest earned on her investments. She apparently never worked."

"In this country," Jake added. "Remember the Spanish-language cookbook and the fact that her fillings didn't appear to be American-made. Was she an immigrant? Have you checked INS records?"

"We're doing that now. Their computers have spit out a few Hogaarths in her age range. They're all German, all accounted for. INS is still looking."

The waitress arrived with their food: one-third-pound bacon and Swiss cheeseburgers with french fries and onion rings. Not a scrap of greenery in sight, not even a pickle.

"Ah, myocardial infarction on a plate." Jake sighed.

Pasquarelli prepared to dive in. "Can you believe my daughter says I ought to start eating tofu burgers?"

"That's what you get for sending her to college in Vermont." Jake bit into the pure nirvana of the Ian's burger, greasy and proud. "So what did this elderly woman, who never talked to anyone, know that was worth torturing her for?"

"How the hell can I find out if I can't locate one person who ever had a conversation with her?"

"You have to go back to this Family Builders place," Jake advised. "Why did she choose that charity to leave her money to, not the Cancer Society or the Red Cross or a home for wayward cats? It's not a high-profile group. There has to be some personal connection there."

Pasquarelli waved a french fry in Jake's direction. "They've been very cooperative. Let us go through their mailing list and financial records. The director, Lydia Martinette, assures me no one named Hogaarth ever adopted or applied to adopt through their agency, and no kid with the surname Hogaarth was ever placed through their agency."

"And you believe her?"

"Why shouldn't I? I checked this place out, Jake. Social Services, family court — they all say Family Builders does great work. You should see the pictures in the waiting room — kids in wheelchairs, mentally challenged kids, kids who've been bouncing around foster care for years, and Mrs. Martinette finds them all homes."

"That may well be, but Mrs. Martinette is just looking for the obvious connections; you might be able to find more subtle ones there in the files," Jake said.

"They're confidential adoption records, Jake. No judge is going to give me a subpoena to go on a fishing expedition when I don't have the slightest evidence that I'll find something relative to Amanda Hogaarth's murder."

Jake sighed. Of course Pasquarelli was right. The only clues they had to Amanda Hogaarth's murder were a Spanish-language cookbook, an adoption agency, and a torture method. They needed more data points here. Suddenly, a vision popped into Jake's head: the clean ring on Hogaarth's coffee table left by an object the criminalists had taken away. "Say, did the crime-scene guys find any prints on that thing they took from the vic's apartment — what was it, a cup, a glass?"

Pasquarelli drained his beer and looked around Ian's.

"You want another beer?" Jake raised his hand to signal. "Our waitress is over there."

The detective yanked Jake's hand down. "No! Don't call her." Pasquarelli leaned forward and Jake did the same, straining to hear his friend's suddenly lowered voice over the clamor of the bar crowd. "I'm not supposed to tell anyone this. They lifted a perfect print from a coffee mug. We sent it off to SAFIS, the national fingerprint database, and the next thing you know, I got a call."

Pasquarelli twisted his head around again.

Jake thought he would have rotated it 360 degrees if that were biologically possible. "I'm to report to Twenty-six Federal Plaza tomorrow to discuss that print with none other than the assistant director in charge of the FBI, David Conroy. He's flying in from Washington, D.C., especially for this meeting."

CHAPTER FIFTEEN

Sam sat at his brother's dining room table, reading the *New York Times,* a cup of steaming coffee before him. Things sure had improved around here since Jake started seeing Manny. Now there was always French-roast coffee and toast made with Portuguese sweet bread in the kitchen, not to mention toilet paper in the bathroom. Ah, the civilizing influence of women! He glared at his brother, also engrossed in the *Times,* across the table. One thing hadn't changed. There was only one copy of the paper delivered, and he, as the uninvited guest, had to content himself with the sections Jake cast off. He'd already read the Arts and Dining Out sections, and he had no interest whatsoever in Business. That left Metro, since Jake was selfishly hogging both Sports and the main section. He picked it up unenthusiastically.

MAYOR VOWS TO RAISE CITY READING

SCORES. Yeah, yeah, they kept that story on file and had been rerunning it every year since he'd been in kindergarten; CITY TO ALLOW PEOPLE TO CHOOSE SEX ON THEIR BIRTH CERTIFICATES — only in New York. Sam turned the page. LONG ISLAND PO-LITICO ACCUSED OF CORRUPTION, like that was news. He glanced over at his brother, who appeared deeply engrossed in the op-ed page. Then why couldn't he have Sports? Sam casually extended his long fingers and slowly drew the Yankees coverage closer.

Slap!

Sports was snatched back.

"C'mon, Jake, you can't read two sections at once. Just let me check the standings."

"No, I won't get it back. I want to read the paper in peace before I leave for work. You have all day to read it. Wait."

Sam sighed and returned to the Metro section. No new stories on the Vampire or the Preppy Terrorist. It really was a slow news day. He turned to the third page of the section and scanned the "Metro Briefs," stories so minor that they didn't merit a by-lined article. A fire in Westchester, a hit-and-run in Connecticut . . . His gaze slid down the column in boredom, then stopped, riveted.

EXECUTION-STYLE SLAYING IN KEARNY

On May 24, police found the body of a twenty-three-year-old man in a litter-strewn lot in Kearny, New Jersey. He had been shot once in the temple, execution style. The victim was identified as Benjamin Hravek, who worked intermittently as a roofer. Police are seeking a ponytailed, tall, thin Caucasian male with silver hair, age approximately thirty-five, known to have had a violent encounter with Hravek at the Gateway Inn several days before his death.

The Metro section slipped onto the table and Sam stared out the window behind his brother's left shoulder.

"Oh, here — take the damn Sports." Jake tossed him the section.

But Sam was already out of the room by the time the newspaper landed.

Manny paced the space in front of her desk with the phone pressed to her ear. She covered the distance in a few strides of her long legs, pivoted at the first of the white Carrera leather chairs she had purchased to inspire the confidence of her clients, and marched back toward the other chair, where Mycroft sat licking his paw.

"I want to talk to your client and find out what the hell's going on." Sam's voice came through the phone loud enough to make Mycroft's ears perk. "This little odd job you recruited me for is going to end up getting me arrested for murder."

"Look on the bright side, Sam. You'll have the best defense counsel on the east coast."

"Damn it, Manny! This isn't funny. There's some serious shit going down here."

"I know there is, Sam. And I'm not sure it has anything to do with the Iqbar case and Islamic terrorism. You know, Brueninger has presided over scores of controversial cases. What if the feds were sidetracked by Travis's reading material? What if they're looking at this all wrong?"

"You've got a point. I can't see a guy like Boo agreeing to work for a bunch of Muslim extremists. He's more of an organized crime kind of guy." Sam paused. "Was, I should say. Did Brueninger preside over any Mafia trials?"

"I've got a list of every case that came before him in the past five years," Manny said. "There was a Mafia money-laundering case a while back where a few mid-level capos got sent to minimum-security prison. I don't see the mob retaliating over that. They take those convictions as the cost of doing business."

"Yeah," Sam agreed. "A little R and R and the boys are back to work. Besides, Boo's not Italian. Hravek is what — Czech, Hungarian, Serbian?"

Manny scanned the list of Brueninger's cases. "Hey, here's something. The judge convicted a bunch of guys from former Soviet-bloc countries for human trafficking — smuggling poor Albanian girls into the country and forcing them into prostitution."

"Sex-slave traders. They sound like the kind of guys who might carry a nice grudge against the man who sent them away."

Manny had done a Google search on the case while she and Sam were talking. "Apparently, he sent them far away. They were deported to serve their sentences in Albania."

"Eeew — that sounds unpleasant. *If* they're still there. But who knows — bribe the right people in the old country and they could very well be back on the streets here in New Jersey."

"And how would we ever know?" Manny asked. "We can't do follow-up in Albania."

"I'm relieved to hear you say so, because I'm not taking a field trip to Tirana."

Manny kicked at the side of her desk in frustration, then hopped up and down in pain. Mycroft studied her mournfully. Since getting expelled from the Little Paws doggy day-care center for fighting with a Boston terrier, he'd been spending long days in the office with Manny. "Somehow we have to find out who hired Boo, and why. Why did the bomber want to involve Travis?"

"Travis and/or Paco," Sam said. "The two guys Boo took with him to Club Epoch aren't going to know anything. We have to find the other guy, Freak."

"Or Deke or Zeke," Manny said. "No one seems clear on his name, where he came from, or where he disappeared to."

"The police maintain a database of nicknames bad guys use on the street," Sam said. "Do you know if the feds tried to find this guy in there?"

Manny dropped into her desk chair and swiveled to look out the window. Twenty floors below, the hustle and flow of lower Manhattan moved silently by. "If you ask me, the feds seem to be doing all they can to pretend our mystery man never existed. And I find that in itself to be very suspicious."

"Ah, Manny — you see conspiracies everywhere. Why not give plain old incompetence credit sometimes?"

"You're right, Sam. It's hard to overestimate that on the federal level. Luckily, I know a guy high up in the New Jersey Bureau of Criminal Justice. I'll suggest he run those names for us — for their investigation."

Manny waved Kenneth into the office. He was wearing a faux tiger-skin shirt topped by a short feather boa jacket. The jacket was a concession to the need for formal law office decorum. Despite his new natural-toned acrylic nails, he'd done an excellent job typing up the Eduardo wrongful death summary judgment brief that had to be filed with the court the next day.

"Thanks, Kenneth. I'll sign that and you can send it off."

"Hello? Are you still there?" Sam demanded.

"Sorry. Where was I?"

"Tracking down Freak."

"Right. If I could find him, the feds would have to accept that Travis didn't plan this. If I can't, I have to find another way to convince them Travis was an unwitting dupe, not an intentional coconspirator."

"Are you sure that's true?"

Manny sighed. "Not entirely. And that's exactly why I'm telling you to stay away from Travis Heaton. He's under house arrest, and I'm sure there are federal marshals keeping an eye on his apartment. If they see you waltzing into his building, a fleet of cruisers will be waiting for you when you come out. I'll talk to him."

This suggestion was met with silence. Finally, Sam spoke again. "Okay, maybe you're right."

Manny smiled. There was a sentence you'd seldom hear any man utter.

"Listen, this is what I want you to find out. Whose idea was it that they go to Club Epoch? Why that place, that night? Did Travis know they were going to be meeting anyone?"

"I want to know those things, too, Sam. And believe me, I intend to find out."

"And what about this Paco kid — are you going to talk to him?" Sam demanded.

Manny switched the phone to her other ear and reached out to stroke Mycroft. He yipped and scooted away from her hand. "Mikey, what's —"

"Manny! What about Paco?"

She wasn't eager to answer this question. The truth was, Paco Sandoval was proving quite elusive and it was really pissing her off. And worrying her. He was hiding behind his diplomatic immunity and letting his friend take the fall. If Paco was just an innocent dupe, as Travis claimed to be, then why wouldn't he at least cooperate in his friend's defense? She suspected that this mysterious caller who'd contacted Boo Hravek was somehow connected to Paco. But how could she prove it if she couldn't even talk to the kid? His family's apartment near the UN was a veritable fortress; the Monet Academy had treated her like a damn pedophile when she tried to reach Paco there. Still, she didn't want Sam to panic. She could handle this.

"Look, Sam, Travis went to school today, and he'll talk to Paco and let him know we need to meet with him. I'll work it out."

"You'd better. Call me as soon as you're done with those kids."

"Fine. Expect to hear from me by five."

As soon as she'd put the phone down, Manny scooped up Mycroft to examine the paw he was licking. The dog held perfectly still as her fingers searched gently. Then he shuddered and yelped when Manny found the swollen wound hidden in his curls. He'd been bitten by that damn terrier! The nip he'd given Kimo had been in self-defense.

"Oh, Mikey, I've got to get you to the vet. You're wounded. And unjustly accused, too."

■ ■ ■ ■

Jake peered at slides through a microscope set up on a small side table in his office. While he'd been obsessed with the Vampire, a multitude of work on other cases had piled up. Stacks of case folders and unproofed autopsy reports teetered on his desk. The medical degrees and awards hanging on his walls seemed to mock him as he worked.

As much as he tried to focus on wrapping up the details of these other cases, thoughts of the Vampire continued to derail his concentration.

A light tap at the door made him look up. Vito Pasquarelli stood on the threshold of his office, looking as gaunt and nervous as Jake had ever seen him.

"What's the matter?"

Vito stepped into the office, shut the door, and leaned on it. "I had my meeting with the FBI this morning." His eyes were half-closed as he spoke. "They want to take over the case."

"That's good news, isn't it?" Jake came out from behind his desk and waved Pasquarelli into a chair beside him. "This Vampire thing has put you in the hot seat. Let them have it."

Pasquarelli shook his head. "The mayor's fighting it. Ever since the FBI fouled up that near-miss subway bombing in Brooklyn and let the conspirators slip away, the mayor never misses a chance to hang the feds out to dry. He says no one does a better job of protecting New Yorkers than the NYPD."

Jake grinned. "His confidence in you is touching."

"Yeah, yeah, tell me about it. He's just grandstanding for reelection, and jabbing our congressmen for not getting New York more federal antiterrorism money. That all looks great on the news, but I'm the one who's gotta figure out how to solve this Vampire thing, and I don't see how I'm going to do it if the FBI gets its knickers in a twist and refuses to help me."

"Why do they want the case? What do they know that you don't?"

"They know whose fingerprint was on that coffee mug, but they don't know how it got there. And neither do I."

"It didn't get there when the person was drinking from the mug?"

Vito leaned back and stared at the warped and grimy ceiling of Jake's office. "Well, maybe. But he sure as hell wasn't having a drink with Ms. Hogaarth."

"Why not? Whose print is it?"

The detective gave up on trying to divine the future by reading the stains in the acoustic tile and met Jake's eye. He spoke the words as distinctly as if he were calling the person forward to accept an award.

"The former president of the United States — Richard Milhous Nixon."

CHAPTER SIXTEEN

Manny stood on the front stoop of the five-story walk-up on West Ninety-seventh Street and pressed the button next to the faded nameplate reading HEATON. When nothing happened in response, she pressed again.

She'd managed to squeeze in a visit to Mycroft's new vet on the way to Travis's apartment, but the detour made her fifteen minutes late for her client. Dr. Costello had been so accommodating, examining Mycroft right away, bandaging him up, and even placing a call to Little Paws to argue, successfully, for Mycroft's readmission. Efficient, kind, and handsome, too. But Dr. Frederic Costello was married, to his receptionist, and she had Jake, so enough of that little daydream.

Manny leaned on the button again and tried shouting into the scratched and dirty speaker. "Mrs. Heaton? It's me, Manny Manfreda."

144

A window on the second floor opened and a woman in a green-and-orange housecoat leaned out. "Bell don't work. You gotta call." The window slammed down.

Manny sighed and dug out her cell phone. But as she dialed, the buzzer opening the outer door sounded and she was admitted to the building. In the small tiled vestibule, Manny was assaulted by the mingled scents of industrial-strength roach spray, cooked cabbage, and ammonia. The stairs ahead were steep and narrow. Manny looked down ruefully at her Chanel wedges and began the long climb to the fourth floor.

On the second floor, the sounds of Spanish-language holy-roller radio blared. *"¡Dios, Dios! ¡Yo te amo Dios!"* over and over, barely muffled by the scratched brown metal door to apartment 2A. This was not the kind of two-bedroom Manhattan apartment most Monet Academy students were familiar with. She wondered if Travis ever brought his friends home. She wondered what he felt when he visited them in their luxury co-ops and town houses.

Manny shifted her purse to her other shoulder and kept climbing, pausing to catch her breath at the next landing, but she was motivated to press on by the intense cooking smells on the third floor. With a stitch in her side, she reached apartment 4A, positioning herself directly in front of the peephole before she knocked, so Mrs. Heaton could see her clearly.

She had barely grazed the door with her knuckles when it flew open. "Thanks for coming. I'm sorry I'm still in my work clothes. I just got in a few minutes ago." Maureen Heaton stepped back to let Manny in. The door opened directly into the kitchen, a room with cracked greenish linoleum and a window that looked out onto a brick wall. Manny hadn't seen such an ancient gas stove since she'd last visited her great-aunt Cecilia.

"Can I get you a drink?" Mrs. Heaton offered. "Lemonade? Tea?"

"Just a glass of water will be fine, thanks." Manny tried not to pant as she spoke.

Mrs. Heaton gave her the water and led her down a long, narrow hall that ran past two closed doors and ended in a small, bright room overlooking Ninety-seventh Street. "Have a seat," Mrs. Heaton directed. "Travis should be home any minute now."

Grateful for the rest, Manny dropped onto the lumpy sofa, which was not completely sheathed by a ready-made slipcover. The room was filled with books. Books, and photos of Travis. Travis as an infant, Travis at his first birthday party, Travis on the shoulders of a tall, thin man who was obviously Mr. Heaton. More recently, Travis playing violin, Travis receiving a science fair award, and Travis in a Monet Academy fencing competition.

"So, Maureen, before Travis gets here, tell me a little about Paco Sandoval. How long have the boys been friends?"

Maureen sighed, the sigh of every mother who's ever disapproved of her kid's friends but can't figure out what to do about it. "Paco. Well, Paco is everything that Travis isn't. Wealthy, worldly, popular, hot with the girls."

Manny arched her eyebrows. "Yet he befriended Travis?" In her experience, that wasn't how high school worked.

"They were placed together in a peer tutoring program," Maureen explained. "Paco was failing math and chemistry. With Travis's help, he got his grades up to *B*'s."

"So, Travis is a chemistry whiz?"

"Oh, yes! He won a special competi—" Maureen stopped mid-gush and turned on Manny. "Don't tell me *you* think Travis built that bomb?"

"No." *Maybe not at this very moment, but try me again tomorrow.* "But, Maureen," Manny continued, "it's important that I

147

know absolutely every detail of Travis's life that the prosecution could possibly use against him."

Maureen rose and paced around the room. "I always knew Paco would manage to get Travis into trouble, but I figured it would be for something like cheating on homework or drinking at a party. Not this — federal terrorism! What could I do? I tried to reason with Travis, but he wouldn't hear one bad word about his friend. Travis was always a little socially backward. He had his own interests, which kept him occupied. Paco ushered him into the circle of cool kids. Travis would do anything for that boy."

"Our goal is to get Paco to do something for Travis. Why is he being so elusive? Can we appeal to his parents? Do you know them?"

Maureen shoved her hands into the pockets of her aqua nurse's smock. "I don't have the free time during the day to volunteer at the Monet Academy the way some of the mothers do. I don't know any of those women well."

Manny felt a flash of sympathy. Poor Maureen was excluded from the Monet in-crowd as surely as her son had been.

"You've never met the Sandovals at school

concerts or sporting events?"

"They're often traveling. I see more of them in the society pages of the Sunday *Times* than at school. But I did see them once at the senior class play. Paco had a small part, but Mrs. Sandoval was carrying on like he was Matthew Broderick. Ambassador Sandoval looked bored and irritated. He's very severe — nothing like Paco, even though there's a physical resemblance."

"So you like Paco?"

Maureen shrugged. "It's hard not to. He's funny and charming and has beautiful manners. Every inch the diplomat's son. At first, I was thrilled that he befriended Travis. Paco helped my son fit in at Monet. Travis's first two years there were rough. He was constantly pressuring me to let him transfer to public school. Then Paco came along, and Travis started to enjoy school."

"And then something happened?" Manny prompted.

Maureen shrugged again. "Nothing dramatic. Just these past few months, Travis hasn't talked to me as much; he's secretive, and I don't always know where he is." She fiddled with the stethoscope that still hung around her neck. "But everyone told me that was normal. 'He's growing up,' they'd say. 'You have to let him go.' And now look what's happened. I —"

Manny jumped up from the couch, hoping to avert another full-scale emotional breakdown. She glanced at her watch. "It's nearly four — shouldn't Travis be home by now?" A twinge of worry rose up in her throat, but she pushed it resolutely down. She was the lawyer, not the overprotective mother of an only child.

Maureen looked at her own watch in alarm. "He's always home by now. He certainly wouldn't have stayed after school without calling. Not with all that's going on." She rose and looked out the window. "Unless there was some delay on the subway . . ." Maureen's upper lip trembled. "What could have happened? Should I call the school?"

"Wait a minute." Manny looked over at the two closed bedroom doors. "Is it possible Travis has been home all this time? You said you just walked in before I arrived. Maybe he's in his room, plugged into his iPod." The worry subsided. That must be it. She suspected Travis was none too eager to talk to her again. He was probably lurking in his room, trying to postpone the inevitable for as long as possible.

Relief flooded the mother's face and she strode down the hall. "You're probably right. I'm always calling him and he never hears me." She rapped sharply on the first door. "Travis, honey, are you in there? Ms. Manfreda is here to talk to us."

She opened the door without waiting for an answer, Manny right on her heels.

For a moment, all Manny could discern by the dim light of the shaded window were papers and clothes. Piles of each covered the floor, the bed, and every other level surface. The next thing she noticed was the electronic hum emitted by not one but three computers — two desktop, one laptop — and assorted other speakers, hard drives, routers, and mice. Was that lump in the bed Travis, or just a tangle of sheets and blankets? Maureen flicked on the wall switch and light flooded the room.

Manny watched as Maureen's eyes darted back and forth, desperately searching for Travis, willing him to be there. She stepped forward to examine the interconnected maze of computers that occupied the desk and a folding table in the corner of the room.

"Quite a bit of equipment he's got here." Manny sized it up — the very latest models. Ironically, the deluxe Apple laptop was one that she had wanted for herself but had passed up in favor of a spree at the Henri

Bendel trunk show new designer event.

"Computers are Travis's passion. He earned the money to buy most of this. Never needed any help getting a job from the school placement office."

Manny estimated the equipment before her added up to about two decades' worth of babysitting. The more she learned about Travis, the more he worried her.

Next to the desk was a bookcase. Three shelves were jammed with books; the top shelf was empty. Maureen saw Manny looking at it. "That's where the police took away Travis's books."

"Maureen, why didn't they take his computers?"

"Well, truth be known, Travis had moved them to a friend's house the day before he was arrested. An old one was here on the desk, and the FBI did take that," Maureen explained.

The more Manny heard the more she worried Travis was guilty.

"It also seems like they took a lot more books than what he had for his comparative religion class."

"Travis got interested in the subject and did more than the required reading." Maureen got huffy. "I've always encouraged his intellectual curiosity."

"Mmm. How long would you say he's had this interest in Islam?"

Maureen turned away and began folding the scattered clothes on the bed. "I don't know. It's not like he talked to me about it. I'm just dumb old mom." Suddenly, her shoulders began to shake. "If his father had lived, none of this would've happened. Travis always talked to his dad."

Maureen was bigger than Manny, which made hugging her awkward. Manny improvised with a few awkward pats on the back. As she administered this aid, something in the tangle of Travis's clothes caught her eye: black-and-white checks, fringe. She pulled at it. An Arab man's head scarf emerged from the pile. A kaffiyeh, the same pattern Yasser Arafat always wore.

Manny held it up. "Does he wear this much?"

Maureen snatched it away. "I've never seen that before. He must've . . . Someone must have given it to him."

Yes, someone. Who?

Manny turned back to the computers and noticed a piece of paper taped to one of the monitors. She squinted to read the teenage scrawl:

Mom —
Don't touch any of this. Don't move the
phone. I'll be back soon.

T

Maureen had been reading along, too, and
as her eyes scanned the words, her fingers
tightened their grip on Manny's arm.
"What? What does he mean, 'back soon'?
He can only be here or in school; that's
what the FBI said."
Manny took in everything before her —
the computers, the phone, the note — but
her ability to process the information stalled.
The last time she had experienced this sense
of slow-motion impending doom, her sports
car had been sliding off an icy road, heading for a massive oak. Now in Travis's room,
the crash came as pieces of the puzzle
clicked together.
"He's rigged some way to override the
monitoring system." Manny's voice, flat and
dead, hung in the air like another of the
apartment building's bad smells.
"What do you mean? That can't be."
Maureen's spiral of panic kept rising. "If
you take off the ankle bracelet, the FBI
knows right away. They explained all that to
us."
"He hasn't taken it off," Manny explained.

154

"The bracelet transmits a signal back to the FBI through the phone line. Travis has figured a way to send that signal using this laptop. He's a kid, understands electronics better than the feds — a Kevin Mitnick devotee. Travis must have figured that as long as he keeps the signal transmitting somehow through wireless relay stations going back only to this phone, it looks like the bracelet signal is coming from this apartment on West Ninety-seventh Street."

Maureen's head swiveled back and forth, searching for an answer, looking for an escape from the truth. "You mean, you mean he's out in the city and we don't know where? But how did he do it?"

"I'm not sure exactly, but it must be working, or there would be a dozen federal agents busting down the door right now." Manny rubbed her temples. "The question is, How long can he keep it up?" Manny glanced at her watch. "I'll give him until seven p.m. to get back in here. Then I'm going to have to report this to the FBI."

"No, you can't!" Maureen pleaded.

"I have no choice, Maureen. I'll be disbarred otherwise."

"But what if he doesn't come back?"

"He'll go back to jail. And nothing I can do will get him out."

CHAPTER SEVENTEEN

Jake stared long and hard at the two people he cared most about in the world. A full thirty seconds passed before he could bring himself to speak. "Let me get this straight. You" — he nodded at Sam — "are under suspicion of murder for a gangland-style slaying in Kearny. And you" — he turned to Manny — "risked disbarment by waiting three hours before reporting your client had broken out of the federal electronic monitoring system while you consoled his mother."

"That's it in a nutshell," Sam said. "I must say, you have a real knack for succinct summary."

"Should have been a lawyer," Manny muttered sheepishly. She was seated at one end of the sofa, and Sam was sprawled at the other end.

"I'm flabbergasted," Jake continued. "There's no question what you have to do. Sam, you've got to go to the Kearny police and explain everything that happened —"

"Not so easy, bro," Sam said, interrupting him. "I didn't hurt Boo Hravek, but I did knock out his bodyguard. I can't risk getting arrested for assault." He grinned at his brother. "Bad for my career."

As Jake was never sure exactly what his brother's career was, he was in no position to argue the point. But he felt fairly confident his brother wasn't an enforcer for the mob, and that was the only job he could think of where an assault conviction would be a résumé plus.

"And what about you, Manny? I suppose you're going to condone Travis's escape from custody by claiming he should never have been in the monitoring program in the first place."

Manny rubbed her tired eyes so hard that her mascara wept onto her cheekbones. "This morning, I would have said he didn't deserve to be in the monitoring program. Now, I'm not so sure. Face it: A kid who's smart enough to override his ankle bracelet is smart enough to have built a bomb."

"So, you've reported his absence to the feds. Let them handle it." Jake spoke in the level, logical tone he used when directing the work of his assistants. He expected to receive the respectful, attentive response he always got from them. Of course he was wrong.

Manny pulled her long legs up and wrapped her arms around them. "I can't," she wailed. "I don't trust them."

She jumped off the sofa, kicking over a pile of Jake's books. "I can't send him back to jail for months, and give the prosecution more damning evidence, without doing something to help him. I'm sure that Travis must have done this so he could meet up with his buddy Paco. But the feds refuse to put pressure on the Sandovals. If I could break through the wall that's been thrown up around Paco, I'd probably find Travis."

"You've tried calling?"

Manny cut him off with an impatient wave. "I've tried everything. I call the parents, I get some social secretary who very politely takes my message, but no one returns my call. I call Paco's cell phone and get rolled over immediately to voice mail. I'm telling you, caller ID is a curse. I go to their apartment building, I can't get past the concierge."

"They must leave the building sometime. Stand outside and wait."

"They come and go in their chauffeur-driven car, which enters and exits through the building's garage," Manny said. "It's one of scores of black Town Cars that come and go from that building all day long."

"Ah, lifestyles of the rich and not quite famous," Sam said. "I think —"

Manny was now pacing around the room. "Sam, you are brilliant. I take back everything I ever said about you."

Sam stood and preened like Mycroft until he realized that Manny's compliment contained a Trojan horse. "What? What have you been saying about me?"

"Lifestyles of the rich — that's how I can get through to the Sandovals. Maureen Heaton said she sees their picture in the society pages of the *Times*." Manny scanned the cluttered room. "Jake, where's your laptop?"

Jake went over to the paper-strewn table under the front window and reluctantly retrieved his computer. He felt like he was handing an alcoholic a bottle of Absolut, but there's was no holding back when Manny was in one of these moods.

"What are you looking for?" Sam asked as Manny pulled up the *New York Times* Web site.

Her mouth slightly open, her fingers flying over the keyboard, her eyes riveted on the screen, Manny didn't answer.

"Sam, you might as well order the takeout.

She won't stop when she gets like this until she's found what she wants." Jake picked up the most recent issue of the *Journal of Forensic Sciences.* "She'll tell us when she's ready."

Jake sat in the worn leather club chair and blocked out Manny, his brother, and the world with the drab blue-and-gray-covered magazine. After ten minutes, he realized he'd read the same paragraph on the relationship between wound patterns and the sexual psychosis of the assailant three times and still didn't have a clue what the author was saying. His mind kept looping back to the Vampire.

What was the killer after? Why had he merely drawn blood from the first few people, then escalated to torture and murder in the case of Amanda Hogaarth? Had he resorted to torture because whatever information he was seeking from the blood wasn't enough for his purposes?

Had the Vampire intended to kill her, or was her death simply an unintended consequence of the torture? How had he gained access to her apartment, when Ms. Hogaarth obviously wasn't the type to open her door to anyone who came knocking?

The only means Jake had to understanding the Vampire was through his victims, but they all seemed such ciphers, especially Ms. Hogaarth. So far as anyone knew, she had never been married. Her body said unequivocally that she had never given birth. She was old and dowdy. So why had the Vampire chosen this particular form of sexual torture?

Jake let the magazine drop, no longer even pretending to read. Manny was still poring over something on the computer. Sam sat text-messaging furiously on his cell phone. Even Mycroft was electronically bewitched, enthralled by an Animal Planet show set on mute. Jake shifted his lanky frame. He didn't need hardware, software, or a wireless connection to do what needed to be done. He just needed to let all the information on this case stored in his brain come together in some coherent form.

He shut his eyes and let his active mind disconnect from the present, willing his subconscious to take over. Victims seemingly without a connection. Except blood. Blood must tie them together. Blood ties . . . Blood is thicker than water. . . .

The doorbell rang. Manny leaped up from the computer. "It's the deliveryman from the Great Wall. C'mon, guys — dinnertime!"

Jake rose and stood rubbing his temples

as his brother, the dog, and Manny rushed past.

Manny glanced back at him. "What's the matter? Did you doze off?"

Jake shook his head. "No. Something is there, just out of my reach. It will come, if I let it."

"I'm telling you, it *will* work." Manny's chopsticks dived into the white cardboard container and pulled out a clump of kung pao chicken. "According to the Style section of the *Times,* three of the last five fundraising events Monserrat Sandoval attended had to do with animal welfare. The Howliday Ball, the World Wildlife Foundation dinner, and the ASPCA Companion Animal Luncheon. Mycroft and I have to get ourselves invited to that one next year."

"Better start accepting cases that actually pay," Sam advised. "You'll need to cough up twenty grand."

"All right, year after next. But don't you see? This is the perfect entrée for me to get in to see her."

"Purr-fect," Sam mimicked.

"Purr-fect," Jake chimed in.

Manny flicked a water chestnut across the table, scoring a direct hit on Jake's beaky nose. "You two need to be separated."

"So, you pose as the representative of some animal lover's charity and you talk your way in to see her." Jake wiped off his face and slipped the water chestnut to Mycroft. "Then what? 'Señora Sandoval, please make a donation to our bark-a-thon, and by the way, can I speak to your son, Paco? Are you harboring any fugitives here?'"

"Scientists!" Manny shook her head. "You have no imagination whatsoever. Just leave the strategy to me. I'll have your part all worked out for you."

"My part? What do you mean, my part?"

Manny's blue eyes opened wide. "Well, of course I can't pull this off alone. It's a two-person operation." She patted Jake on the knee. "And *you* are coming with me."

He nudged her away. "I can't. I have a lot of work to do."

"Oh, real nice, Jake. After all the times I've saved your ass at work, now when I need you, you're too damn busy."

Jake bristled. "When have you ever saved my ass at work?"

"Let's see. . . . How about two weeks ago, when you were all set to declare that naked NYU coed's nosedive off a balcony the work of a sadistic killer because of the way her pubic hair had been plucked out. I took one look at the autopsy photo and clued you in:

Brazilian bikini wax. No killer involved. Although those wax jobs are sadistic."

"Okay, that was a good call. I'm happy to repay you for services rendered, but not tomorrow."

"Nonsense. This won't take long." Manny pulled a fortune cookie from the pile left in the center of the table and cracked it open. " 'A journey of a million miles begins with one step.' See? You're destined to do this." She tossed a cookie to him. "Read what yours says."

Jake snapped the brittle cookie and pulled out the white slip of paper.

" 'Blood debts must be repaid in blood.' "

CHAPTER EIGHTEEN

"You know what your problem is? You spend entirely too much time with dead people." Manny and Jake were under one umbrella, striding toward First Avenue, heading for the Sandovals' building on the East River. "You've totally lost touch with how living, breathing human beings react."

True to Manny's prediction, the elusive Señora Sandoval had been immediately responsive to the plea, delivered over the phone by Kenneth in one of his most breathless performances, to discuss the rehabilitation of pets lost and injured every year during hurricane season on the Gulf Coast. The social secretary had only to hear the words *homeless pets* and Kenneth had been put through directly to the ambassador's wife. Within minutes, he'd succeeded in getting this appointment for "Jack Rose" and "Franny Medford," representatives of Home Again, who were in New York for just a few days, trying to raise money for the desperately needy animals in their care.

"There's probably some clause in the Patriot Act that makes impersonating an animal activist a federal offense," Jake complained.

"Look on the bright side — we'll be sent to Club Fed together."

"Great. We can brush up our doubles tennis game. Me and you versus whichever corrupt politicians and bankrupt CEOs are on our cell block."

Manny grinned. "I knew you'd come to see the upside of this project."

Jake stepped off the curb into the path of a turning taxi and stopped it with his glare. "Anyone with half a brain in her head will see through this ruse in an instant. And then how are we going to talk our way out of there?"

"The pictures, Jake, the key is in the pictures." Manny flourished a thick black binder. "I tell you, I had myself in tears putting this together."

Following advice gleaned from her more successful criminal clients, Manny had chosen to create a lie as close to the truth as possible. There really was a small organization in Mississippi dedicated to rehabilitating storm refugees, and their Web site was full of heartbreaking pictures of wet, starving, broken-limbed dogs and cats. Inspired by the group's work, Manny had found other photos along the same lines and combined them to create a presentation to sell Señora Sandoval. Then she'd written a letter of introduction for Jack and Franny on a letterhead she'd created by duplicating Home Again's logo with a graphics program, and printed out business cards on stock from the office-supply store. The lawyer in her experienced a brief moment of squeamishness as she studied the perfection of her counterfeit, and she considered tweaking the logo a bit to get around the copyright laws. Then she laughed — trademark infringement would be the least of her worries if she got caught in this charade.

"Here're your cards." She handed a few to Jake as they came in sight of the Sandovals' building. "Start assuming your identity."

Jake scrutinized them. "They look cheap," he complained. "She'll know they're fake."

"We're not trying to pass ourselves off as investment bankers. We're a low-budget charity — frugality is part of our persona."

"Okay, say she believes we really are from Home Again. How am I going to keep her occupied when you go off exploring?"

"We've been over this. Just keep showing her the photos. Talk about how each animal is being treated."

"But I don't know that," Jake protested. "I'm not a vet."

Manny stopped in the middle of the sidewalk and grabbed Jake by the shoulders. "Listen to me: Make. It. Up. You're not writing an autopsy report. It doesn't have to be true; it just has to be plausible. Talk about infections; talk about parasites. Talk, and don't stop until I'm back. Got it?"

"Got it. Pretend I'm a lawyer and lie."

"Won't cause your hair to stand out any more." Manny remembered the first time she saw Jake, who had been alighting from a helicopter. An unkempt head of salt-and-pepper hair brought to mind a cross between Albert Einstein and Dr. Frankenstein. Love at first sight.

They stood on the east side of First Avenue with crowds surging around them and for a moment Manny worried that she had gone too far, that Jake was going to turn on his heel and leave her there. But then he rolled his eyes, shook his head, and resumed walking toward their destination.

As they approached the canopy where the uniformed doorman stood, Manny squeezed his hand. "Thanks, Jake. You're a real trouper."

"¡Ay! ¡Pobrecito!"

Monserrat Sandoval's elegantly manicured hands traced the matted fur of a rescued mutt lying on a bed of rags at the Home Again shelter. The photo was one of the best in Manny's binder and it was having the desired effect. Manny saw Señora Sandoval's eyes brimming with tears as Jake, sitting next to her on the plush brocade sofa, offered his commentary.

"Yes, Comet was found swimming in a polluted canal. He contracted a terrible case of giardiasis from drinking contaminated water."

"He would drink this dirty water even though it must taste bad to him?" Señora Sandoval's English was fluent but strongly accented.

Jake reached out and stroked the pristine Maltese in Señora Sandoval's lap. Here was a dog who'd never tasted anything other than sparkling springwater, a pet every bit as well groomed as its mistress. "Desperation," Jake said. "We all do what we have to do to survive."

Manny prevented her smile from reaching her lips. For a man who claimed to have no acting ability, Jake was doing a mighty fine job. Robert De Niro, hang on to your Oscars; Jake Rosen's nipping at your heels.

Things were going even better than she had expected. It was Friday, and Paco was at school, or, more accurately, on a daylong senior class field trip. In the next half hour, Manny had to find some clue to her client's whereabouts.

Now that Jake had fully engaged Señora Sandoval's attention, Manny was free to scope out the apartment. The foyer separated the living area from the bedrooms. There were two closed doors in the foyer; Manny figured one must be a closet, the other a powder room. Luckily, the Sandovals didn't subscribe to the minimalist school of home decor. The apartment, while elegant, was quite crowded with art and antiques the family had acquired on their world travels. A large étagère packed with china and figurines partially blocked the view of the bedroom hallway from where they were sitting in the living room. Once she excused herself to go to the powder room, Manny was sure she could slip down that hallway unnoticed, as long as Jake kept Señora Sandoval occupied with the photos.

Jake was turning a page in the binder and Manny made her move.

"Excuse me, ma'am, but could I trouble

you to use your powder room?"

"Of course. Let me show you." Señora Sandoval moved to escort her guest there, but Manny motioned for her not to get up.

"You just keep talking. Is it there in the hall?"

"Yes, the second door."

Manny crossed the room quickly, and when she reached the powder room, she glanced back and saw both heads bent over the book of photos. She reached into the powder room, switched on the light and the fan, shut the door, and slipped down the hallway. Dressing the part of the committed animal welfare worker, she had worn flat black Crocs — adorned with numerous multicolored Jibbitz poodles, of course — so she didn't make her usual high-heeled clatter.

She suspected the door at the far end of the hall must be the master suite. That left a door on the left or the one on the right to be Paco's. She opened the door on the left and was about to back out, thinking that such an orderly, uncluttered space must be a guest room. Then she spotted the Monet Academy logo on a throw pillow and realized she was, in fact, in Paco's room.

Manny stepped in and shut the door quietly behind her.

What a difference from Travis's bedroom! No piles of clothes and unmade bed — the Sandovals had a maid to take care of that. But neither was there any sign of the occupant's personality. The crisply color-coordinated curtains and bedding revealed only the taste of an expensive decorator. Antique prints of sailboats hung in lieu of rock star and sports posters. And the desk looked like it belonged to the receptionist at a swanky Park Avenue law firm — no paper, no pens, just a perfectly placed computer and a phone. Kind of weird, really. What kind of kid lived like this?

Her eyes lighted on a framed photo, the only personal touch in the room. It showed a smiling Paco with his arm around a man who looked to be about ten years older. Manny figured he must be an older brother, or maybe a cousin. They both had dark hair, wide smiles, and snappy blue blazers. A sparkling blue sea and brilliant sailboats formed the backdrop. A happy family vacation shot, no doubt.

She began searching the bureau. Neatly folded sweaters and polo shirts, stacks of boxers and tees, a sock drawer that would make a drill sergeant weep with joy. The closet: no junk, no hiding places — just two poles of hanging shirts, jackets, and pants.

The desk drawers were just as unrevealing — they looked like an advertisement for an office-supply store. *Shit!* All the effort she'd made to get herself in here, and this is what she'd found — an Ethan Allen model room.

All that was left was the computer. Manny glanced at her watch. She'd been gone exactly two and one half minutes. Jake had instructions to explain her prolonged trip to the powder room by saying she had contracted a digestive disorder from the animals, which made her prone to episodes of nausea. Did she have enough time to boot up the computer and sort through Paco's documents? She had come this far. She might as well go whole hog.

Unlike Travis, Paco had a standard-issue desktop computer with no bells and whistles. Manny moved the mouse and the screen sprang to life. Good, it had only been in sleep mode. She clicked on the documents icon. Would it be password-protected? No, it opened right up.

There were folders labeled for every subject he took at school, as well as one for college essays and another for cover letters. Geez, the kid was really anal-retentive. She didn't have time to open every folder — she had to assume that they were what they claimed to be. Near the bottom of the alphabetical list of folders was one called "Stuff." That sounded more promising. Manny double-clicked and discovered three documents, each identified only with initials. One was entitled "TAH." Travis Andrew Heaton? She opened it.

It was single-spaced, as a letter would be, but contained no salutation or closing. Was it the draft of a letter, some sort of plan? Manny's heart rate kicked up. Sure enough, Travis's name was repeated throughout the document. Unfortunately, the rest of the words were in Spanish. She could translate a few: *problema, ayuda, solamente.*

Something about a problem and needing help. She needed a native speaker, or at least a good dictionary, to really understand what Paco was saying. She'd have to print this document out and take it with her.

Manny crossed to the door and listened. She couldn't hear Jake and Señora Sandoval, so presumably they wouldn't be able to hear the printer. Time check: Five minutes had passed.

She ran back to the computer and gave the command to print. The printer, a low-end ink-jet one, buzzed and clanked to life. A message appeared in a window on the monitor: "Printing page one of three." The printer made a strange digesting sound and laboriously pulled a sheet of paper into its maw. Slowly, slowly words began to appear. Manny stood anxiously by, silently urging it to hurry. *C'mon, c'mon.* You'd think the Sandovals could spring for a high-speed laser printer for their baby.

Finally, the first page slid into the tray. Manny snatched it up and looked for the next page. The printer fell silent.

What the hell? She sat down in front of the screen, trying to detect what was wrong. Just as she doubled-clicked the printer icon again, the printer lurched back to life, made the digesting sound, and pulled another sheet of paper through its feeder. Now she had commanded it to print again and she'd have to stay here while it coughed out six pages instead of three. Frantically, she began to look for a way to cancel the second print order.

While she searched the control panel folder, the printer disgorged the second sheet. It paused, but now Manny knew it was just catching its breath. She took her eyes off the printer and went back to canceling the second print order. The digesting sound came again, followed by a horrible crackling and crunching. She looked up at the printer in time to see the final sheet of paper being sucked into the machine at a thirty-degree angle. The computer began to beep and a message window appeared. "A paper jam has occurred. Clear the paper path and resume printing."

She glanced at her watch. Eight minutes gone, and now she had to repair a friggin' computer.

She took a deep breath. *You can do this. You're good with electronics. A woman who's figured out every feature on her cell phone can figure out this printer.* But the stupid machine was nothing like the printer she had at home, or the one in her office. She couldn't even see how to open it up. She tugged at the jammed paper and only succeeded in tearing it. Another deep breath. *Focus. Look at it. See how it's put together.*

And then, for the first time since she had entered Paco's room, Manny heard a sound from outside the door.

"Hi, Mama! I'm home!"

CHAPTER NINETEEN

For at least the hundredth time since Manny had left the room, Jake checked his watch. Eight minutes and forty-three seconds had passed. At the five-minute mark, Señora Sandoval had glanced up from the binder of animal photos and cast a quizzical look at the powder room's door. Jake had delivered the explanation about Manny's sudden bouts of nausea, and, amazingly, Señora Sandoval had murmured sympathy and gone right back to perusing the photos. Now, the sound of a door opening made both of them pause.

Jake immediately focused on the dimly lighted hallway that led back to the bedrooms. If Manny emerged from there, he hoped to hell she'd have a plausible explanation to offer their hostess. But there was no movement from that direction, giving him hope that she'd already made it out of Paco's room and was about to make her grand reentry from the powder room. But when his glance flicked to the powder room's door, he saw that it was still closed, a band of light visible at the bottom.

So what door had opened?

"Hi, Mama! I'm home!"

Jake felt sudden chest pain and tensing of his leg muscles, a spontaneous headache on his left side, and a racing heart. This was not supposed to happen. Paco was supposed to be on the senior social studies field trip all day.

A slender young man with dark, wavy hair appeared in the foyer and looked into the living room.

"Paco, darling. This is a surprise. Why are you home so early?"

"The field trip was dismissed early because of the rain."

"*Ah, que malo.* Come here and meet Mr. Rose. He is talking to me about the animal-rescue efforts on the Gulf Coast. You must see these photos, darling. They are so tragic!"

Jake locked eyes with Paco, willing him to come into the living room and join them on the sofa. "So many young people volunteer in our organization," Jake said, trying to keep his voice casual. "Paco might like to learn about the opportunities we offer."

Paco smiled, a dazzling flash of white in his handsome olive-toned face. "Oh, yes. I love animals. I would like to hear all about it."

Jake's heart rate began to slow down.

Paco extended one foot. "Just let me put away my school things and change my socks. I stepped in a puddle on the way home."

It took every ounce of self-control Jake possessed to keep from leaping up and shouting, "No! Come here right now."

He watched in dread as Paco turned toward the long hallway. What would the kid do when he discovered a strange woman in his bedroom? What would Manny do when that bedroom door opened? Was she even aware that Paco had arrived home? Did she have some lame explanation to offer up, or, cornered, would she just blurt out the truth?

The truth might work for her. Señora Sandoval was clearly kindhearted. Manny could throw herself on the woman's mercy and explain that she was an overly dedicated defense attorney just trying to save her client from harm. But what excuse could he possibly offer for why a deputy medical examiner of the City of New York was aiding and abetting her? He was already skating on thin ice with Pederson. This would be all the justification his boss would need to get rid of a troublesome employee who brought shame on the ME's office.

He could no longer see Paco, but he heard the click of a door opening. He held his breath and waited for the calamity to follow.

This was the spot in the movies where the intrepid heroine would duck behind the flowing draperies to hide out. Except the rooms on movie sets never had simple tailored valances and matching Roman shades. Manny glanced around the ridiculously tidy room for another place to hide. The bed was a platform-style one with a solid base that sat directly on the carpet. She considered diving into the closet, but what good would that do? Paco would notice his computer was on, see the paper jammed in the printer. When he opened the closet door, she would be right there, cowering like a trapped animal, with no justifiable excuse for her behavior.

More was at stake here than just being embarrassed. If Señora Sandoval suspected she and Jake were scam artists, she'd call the police. And when she found out who they were, the shit would really hit the fan. The vision of a disciplinary hearing before the Bar Association appeared in startling detail in her mind's eye. Then she saw herself in prison garb. Even though they'd discontinued the old black and white horizontal stripes — a nightmare for the hips — the new neon orange jumpsuits just wouldn't accessorize with her Chanel.

There were no workable defensive positions open to her. Her only option was a bold offense.

Manny flattened herself against the wall next to the bedroom door and waited.

The seconds crawled by. She heard voices but couldn't make out what they were saying. Maybe Paco wasn't going to come into the room after all. Maybe Jake had found some way to keep him out there. Maybe she was squandering the few seconds she had to get out of the room unseen. What to do? Her heart felt huge in her chest, hammering against her ribs, pressing the air out of her lungs.

Indecision was intolerable to her. Manny decided she would open the door a crack and see what was happening out there. Anything was better than just standing here waiting.

Manny stepped forward and faced the door. Tentatively, she reached out and touched the knob.

A floorboard creaked on the other side of the wall. Instantly, she pressed herself against the wall beside the door again.

The door opened.

Paco stood two steps in front of Manny, oblivious to her presence. She estimated that he was only three inches taller than she, and very lean. Still, a young athletic man would be stronger than a female lawyer who visited the gym half as often as she intended to. All she had in her favor was the element of surprise. Hesitate, and all would be lost.

Paco closed the door behind him. Manny sprang.

She jumped right on his back and wrapped her legs around his hips, like a kid playing piggyback. Placing one hand tightly over his mouth, she steadied herself with the other across his chest. He staggered slightly under her weight but kept his balance. "Don't say a word," Manny whispered into his ear. "I read the document you wrote about Travis. I want to know where he is. When I let you go, you're not going to scream. If you do, I'll show the letter to your mother. Understand?"

Paco nodded.

"All right. I'm going to get off you. Don't say a word until you've turned on some music. Go." She slipped off his back.

Paco headed toward the music system on his bookshelf, glancing over his shoulder as if trying to keep an eye on the unpredictable three-headed alien threatening to abduct him.

"I'm Travis Heaton's defense attorney," Manny said, once the music was playing. "I want to know why you've been refusing to cooperate with me. Who planted that bomb? Where is Travis now?" There was so much to find out and so little time.

Manny saw the expression on Paco's face change from fearful to merely cautious. "It's too complicated to explain it all right now. Let's make a plan to meet somewhere else."

"Yeah, right. You talk here or I'll show your mother the document."

Even though she didn't understand everything the document said, Manny could tell she possessed a powerful weapon. She watched as Paco weighed his risks, his eyes darting back and forth.

"No!" His fingers, slender but strong, pressed into her forearm. "Travis is at an apartment in Brooklyn. Three twenty-nine Rosamond Street, 4E. He called me from there yesterday, but he couldn't talk."

"What —" But Manny was interrupted by a high-pitched voice nearby.

"Ms. Medford? Are you ill? Do you need help?"

Manny pushed Paco toward the door. "Get your mother back in the living room. Tell her you ran into me in the hall and sent me to the kitchen for a drink. I'll follow you out there in a few seconds."

The rain had stopped. Jake loped down First Avenue, trying to put as much Manhattan real estate between himself and the Sandovals' apartment building as possible.

As he walked, he delivered a diatribe. "Totally irresponsible . . . reckless and immature . . . only concerned with what's important to you . . ."

From where she trotted four steps behind him, Manny could hear only parts of the harangue, but she caught the drift. She didn't attempt to defend herself. Jake was right: She had put him at terrible professional risk. She should have thought of the long-term consequences had they been caught. But the bottom line was, they had pulled it off. So why all the outrage? She hated when he pulled this indignant father crap. "Slow down," she gasped. "You're more of a workout than spinning class."

"Take your time. No need to keep up with me. I've served my purpose, so let me go."

Oh, now we've switched to used and abused boy toy. "Why are you so touchy? Everything worked out brilliantly. I have this document, which is going to help me figure out what's happening here, and I found out where Travis is. And" — Manny reached into her pocket and pulled out a small yellow rectangle — "we even got a check for five thousand dollars."

"What the hell are you going to do with that?"

"I'm going to send it to Home Again. When I tell them what a great fund-raiser you are, I bet they'll put you on their board."

Not even a glimmer of a smile. Geez, he really was pissed. Manny tried again.

"Jake, look! Souvlaki King." She grabbed his arm and dragged him to a halt. "Let's stop and eat. I'm starving."

"Eat! How can you even think about food at a time like this? I've got so much adrenaline pumping through my body, I won't be able to eat or sleep until next Tuesday."

"I have a parasitic infestation, remember? It must be a tapeworm."

Jake stared at her for a long moment. Then his upper lip twitched. Soon, his shoulders were shaking. By the time they stumbled into Souvlaki King, they were both laughing so hard, all they could do was point to the

gyro special and collapse in the red vinyl
booth.

CHAPTER TWENTY

"You have tzatziki sauce on your chin." Jake smiled at Manny and indicated the location on his own face.

She grinned and wiped her mouth with a handful of the Greek diner's flimsy napkins. Jake never stopped marveling at how totally unflappable Manny was. If he had told his ex-wife, Marianna, that, she would have leaped up from the table in a huff and spent twenty minutes in the ladies' room repairing the damage. Not that Marianna would ever have agreed to eat at Souvlaki King. But if she had found herself in such a place, she would never have ordered the gyro special. His ex-wife did not eat messy food — no ribs, no lobster in the shell, no corn on the cob, ever. No wonder his work had repulsed her.

Manny leaned back in the booth. "Wow, that hit the spot. Just what I needed before a long drive to Brooklyn."

Jake's benevolent mood dissolved. "Brooklyn? We can't go out there right now. I have to get back to the office."

"What's this 'we,' Kemo Sabe? I don't recall asking you to go."

Jake glared at her. "You can't go out to some strange apartment in Brooklyn alone. There's no telling what you'll find there, or whom Travis is with."

"I'll be fine." Manny stood and straightened the demure skirt she'd chosen for her animal activist charade. "Look how I'm dressed — drab as a dormouse. No one will take the slightest interest in me."

Jake slid out of the booth to block her exit, causing the worried waiter to rush over with the check. "Manny, please. This is needlessly risky. Just wait until five-thirty and we'll go out there together."

Manny dodged around him. "I don't need a chaperone. Every minute that Travis is away from his apartment, he digs himself deeper in the hole with the feds. I've got to talk to him and figure out what's going on, then bring him back on my terms, not the government's."

"Don't be reckless!" Jake grabbed her shoulder, but she pulled away and strode down the center aisle of the diner. Jake followed. *Groundhog Day* — shades of *Il Postino.*

"You pay! You pay bill now!" the waiter shouted.

"Give the man his money, Jake," Manny instructed as she reached the door of the restaurant.

"At least call Sam to go with you," Jake shouted after her as he fumbled with his wallet.

"Okay, sure. Bye — thanks for lunch!"

And she was gone.

Jake stood at the cash register and watched her red hair disappear into the crowd. He knew damn well she wouldn't call Sam. Should he follow her to Brooklyn? By the time she got her car and drove through midday traffic, he could make it out to Rosamond Street on the subway. He thought of the pile of work on his desk, the hours this morning that he'd been missing in action. Pederson was probably already foaming at the mouth.

Well, screw Pederson. He wasn't going to let Manny get killed just to avoid a confrontation with his boss. Now, what was the address and apartment number Paco had given her? Jake closed his eyes and tried to relax his mind so it would come to him.

"Hey." The waiter poked him. "Here's

your change. Whaddaya, some kinda horse? You sleep standing up?"

Jake scowled. No one could accuse this guy of groveling for tips. If the address had been about to come to him, it was lost now. He suspected Rosamond Street was one of those short blocks in Carroll Gardens, but he'd have to check a map to be sure. He figured maybe he should just hang out on the street and wait for Manny's high-profile black convertible to arrive.

Damn it — he didn't need this aggravation. Manny was a complication in his life, a complication that took him away from concentrating 100 percent on his work.

His cell phone rang. The knot of tension within him unwound. He assumed it must be Manny, telling him she'd changed her mind and that she'd wait until five-thirty and go to Brooklyn with him.

"Hello."

"Rosen, get over to 233 1/2 West 164th Street." Pederson's snarl came through the airwaves. "There's another body waiting for you. Your Vampire has struck again."

Jake stepped out onto the sidewalk, looking in the direction Manny had charged off. Then he turned and walked the other way. Whatever awaited Manny on Rosamond Street, she'd have to face it alone.

Jake arrived on an upper Harlem street packed with police vehicles to find a gray-faced Pasquarelli pacing outside the door to a boarded-up storefront church. TABERNACLE OF LIVING PRAISE was painted on the filthy window, just barely visible behind a rusty metal grate permanently fused in the closed position. The gentrification that had swept through the brownstone blocks of central Harlem hadn't reached this grim little enclave of tenements, liquor stores, and check-cashing shops. The neighbors sat on their front stoops and leaned out their windows, watching the unfolding drama with about as much interest as they would give to a repeat of *Beverly Hills, 90210*.

"I'll take you to the body," Pasquarelli told Jake. "I got a feeling I know what you're going to say. I'm hoping to hell I'm wrong."

Jake followed him into a dim hallway. A large rat sat on the stairs leading to the second floor, utterly unperturbed by all the commotion, attentive to the prospect of food that this incursion of humans might bring. As the men passed, the rat emitted a noise that sounded for all the world like a sarcastic snicker.

Pasquarelli flinched. "Fuckin' rats — the place is crawling with them. They say for every one you see, there're three more hiding." Jake, whose nose was as sensitive to anything involving death as a bloodhound's was to the living, didn't have to be told that. He could smell their presence — their droppings, their dander, their decomposing bodies — all around him. The scent of rodents was mixed with something much worse: human excrement, human decay, human fear.

The hall led straight from front to back, passing two rooms. The front main room was filled with a clutter of old chairs and a small lectern, illuminated slightly by the dusty sunlight that penetrated the window and grate. Although a few crime-scene techs worked that space, the real beehive of activity was in the small, windowless rear room.

The building's power had been shut off long ago, and an orange electrical cable snaked out to a police generator on the street. Brilliant work lights showed up every detail of the room in harsh relief.

A man's naked body was spread-eagled on a wide, old wooden door that had been set up across two sturdy sawhorses, apparently lifted from a construction site. The man had been tightly secured to the door with rope tied to large metal rings screwed directly into the wood. Each hand and foot was tied to a ring, and the rope crossed his torso in two places, tied with no slack on both sides.

Jake turned to Pasquarelli. "What makes you think this is the work of the Vampire? All the other victims were attacked in their homes."

The detective pointed.

Inside the crook of the victim's left arm was a Band-Aid with a cotton ball beneath it, the kind of remedy a nurse applies after drawing blood. Printed neatly in black ink on the Band-Aid were the words *Look here.* Jake did as directed and saw the single puncture mark of a blood draw.

A man's tasteful plaid suit was draped neatly on a hanger; a shirt and underwear were folded on a chair, with a pair of vintage Weejun penny loafers lined up underneath. The victim's clothes — this was no homeless derelict. Still, Jake was not entirely convinced.

"Could be a copycat."

Pasquarelli gestured uncomfortably toward the midsection of the body. "You're the expert, Doc, but aren't those burn marks like on Ms. Hogaarth? And that detail wasn't released to the public."

Jake pulled out his magnifying glass.

"Can't be positive until the autopsy, but I think you're right. You've ID'd him?" he asked Pasquarelli.

"He's a Dr. Raymond Fortes. Works for a small pharmaceutical firm. They reported him missing on Wednesday."

Jake shook his head. "He's been here quite a bit longer than that." He began to examine the body and spoke aloud as he worked. "Numerous small flesh wounds and bruises. The bruises have various coloration — these yellowish ones are older, the purplish ones are more recent. Rat bites — inflicted over a period of days."

"What's that muddy-looking brown stuff in his chest hair and on his leg there?" Pasquarelli asked.

Jake touched it and raised his gloved hand to his nose. Just as he suspected. "Peanut butter."

"Wha—" Understanding crept into Pasquarelli's mournful brown eyes. "Ah, Jesus. They spread peanut butter on him to attract the rats."

"Have you contacted the next of kin?" Jake asked. "This won't be an easy thing to tell them."

"The vic was a widower, not many friends. When he didn't show at the office on Monday, they didn't think much of it. Sometimes he worked from home and didn't like to be disturbed. Guess Dr. Fortes wasn't their most popular employee. But by Wednesday, they started calling him, and when they couldn't turn him up, they filed a missing person report."

"And the police tracked him to here?"

"Hell no. A middle-aged man with no family to make a fuss goes missing, we don't bother much. We checked to see if he was at the morgue. A couple uniforms went over to his apartment. No signs of trouble there, so they figured he decided to walk out on his life in New York. Happens all the time."

"So who found him?"

"City rodent-control officer. People from the building next door been complaining that the rats are invading them from over here. Baby got bit, so the rat guy comes over here to see about spreading the poison and sealing up the holes." Pasquarelli shoved his fists into the already-misshapen pockets of his brown sports coat. "He's got a truly sucky job, and today it got even worse."

Jake nodded as he continued to study the body. In places, the loss of flesh was quite extensive. Some of the older wounds were inflamed and covered in pus. Pasquarelli grew restless at Jake's silent examination.

"How long ago did he die?" the detective asked.

"I'd say his heart stopped about two days ago. But he started the process of dying many days before that."

"What finally killed him?"

"I can't tell until I open him up. Probably a combination of things — shock, dehydration, blood loss, infection. He wasn't a young man — probably in his early sixties."

"Days of suffering," Pasquarelli said. "How could one human being do that to another? I've seen homicide, suicide, fratricide, patricide, and every other kind of cide, but I've never seen anything like this before. It's starting to feel like this Vampire really is some supernaturally evil creature."

Jake shook his head. "Don't let your imagination run away with you, Vito. When we catch this guy, he'll be as average as you or me. Not an obvious monster, but a person with a regular life, like the Nazi death camp guards or the soldiers at Abu Ghraib."

Pasquarelli was not persuaded. "But those guys justified what they did by saying they were just following orders in a time of war. That's not what's happening here."

"Maybe he's fighting his own private war, Vito. Our job is to figure out what it is."

CHAPTER
TWENTY-ONE

Trapped.

Manny took a deep breath to steady her pounding heart. For at least the tenth time since she'd gotten into this mess, she looked for a way out.

Hopeless. A Moishe the Bagel Man truck in front of her, black livery cab beside her, overbearing SUV right on her tail. And beneath her, the waters of New York Harbor. She hated to admit that Jake had been right, but the subway to Rosamond Street would've been much faster. Bumper-to-bumper traffic on the Brooklyn Bridge at midday should not have come as a surprise.

Still, driving her Porsche hadn't been a totally stupid idea. Once she found Travis, she wanted the option of getting him out of that apartment fast. Standing on the subway platform waiting for the B train didn't really fit her plan for a quick escape.

Manny squirmed in the driver's seat

without taking her feet off the clutch or the brake pedals. What awaited her on Rosamond Street? Would Travis be alone in the apartment? Would he listen to reason, come with her willingly? What would she do if he refused, or if whoever lived in the apartment refused for him? The possibilities for trouble seemed a lot more numerous stuck here in traffic than they had in the diner with Jake.

The driver of the livery cab, distracted by talking on his cell phone headset, allowed a small gap to open up in front of him. Manny jerked the wheel and accelerated, shoehorning her way into the space and inching past the bagel delivery truck. The maneuver gave her a sense of accomplishment until she saw the broader vista of jammed traffic ahead of her. Out of one tight spot and into another — an uncomfortable metaphor for her behavior today. She didn't think of herself as reckless. As a lawyer, she was trained to be logical. But somehow, Jake, with his methodical and painstaking approach to every problem, made her seem impulsive.

A sudden cavalcade of horn blowing interrupted her reverie. Manny leaned on her horn, too. What the hell — it didn't change the pileup of cars, but it felt good.

When the horns subsided, a chirping

sound remained. Manny cocked her ear, then pawed through her purse for her Black-Berry. It was chirping to remind her of an appointment. She didn't remember scheduling anything for today — certainly no court dates. Her hand closed around the gadget and she scrolled to the calendar function. "Mycroft to vet 3:00" flashed before her eyes.

Oh shit! Because Kenneth was filing papers in court, she was supposed to take Mycroft in to Dr. Costello for a follow-up to make sure the bite he'd received from Kimo was healing properly. Even if she turned around — even if she *could* turn around — she'd never make it to collect the dog and get to Dr. Costello's office by three o'clock. Better just to call and reschedule.

Manny expected to get the receptionist, but the voice coming over the line was male and familiar. "Dr. Costello? It's Manny Manfreda."

"Ah, hello, Ms. Manfreda. How are you? And how is Mycroft?"

"At the moment, I'm not so good. I'm stuck in traffic on the Brooklyn Bridge, pointed away from your office, so I'm afraid I have to reschedule Mycroft's appointment. I'm sorry it's at the last minute, but could we come in tomorrow?"

"I don't have the appointment book — it's on my wife's computer. Let me go and check."

Manny could hear rustling and shuffling over the line, but Dr. Costello kept talking as he worked. "I see we have a celebrity in our midst. TV news in the taxi on the way in kept repeating you were representing some kids in that case out of New Jersey. It sounds like it is an interesting matter."

"Well, the government's case is shaky." Manny figured she might as well practice projecting the cocky air of confidence all prominent defense attorneys had mastered, even if she was just talking to her dog's vet.

"Good. It's up to lawyers like you to keep the government from overstepping its boundaries."

Manny smiled. Not only was her new vet very attentive to Mycroft but he also shared her own libertarian views. It wasn't essential to be in political harmony with your pet's doctor, but it was a nice bonus. "It's refreshing to hear you say so, Dr. Costello. I think there are a lot of people who think the Preppy Terrorists deserve to be locked up."

The doctor made heavy breathing sounds, which came over the line along with the pinging of a computer program being launched. "Ah, finally I come to tomorrow's schedule. It seems we can fit you in at two or at three-thirty."

"I'll take three-thirty."

Dr. Costello sighed. "It doesn't seem fair."

"Oh, really, I appreciate your squeezing me in. Three-thirty is just fine."

Dr. Costello laughed. "Can I have your autograph tomorrow?"

Manny accelerated and drew two car lengths closer to the end of the bridge. She repeated now what her professors had pounded into her in her fist year of law school. "Justice is never perfect. As long as I'm allowed to be heard, the system is working."

"I hope you're right."

For no discernible reason, the cars ahead of Manny began to move. She pulled onto the BQE, thrilled with the sensation of traveling at fifty miles per hour. She now understood why in California they called a high-speed chase anything approaching double digits. "I know I am."

CHAPTER
TWENTY-TWO

Manny pulled up beside the last parking spot on Rosamond Street. A man walking by shook his head, doubtful she could squeeze the Porsche into such a tight space. But with a few deft pulls of the steering wheel, Manny had her car snugly aligned with the curb. Success in parallel parking, as so much in life and the law, all hinged on your approach.

She relaxed as she sized up her surroundings. Rosamond Street was a nice middle-class block, lined with nondescript low-rise redbrick apartment buildings. Not fancy, not funky, not scary — the kind of place where schoolteachers and firefighters and mail carriers raised families, avoiding the drama of the highest and lowest ends of New York society.

She found number 329 and stood on the stoop for a moment, considering her approach. If she buzzed apartment 4E and announced herself, would Travis let her in? Her problem solved itself when a man exited the building and obligingly held the door open for her.

Trusting soul, Manny thought. *Guess I don't look too threatening.* Inside the building's small lobby, Manny hesitated: ancient claustrophobic elevator or dark, steep stairs? Figuring she wouldn't come across as masterful if she arrived at Travis's hideout gasping for breath, Manny reluctantly stepped into the tiny elevator.

Several lurching, grinding minutes later, she stepped out on the fourth floor. As she looked down the L-shaped hall to get her bearings, a slim figure in a baseball cap and denim jacket appeared from around the corner and slipped quickly down the stairs.

"Travis!" Manny shouted, and raced toward the stairs. She got to the railing and peered down at the person on the landing one floor below. She saw a ponytail protruding from under the baseball cap and heaved a sigh of relief. Not Travis after all.

Continuing down the hall, Manny saw the third door on the left was ajar: 4E. The gyro special gave an unhappy lurch in her stomach. New Yorkers, even ones who lived in safe middle-class neighborhoods, did not leave their apartment doors hanging open.

Manny hugged the left wall of the hallway and cautiously approached the door. It was dark inside, too dark to tell if someone was standing there watching her. When Manny got within a foot of the door, she reached out, quickly shoved the door open, and flattened herself back against the wall.

Nothing happened.

"Travis?" she called. "Travis, it's Manny Manfreda, your lawyer. I'm here to help you. Can you hear me?"

No sound. No movement.

Now what? Call 911? And tell them what? "Hi, my client is an escaped federal prisoner and he was supposed to be in this apartment, but he's not, and the door's wide open, so can you send someone right over?" She'd get help all right — two attendants from the psych ward at Kings County Hospital and a syringeful of sedative.

Could she just walk in there and check out the apartment? No, it seemed too much like those teen slasher movies where the girl hears a sound in the basement and goes down alone to investigate even though she knows there's a crazed killer on the loose. TSTL: too stupid to live.

Manny suddenly heard loud voices through the wall, but they weren't raised in anger. She listened. A woman's voice: "You wanna soup?" A man: "Not now. Maybe later." "Oh, later. You letta me know, prince."

She inhaled. The smell took her back to her parents' kitchen in Red Bank. Pasta fagioli, definitely. She could make friends with the people in 4D.

She knocked on the door and heard approaching footsteps.

"Who that gonna be?" the woman inside muttered.

Manny stood in front of the peephole for inspection, smiling and waving like Queen Elizabeth. The door opened a crack on the chain and one dark eye peered out.

"Hi! I wonder if you could help me? I'm looking for your neighbors here."

"Maria and the kids? They move-a last month. Buy a house in Jersey."

"No, not Maria. The people who live there now."

"No one live there now. Landlord gonna fix nice, jack up the rent."

Manny relaxed a bit after the woman introduced herself as Lena Castigliore. Mrs. Castigliore spoke with the same broken-English accent of Manny's beloved grandmother Adeline. Maybe that's why the door was open — workmen coming and going.

"Oh, I was just worried because the door is open."

Now the woman in 4D opened her door and shuffled into the hall in her blue quilted slippers, unable to resist investigating this impropriety in her building. "That no good. I call-a da super."

"Good idea."

Manny used the interminable minutes waiting for the super's arrival to befriend Mrs. Castigliore. Compliments on the aroma of her soup got the old lady talking. At her age, she welcomed the opportunity to talk to anyone about anything and wasn't too particular about the reason she was being asked.

Yes, she had heard the door of 4E open and close a couple of times these past few days. She had assumed it was contractors. No, she hadn't actually seen them. But wait, once she had seen a man go in. Yes, a young man. Oh, no, not eighteen; more like thirty, thirty-five. No, she hadn't heard any talking — no noise at all.

Now the super arrived, a small Hispanic man with a mop of dark hair and the requisite large bunch of keys. Despite the fact that Mrs. C. had called to report the door being open, he stood in front of the apartment with his head cocked and his eyes narrowed, obviously very puzzled to see that the door was indeed open. Manny's uneasiness returned.

"So, have there been workmen here the last few days?"

"No, no guys yet. The boss, he say they coming *miercoles,* Wednesday." Cautiously, the super stepped into the apartment. Manny and Mrs. C. trailed behind him. Manny was all prepared with a story of how her sister was moving to New York and needed an apartment, but no one thought to ask why she was there.

The front door opened directly into a large living room. Scratches on the floor showed where the furniture had been, but the room was empty except for a child's partially deflated ball. They proceeded in a line across the room to a hallway leading to the bedrooms. The wood trim around the first bedroom door was deeply scratched. The super shook his head and muttered, *"El gato."* Inside the room lay a crumpled sleeping bag.

"Did Maria leave that?" Manny asked.

Mrs. C. shook her head. "I went over to say good-bye the day she moved. I see her check every room. She no leave this behind."

They peeked in the bathroom — a paper

cup, a flattened tube of toothpaste, and a dirty towel.

"No," Mrs. C. said. "Maria leave-a the place clean. Someone been staying here."

Manny's eyes darted back and forth, searching for a sign that the someone had been Travis. There were no papers or clothing out in the open. Could she press her luck and start opening closets?

Now the super and Mrs. C. moved into the tiny kitchen. At the doorway, the old lady stopped short. Manny, following, bumped into her. The room erupted into a Tower of Babel, cascades of Spanish pouring from the super, a competing torrent of Italian from Mrs. C. Manny elbowed her way past them and added her own contribution to the mix.

"Oh, dear God!"

CHAPTER
TWENTY-THREE

Blood, lots of it — dried, brown, but still unmistakably blood. It had spattered the kitchen counter, dripped down the cabinets, and smeared on the floor. When it had been fresh, someone had stepped in it, leaving a trail of smeary footprints to the refrigerator. Bloody prints marked the fridge handle, a ghoulish version of the sticky smudges the kids who used to live here must have once left.

Manny could feel her own blood surging through her arteries, propelled by a heart beating twice as fast as normal. Was this Travis's blood? What if he had died because the feds had refused to question the Sandovals?

"We gotta call-a da nine-one-one." Mrs. C.'s English had come back to her as she backed away from the gruesome scene.

"Yes, call them from your apartment," Manny said. "We'll wait here." She grabbed the super's elbow, pulling him toward the hall. "We shouldn't touch anything. The police won't want us in here."

"I'm going downstairs," he said. "I don't know nothin' about this anyway, and I don't like blood. Cops can come see me there."

Manny was happy to see him go. She knew she should go out in the hall to wait for the cops, but she couldn't resist looking around a little more. She'd already contaminated the crime scene by walking through each room. Walking through again wouldn't make matters any worse, would it? She knew how Jake would answer that question, but she shut his voice out of her head.

But as she prowled through the apartment, Jake's voice continued to follow her. *Don't touch anything,* it said.

"I won't, I won't," Manny murmured, barely realizing she was speaking aloud. "I'm just going to look in the bathroom again. Isn't that one of the first places you check out?"

She poked her head in that door again. The toilet seat was up, confirming a man's presence. She looked in the bowl in case something had been carelessly discarded there, but it was empty. She knew this room could be a trove of fingerprints — you wouldn't wear gloves in the john. She didn't want to smudge anything, or add her own prints to the mix. Still, the medicine cabinet tempted her. "Oh, like you wouldn't open this? I'll be careful," she assured her inner Jake.

Rooting through her purse, Manny produced a pencil. Placing the eraser end under the edge of the cabinet door, she clicked it open. Rusty, dusty, and empty, except for two paper-wrapped tubes. Tampons. Left over from Maria's occupancy, or had there been a woman here, too?

She went back into the bedroom. *Don't even think of touching that sleeping bag!* Jake's voice cautioned.

"Don't worry. I know it's full of fibers and hairs and skin flakes. I'm just going to peek in the closet." But the closets in both bedrooms were empty, and Manny felt herself drawn back toward the kitchen. She swore she could feel Jake dragging her back.

She shook him off. "The police will be here any minute. This is my last chance. I'll be careful."

Manny stood on the threshold and surveyed the kitchen carnage. She thought of all the hours she had spent with Jake in his lab, reviewing crime-scene photos . . . all the things he'd taught her about blood-spatter patterns. Low velocity: Large round symmetrical drops meant someone was dripping blood while moving very slowly or standing still. Medium velocity: More elliptical drops with a tail showing the direction the blood drop was traveling. High velocity: usually from a weapon exerting force, a multitude of tiny, fine particles. This blood didn't seem to fit any of those patterns.

"There's something weird about this, don't you think?" she whispered.

Why was most of the blood on the counter, not the floor? She tried to imagine a scenario that would account for this. The victim was shot and fell against the counter? Then where was the bullet hole? And why hadn't Mrs. C. heard anything? Okay, not shot — knifed. But if the victim fell onto the counter, that would indicate the attacker came at him from the middle of the kitchen. The blood would spurt out and spatter across the kitchen, not drain out the victim's back onto the counter. And why those perfect drips down the front of the cabinets? If the victim had slumped to the floor, that blood would be smeared.

This pattern looked familiar all right, but not from crime-scene photos. It reminded her of something that had happened in her own kitchen last week. She'd knocked over a glass of orange juice; it had formed a puddle on the counter, then dripped down the cabinets and formed a smaller puddle on the floor. Then Mycroft had come in to sniff, and tracked juice across the floor.

"Look at that, Jake. Doesn't it seem like that blood has been spilled, literally? Like from a container? But who has a container of blood?"

A tingle pricked Manny's scalp. Her gaze shifted to the bloody prints on the fridge. "C'mon, Jake, I've got to. I can't *not* open it." Manny dug through her purse again, this time producing a silk scarf. She sighed. "Oh well, at least it's not the Hermès." Wrapping it around her hand and using just two fingers, she opened the refrigerator.

Inside, more blood. Not spilled, but stored neatly in vials. Manny counted seven. One for each of the Vampire's victims.

CHAPTER
TWENTY-FOUR

Jake and Mycroft surveyed the limp form on the couch. Whimpering, Mycroft licked the slack hand dangling near the floor. Jake massaged the blistered feet.

"Are you sure you don't want me to send out for food?" he asked.

Manny raised her hand in protest and turned her head. "I'm too exhausted to eat."

About seventeen hours had passed since Manny and Jake had infiltrated the Sandovals' apartment. Over fifteen since she had headed to Brooklyn searching for Travis and Jake had been called to the scene of the Vampire's latest victim. To Jake, it felt like enough had happened to fill three weeks. To Manny, it must have felt more like three lifetimes.

He moved to sit beside her and smoothed the hair away from her brow. "Stop blaming yourself. No one could have anticipated this."

Manny pushed off his hand and sat up. "You're right. No one could have anticipated that of all the millions of apartments in New York, Paco Sandoval would send me to look for my client in the one that's apparently being used by the Vampire." Manny jumped off the sofa with a jolt of energy that sent Mycroft scampering for cover. "No one could have anticipated that a kid who was already in a ridiculous amount of trouble for being in the vicinity when a mailbox blew up is now in an absolutely mind-boggling amount of trouble for being an escaped federal prisoner and a suspect in the most bizarre murder case New York has seen since the Son of Sam."

Manny kicked at a pile of magazines that blocked her restless pacing. "You're absolutely spot-on, dear. Even someone with an imagination as overactive as mine couldn't have predicted this!"

Jake observed her with mounting concern. The hours of interrogation she had been subjected to by the New York police, the federal prosecutor, and the FBI had taken a toll. Manny was teetering on the edge of total exhaustion.

"You need to sleep. What can I get you to help you relax?"

"How about a rag soaked in ether? That

215

ought to do the trick." Manny plopped back onto the sofa. "What the hell is going on here? How can it be that your case and my case are related? That completely shatters the limits of coincidence."

He nodded. He'd been agonizing over the same question ever since Manny had called him from the apartment in Brooklyn to report her discovery. The previous morning, they had been following two distinctly separate paths in pursuit of two very different criminals. Now they were apparently on the same road, searching for what? A killer and his accomplice? Or a killer and his victim? Because Jake didn't believe for one moment that Travis was the Vampire. No eighteen-year-old, no matter how clever, could have masterminded these attacks.

And what were his and Manny's roles in this drama? It made sense that he, the most experienced member of the ME's staff, would be working on the Vampire case. But what was the significance of that stupid argument with Pederson when he seemed to be warning Jake away? And why, of all the criminal lawyers in New York, was the woman he happened to be involved with chosen to represent Travis Heaton? No matter how insulted Manny might be to hear him say it, she wasn't the obvious first choice to defend the Preppy Terrorist. So how had she gotten the job? Who had recommended her? They needed to get to the bottom of this connection.

Jake walked over to Manny and pulled her gently to her feet. "For some reason that I can't fathom, someone wants us both on this case. Now we're going to start figuring out why."

Manny sat bleary-eyed at the kitchen table, trying to focus on the typewritten words swimming across the piece of paper Jake had set before her. "How can you be so perky at six in the morning? You didn't get any more sleep than I did."

"I did my internship at Bellevue. Learning to function on three hours' sleep was part of the training back then." Jake placed a mug of coffee in her hands and let her take the first sip before he continued. "These are the questions we need answered by the end of the day. The first two items concern your matter."

The first half cup of scalding French roast was having its effect. Manny had acquired enough mental clarity to read aloud. " 'Who recommended Manny to represent Travis Heaton?' You remember . . . you were there when Kenneth called me to tell me about the case."

"Yes, but who called Kenneth? Maureen Heaton herself?"

Manny took another gulp of coffee. "No, some friend of hers. But I don't know who. Kenneth was excited and I was excited. I don't recall what he told me. He was supposed to type an intake sheet, but he'd just had his nails manicured and . . ."

"Let's call him now and disturb his beauty sleep," Jake said.

"Can't. He's gone away for a romantic getaway with a new friend. He told me he wouldn't be answering his cell for a few days."

"I'm not walking him down the aisle." Jake rolled his eyes. "Can you ask Mrs. Heaton directly?"

"I will." Manny let the paper slip from her fingers. Something floated on the edge of her memory, but she couldn't quite pin it down.

"What's the matter?" Jake asked.

"I'm trying to remember. . . . The day I won that bail hearing in court and got Travis out of jail, Maureen hugged me and said, 'I'm so glad Tracy sent you to me.' At the time, I didn't think much of it, but I don't know anyone named Tracy, man or woman."

"You know a million people." Jake handed

Manny the phone. Manny started to dial, then abruptly hung up. "No, I can't. Maureen's going to be ballistic with this new development. Since it's only six a.m., I can't talk to her yet. What's second on the list?"

She picked up the paper and read, " 'Follow-up with Jersey police contact re street name Freak.' Oh, I already did that yesterday morning. I forgot to tell you about it in all the excitement. Apparently, Freak is a rather popular street name. There were three in the database. One was black, and we know our guy is Caucasian. One's in prison upstate. And one recently completed a short jail term for promoting and participating in dog fights in Paterson." Manny shuddered. "Slimeball. They should have locked him up and thrown away the key. He could possibly be our guy."

"You're not prowling around the back alleys of Paterson looking for dog fights," Jake warned. "We'll let Sam handle it. And before he does that, he can translate that letter from Paco's computer."

"Sam speaks Spanish?"

"Fluently. Learned in the jungles of Guatemala."

"What was he doing there?"

Jake shrugged. "Don't ask, don't tell."

For a split second, Manny fantasized that

Sam was an undercover CIA mercenary. "Didn't he spend the night here? I'll go wake him up."

"No need, my dear woman." Sam entered the kitchen, followed by Mycroft, whose leash was trailing behind him. "I dreamed I was being kissed awake by a striking red-head. Turned out it was no dream, just Mycroft having a bladder emergency."

"Thanks for walking him, Sam." Manny squinted at him. "You just stayed in the neighborhood, right?"

"Yeah, why?"

"Last time your brother took Mycroft for a walk, he used him as a pimp," Manny told Jake. "Took him to Fifty-fourth in front of Manolo Blahnik to pick up well-heeled women. However, I have a way for him to make up for that little indiscretion."

Manny patted the chair beside her, inviting Sam to sit. "I have a translation job for you. Jake, hand me my purse, please."

Jake hoisted the large leather Fendi purse from the spot by the door where Manny had dropped it the night before. "Geez, what's in here? A lead vest in case you encounter plutonium on your daily rounds?"

"Just the bare essentials." Manny unzipped the bag and began rooting around for the sheets of paper she had printed from Paco's computer. The bag had multiple compartments, but she was sure she had quickly stuffed the letter in the main one on her way out of the Sandovals' apartment. In the course of the day, it must have worked its way down to the bottom of the bag. Out from the leathery depths came her Black-Berry, wallet, keys, and checkbook. With the major obstacles cleared, she peered in. There was a glimmer of white! Manny pulled. A receipt for the Chrome Hearts sunglasses she had purchased two months ago.

Jake eyed the total. "Surely the decimal point's in the wrong place?"

"I'm too law-abiding to buy cheap knock-offs." Manny kept digging. "Oh hell — I never mailed Aunt Joan's birthday card."

Jake shook his head as he poured his brother a cup of coffee. "You might want to scramble yourself some eggs. This could take a while."

"It must be in the side compartment," Manny said. Out came her makeup bag, the latest *Vogue,* a bag of dried apricots, and a hairbrush the size of a Ping-Pong paddle.

"Dried apricots?" Sam asked.

"I'm trying to snack healthy. They're loaded with antioxidants."

"They're also unopened."

"Ah! Here it is." Manny grinned with relief as she unfolded a bundle of white paper. Then the smile faded away as she read, " 'You are cordially invited to attend a trunk show for Barry Kieselstein-Cord at Bergdorf Goodman.' "

"This is ridiculous. It has to be in here." Manny undid every zipper and snap on the huge purse, turned it upside down, and shook. Sam snatched up his coffee cup to protect it from the cascade of flotsam and jetsam.

When the dust had settled, the two men surveyed the kitchen table with the awe of archaeologists entering an unsealed tomb.

"A socket wrench?"

"A lacrosse ball?"

"I had to tighten the bolt on Kenneth's office chair. And that ball came this close to hitting Mycroft — twice. I wouldn't give it back to those girls in the park."

With every item in the purse spread out on the table, Manny searched systematically, her panic rising with each dry-cleaning receipt and Chinese take-out menu, none of these items proving to be the missing letter.

Finally, she grabbed the kitchen trash can and swept a pile of junk into it. "The letter's gone." She whirled on Jake. "And I did *not* lose it. What goes in the bag stays in the bag. Until it is moved to another bag. Someone stole it."

CHAPTER
TWENTY-FIVE

"Was the bag ever out of your sight yesterday?" Jake asked.

Manny paused to think. "It was beside me in the booth at the diner. I never set it down while I was in the apartment in Brooklyn. Then I talked to all those cops and lawyers and FBI agents." Manny twirled her hair around her fingers. "I don't think it was ever away from me, but there were times it was hooked on the back of my chair, or lying under the table. Someone could have slipped the letter out then."

"But who?" Jake protested. "I thought you left the part about the letter out of the story you told the cops and the feds. No one but Paco knew you had it."

Manny nodded slowly, trying to process the implications. "I intentionally kept the part about the letter to myself. I knew if I gave it up to them, I'd never find out what it said. I figured after I read it, I could always take it back to them if I thought it contained information I'd get in trouble for withholding. Say I forgot about it in all the excitement."

She locked eyes with Jake. "So that means whoever stole it from my bag was tipped off by Paco."

"That leaves out the authorities," Jake said.

"Does it?"

Jake developed a sudden interest in loading the dishwasher, something he never saw the need for until every dish in the house was dirty. Manny knew he was using the time to form a calm response. Always the scientist, always in control of himself.

"Jake, think about it." Manny stood up and started firing items back into her purse. "There's something very fishy about the way Paco has drawn Travis into his circle. And the government's hands-off attitude toward the Sandovals is stranger still. How do we know the Sandovals aren't cooperating with the FBI in some sort of terrorism sting?"

Jake slowly closed the dishwasher. "What empirical evidence do you have?"

"I just told you."

"You take two unexplained phenomena, put them together, and come up with a conspiracy. As a scientist, I look for the most likely explanation first. After that's been eliminated — and only after it's eliminated — I move on to consider the more remote possibilities. When you hear hoofbeats, think horses —"

"Yeah, yeah, yeah, not zebras," Manny said, finishing the old adage. "Your problem is, you automatically trust authority unless you see overwhelming evidence that the system isn't working. I automatically question authority, unless the person wielding it has proven to me that he's above reproach. And frankly, federal prosecutor Brian Lisnek, Ambassador Sandoval, and the merry crew of FBI agents questioning me last night have not cleared the bar."

Sam had been watching the exchange like a fan with center court seats at the U.S. Open. Now he intervened before his brother could respond. "I don't think Manny's totally out in left field. But, *but*" — Sam held up his hand for silence as Jake opened his mouth to protest — "you can't fault Jake's methodology. Assume the most plausible explanation until it's proven wrong.

"So, Manny," Sam continued. "Let's run through the possibilities of when the letter could have been lifted from your purse. Paco knew you'd head for Rosamond Street, but he couldn't know who you'd encounter there. You're sure you initiated the contact with the neighbor and the super?"

"Of course I'm sure. And I wasn't close to anyone else that whole time . . . except —" She broke off, thinking about the way she had entered the apartment building.

"Except what?"

"When I got there, before I could ring the bell, a man came out of the building and held the door open for me. At the time, I thought he was just a friendly neighbor, but maybe he'd been waiting for me."

"And you think he could've reached into your bag and taken the letter in the few seconds that you walked past him through the door?" Sam rose and refilled his coffee cup. "If they really wanted to get the letter back, it would be too risky to put all their hope on that brief encounter. Pickpocketing is most successful on a crowded elevator, a street corner, a subway — somewhere where the victim expects to be jostled, and the perp can disappear into a crowd."

Manny appraised him suspiciously. "You seem to know quite a bit about the subject. If we searched your room, would we find a collection of wallets?"

"Nah." Sam grinned. "I take the cash and ditch the leather. Seriously, though, can you think of a time during the day when you were surrounded by people?"

Manny chewed her lower lip, replaying every scene of the long action-packed day. "When I went to my parking garage to get my car, there were four or five people waiting for their cars to be driven down. There's not much space, so we were crammed together."

"That's a more likely spot for the grab," Sam said. "So, it may be that the person Paco tipped off is familiar enough with your routine to know where you garage your car."

"And that you'd be driving it to Brooklyn," Jake added, "not taking the subway."

"You mean it's someone I know?"

"Or someone who's been keeping an eye on you for a while," Jake said. "Which brings us back to the matter of how you got involved in this case in the first place." He handed Manny the phone again. "You've warmed up on me. I think you're ready to handle Maureen Heaton."

Manny took a deep breath and dialed. As anticipated, the first five minutes of the call passed in a storm of Maureen's panicky speculations. Eventually, Manny was able to bring the conversation around to the matter at hand. "Maureen, refresh my memory: Who was it who recommended that you hire me to represent Travis?"

"Her name is Tracy. I don't know her last name. She's a nurse at the Chelsea Extended Care Center. I was working private duty there the night I got the call that Travis had been arrested. I was in a panic. I needed to leave right away, but I couldn't abandon my patient. Tracy was so understanding. She told me to leave, that it was slow that night and she could spend extra time with my patient.

"And then she showed me your card, said she'd call and have you get in touch with me in case Travis needed a lawyer. You helped her nephew . . . or was it her cousin? Anyway, you called while I was at the jail, and by then I really knew I needed you. And people say New Yorkers are cold, but you know, I've never found that to be true."

Manny murmured a few more words of encouragement and extricated herself from the conversation.

As she dialed the Chelsea Extended Care Center, she relayed the details of her conversation to Jake and Sam.

"How can I know which of my clients has an aunt or a cousin who's a nurse named Tracy?" Manny spent the next fifteen minutes speaking to the receptionist, the human resources manager, the nursing director, and anyone else she could get to answer the phone at the small private nursing home. Each conversation left her more frustrated than the last. Finally, she hung up. Sam and Jake watched her expectantly.

"There's no one named Tracy who works at the Chelsea Extended Care Center."

CHAPTER
TWENTY-SIX

Leaving Manny to deal with her missing client and the puzzle of who had recommended her for the case, Jake retreated to the black cave that was his home office. He had resisted all Manny's efforts to spruce the place up. Black leather chairs, framed antique prints, mahogany and glass display case — all her suggestions were met with a resounding no.

He liked the place just as it was. He didn't need pleasant surroundings in order to concentrate, something that Manny just didn't understand. All he craved was familiarity — the security of knowing that every tool, reference, and resource he might possibly need could be reached with one spin of his decrepit desk chair.

Seen through a visitor's eyes, the office looked hopelessly chaotic. But Jake could plunge his hand into a tower of seemingly random papers and pull out just what he needed. To his way of thinking, filing cabinet equaled trash can.

Today, Jake sat amid an avalanche of information about the Vampire, making notes on a yellow pad in the appalling scrawl that no one but he could decipher. A short list of questions he wanted answered appeared on the page.

1. Coffee mug with Nixon's fingerprints . . . owned by Amanda Hogaarth or left behind by killer? How acquired? Why?
2. Family Builders adoption agency — what is the connection to Hogaarth?
3. Hogaarth and Fortes — why tortured and killed? How are they different from earlier victims?
4. What is the significance of the *blood?*

The intercom buzzed. "Ridley here to see you," the department secretary announced.

"Send him in."

Paul Ridley loped into the room, ducking his head to clear the nearly seven-foot-high door opening. Tall and thin didn't begin to describe the leading crime-scene technician from the police department's CSI team; Ridley looked like he'd been captured by a rogue computer animation program, stretched, and released back into society.

"Have a seat," Jake said. "Just toss that stuff on the floor."

Ridley telescoped his gaunt frame into a chair. "I've got some information on that coffee mug from Hogaarth's apartment."

Jake grinned. Maybe the first item on his list was about to be taken care of. "I know the FBI's been agitating to get custody of that piece of evidence. I was worried you wouldn't be able to discover much before you had to give it up."

"Yeah, we might lose it by the end of the day, but I think I have what you want." Ridley pulled a file folder from his briefcase and began talking from his notes. "Cup was cheap porcelain glazed black, with the initials SCFR printed in silver. Manufacturer's mark on the bottom said 'Cayo.' We traced this to a distributor based in suburban Boston who buys mugs wholesale from a manufacturer in China, then imprints them here for customers who give them away as sales promotions." He pointed at a blue mug on Jake's desk crammed with pens printed with the name LABTECH in red. "Like that — you probably got it from the salesman who handles your lab equipment, right?"

Jake's satisfied smile faded a bit. "There must be a hundred million promotional mugs distributed in this country every year. You're not going to tell me you know how this one once got into the hands of President Nixon?"

Ridley peered at Jake over wire glasses perched on his pointy nose. "Uhm . . . actually, yes."

Jake slapped his desk. "Ridley, don't take this the wrong way. But I love you."

Ridley coughed. "Yes, er, as I was saying, we analyzed the chemical makeup of the glaze, which allowed us to date the mug to a ten-year period when Cayo, the manufacturer, was using this particular formulation. This time frame, 1975 to 1985, corresponds to a period after Nixon's resignation but before his health began to fail, when he was actively accepting speaking engagements. We reviewed the distributor's sales records for this period and found the customer who ordered these mugs: the Scanlon Center on Foreign Relations, a right-wing think tank on foreign affairs. We believe that Nixon delivered an address there in 1977."

"Amazing work, Ridley. So you're saying Nixon drank from this mug during his speech more than thirty years ago, and the prints are still there?"

"Oh yes, glazed porcelain is a perfect medium for accepting fingerprints. As long as the mug was never wiped clean or exposed to moisture or extreme heat, the prints would last. Collectors of presidential memorabilia usually handle this stuff more carefully than cops handle crucial evidence at a murder scene. Don't touch it; keep the items in brown paper bags. Ya know, all the stuff we teach that's generally ignored."

"Were there any other prints on the mug?" Jake asked.

"None. I'd say that rules out the possibility that the former president was in the habit of saving giveaway mugs and taking them home to his wife to use at breakfast."

"So, we have to assume that someone who attended this speech wanted a souvenir. Got a thrill from possessing a mug that Richard Nixon had drunk from." Jake pursed his lips. "Doesn't appeal to me, but I guess it falls into the same category as keeping the sweat-soaked shirt that a rock star throws into the crowd."

Jake picked up a squishy rubber brain given to him by a salesman at the annual forensic science conference and started to squeeze it. "Amazing work, Ridley. You've tracked that mug to the one day in eighty-some years of the president's life when it could have picked up those fingerprints. Unfortunately, it doesn't seem to bring us any closer to figuring out how or why it got into Amanda Hogaarth's apartment. Anyone in the lecture hall that day could have taken it." He flung the brain back onto the desk, where it bounced over an autopsy report. "Do you know how many people attended his speech?"

"Apparently, it was by invitation only. One hundred and twenty academics, journalists, and government policy wonks." Ridley pulled two typed sheets from his folder and handed them to Jake. "The Scanlon Center very generously shared the attendee list with me. You gotta love interns."

"Excellent! You've shared this with Detective Pasquarelli?"

"Yeah, but he didn't seem quite as excited by it as you."

Jake gripped the papers. "I think it's significant. Someone on this list may have killed Amanda Hogaarth."

Ridley unfolded himself from the chair. "I leave it to you and the detective to figure out who." He raised his hand in a farewell salute. "Happy to be of service."

"Thanks, Ridley." He watched as the criminalist looked for area on the cluttered floor to place his size-sixteen feet. "Say, one more thing. Do you know the topic of Nixon's speech?"

"Tactics to destabilize leftist opposition in Argentina."

CHAPTER
TWENTY-SEVEN

"Hello?" Manny answered her phone as she pulled her Porsche Cabriolet into traffic, ready to drive downtown to her office.

"Manny, it's Sam. I just set up a meeting with Deanie Slade, the girl who connected me with Boo Hravek. She's a regular at Club Epoch, where Paco and Travis partied before the bombing. She wants me to meet her there. I think you might want to hear what she has to say."

"When? Tonight?"

"No, right now. I'm about to get on the PATH train to Hoboken. Meet me there."

Manny checked her watch. "Isn't ten a.m. a little early for clubbing?"

"She said the side door would be open. She must know the staff. It's Franklin Street. I'll see you there at eleven."

Deciding that the Lincoln Tunnel would be suicide at this time of day, Manny headed uptown, cruising across the GW

Bridge to make her way south to Hoboken on the Jersey side of the Hudson.

The sky was a rare blue, marred by neither clouds nor haze, and Manny took her eyes off the road ahead a few times to steal glimpses of the city skyline out the driver's side window. Impossible to worry on a day like today!

She had been too busy and preoccupied to check in with Sam on the Boo Hravek angle of the case, but clearly he'd been working on it. Maybe this was the missing piece that would make the other disjointed pieces of the puzzle form into a recognizable picture. Trust Sam to produce it.

Manny stopped at a traffic light. She hadn't driven south along the river from Fort Lee in a long time. Traffic was worse than she remembered. Luxury condominiums with river views were sprouting up everywhere, replacing the old warehouses and factories that used to jam the industrial waterfront. But a few old relics still remained, waiting for developers to pounce.

Manny glanced at her watch. She thought she would have been in Hoboken by now, but she was still one town away, in West New York. Her view of the river appeared and disappeared as she wound through the town's congested streets. West New York was what Hoboken had been twenty years ago — just on the cusp of trendy, still loaded with plenty of grit. A shadow fell over the car, cast by a large abandoned building with the ghostly letters FIREPROOF APPAREL still visible on the side. That would probably be the next factory to be converted into loft apartments. She could get a place five times the size of her Manhattan studio for the same price.

Finally, Manny saw a WELCOME TO HOBOKEN sign. Club Epoch was located close by, on the northern edge of town, and Manny pulled into a parking spot just as the clock in her car hit 11:00. She got out and looked around for Sam. The street was deserted. She dialed Sam's phone, which rolled immediately to voice mail.

The only activity on the street centered on a minimart on the corner. Maybe someone in there had noticed Sam out on the sidewalk in front of the club. The smell of scorched coffee kept hot 24/7 clobbered Manny as soon as she entered. The bleached blonde behind the counter labored over the lottery ticket machine while two shabbily dressed men waited impatiently to lose their money. No use trying to get in the middle of that transaction even to ask a simple question. Manny occupied herself by reading the headlines of the newspapers arrayed in front of the counter. From the *New York Times*'s discreet POLICE PROBE LATEST TWIST IN VAMPIRE CASE to the *New York Post*'s VAMP TO PREP: COME INTO MY LAIR, all three New York papers and the *Newark Star-Ledger* featured the Vampire case on the front page.

A large woman with a head full of braids grabbed the *Post* and struck up a conversation. "Uhm, uhm," she said. "That's one nasty dude. Goin' round stickin' needles in people." She closed her eyes and shuddered.

Manny nodded vaguely, preoccupied with getting the clerk's attention so she could ask if she'd seen Sam strolling the area or entering the club.

"Why can't the cops catch him?" the lady continued. "All that DNA stuff they got nowadays still don't do them no good. 'Member the Son of Sam? They caught that guy 'cause of a parking ticket. I bet this be the same."

Another man joined the line and the conversation, relieving Manny of the obligation to chat. "They better catch him soon, because this shit is freakin' me out. Man, there's nothing I hate worse than needles. Guns I can deal with, but not this."

Manny glanced up. The man who spoke

had hands the size of grizzly paws and a sumo-wrestler-thick neck. Yet she could see from the revulsion on his face that the Vampire really did scare him.

"And what about the guy he killed with the rat bites," the first woman reminded the man.

"Ah, Jesus, don't even go there! What they really oughta do to catch him is —"

The two of them continued in a weird one-upmanship of fear and advice. Manny eavesdropped, amazed by their extensive knowledge of the case. She was sure if she asked either of them to name their congressman or to say what was going on between the Israelis and the Palestinians at the moment, they'd be flummoxed, but on the subject of the Vampire, they were experts. The total media saturation had produced millions of people who saw themselves as prospective victims, prospective detectives, or both.

Finally, Manny reached the head of the line and plunked a pack of gum on the counter. "Have you seen a tall, thin man with a ponytail in the area around here in the past half hour? He may have been headed to Club Epoch," she said to the clerk as she paid.

The woman shook her head. "It's been

quiet all morning, till now."

Manny went back outside and looked across the street at the warehouse-shaped building painted black, with a large silver *E* on the door. That had to be it. She wrinkled her nose — not her idea of a hot nightspot. Was Deanie waiting all alone in there? Manny's sunshine-induced optimism began to ebb away. Why had Deanie suddenly called Sam? She had to realize he was a suspect in Boo's murder. Was this some kind of setup?

She dialed Sam again, and again got voice mail. Then she dialed Jake. "I think Sam's in some kind of trouble," Manny said, not bothering with a greeting. "I'm not sure what to do."

Quickly, Manny explained the situation.

"I'll be right there," Jake said. "Do *not* go into that place alone, understand me?"

"I won't. Not after yesterday. But, Jake, it'll take you over an hour to get across town and over to Hoboken."

"You're in luck. I'm not in my office. I got called to a suspicious death on Forty-fourth and Ninth. I just finished up, and there's a department car here."

"Right around the corner from the Lincoln Tunnel. There is a God!"

■ ■ ■ ■

"How many laws did you break to get here so fast?" Manny asked as Jake pulled up twenty minutes later.

"I had to pass on the right, but that was only because I got stuck behind some guy who kept stopping at yellow lights. Iowa plates. Guess he didn't know that in a blue state, yellow means accelerate."

"The Turnpike Authority ought to post those rules." Manny took Jake's elbow and guided him to the right. "See that black warehouse? That's Club E. Sam said Deanie called him this morning, sounding very nervous. Told him she had some information on what went down with Boo, but she didn't want to talk about it on the phone."

"Any clue why she had a sudden change of heart?" Jake asked.

Manny shook her head. "That's what's worrying me. What if it's a trap?"

"You stay here and I'll go in and check it out," Jake said.

"No way!"

"Manny, it's safer that way. If I don't come out, you can call the police."

"What if it's the police who've set the trap? They're looking for Boo's killer. There could be incriminating evidence in there waiting for you. If the police happen to show up two minutes after you get in there, you'll need a witness to corroborate your story."

Jake glared at her for a moment, then turned to cross the street. "Come on, Manny. Let's get this over with."

Jake tugged on the unmarked black door on the side of the building. It opened, releasing a gust of cold, rancid air. The air-conditioning kept the temperature low, but it didn't do much to eradicate the aftermath of Club E's nightly hordes of sweating, drink-spilling, puking customers.

Jake gestured Manny to the side and peered into the dimly lighted interior. A long hallway, illuminated only by the emergency exit sign, extended to the right. Looking straight ahead, he could see the cavernous dance floor and the outline of one of the three long bars. From his breast pocket Jake pulled a small, bright flashlight. Its beam extended only a few feet, but it was better than walking into the abyss.

"Deanie! It's Sam Rosen," said Jake, lying.

Jake and Manny stood on the threshold, listening.

"I think I heard something," Manny said.

"A voice, but I couldn't make out words."

Jake frowned. "Your hearing must be keener than mine. What direction?"

"Down the hall, I think."

Just inside the door, Jake spotted a heavy stanchion, which he assumed the bouncers must use to prop this door open when the club got too crowded. He dragged it out to hold the door wide open, admitting as much of the day's brilliant sunshine as possible.

"You sure you don't want to wait here?" Jake asked.

"Hell no! I go where you go." Manny followed Jake through the door and down the hall.

"Deanie?" Jake shouted again.

This time, they both heard it. A whimper or moan, unmistakably coming from one of the rooms off the hall.

Jake quickened his pace.

"Be careful," Manny warned. "It could still be a trap. Don't charge through any doors."

Jake stopped outside a door marked OFFICE. "Deanie? Are you in there?"

The faint muffled sound came again. "I think it's that door." Manny pointed to the next door on the hallway.

Jake tried the door, but the knob didn't turn. Inside, the moans increased.

"I don't like this." Manny reached inside her bag. "Let's call the police."

Jake pulled the phone from her hand and dropped it back into the bag. "And how would we explain our presence here? We'd have to tell them about the connection to Sam. We either open this door ourselves and talk to Deanie or leave now and call for help anonymously."

Manny bit her lip. "That door looks pretty solid. The lock's a Yale. Any bright ideas?"

Jake looked around. A large fire extinguisher hung on the wall a few steps farther down the hall. "I could use that as a battering ram." He went to unhook it.

Manny followed, whispering, "But, Jake, what if she's not alone in there? You'll go sailing in, unprotected."

His eyes met hers. He was surprised, and touched, by the concern he saw there. Jake knew she was right, but he chose not to dwell on the risks. If his brother was in trouble, he was going in. Jake squeezed Manny's hand. "You be my backup."

Then he turned, took three running steps, and crashed through the door.

Jake moved so quickly, Manny didn't have time to be terrified. The door splintering open made a tremendous noise, drowning out any other sound from within the room.

Manny stepped up to the opening, clutching the frame with her trembling hand.

Jake jumped up from the floor. Shadowy figures surrounded him. The windowless room seemed to extend endlessly. From the pitch-black interior, the moans had changed to high-pitched, muffled squeals. Manny searched by the door frame for a light switch.

The room sprang to life — a storeroom stacked high with cases of paper towels, cleaning supplies, and glassware. Random paths led between the pillars, like a Halloween corn maze. Except at the center, there wasn't a dummy emitting a sound track of scary sounds; there was a real person, terrified and in pain.

Jake headed into the maze, pursuing the sound. Manny followed. They dodged left past a column of boxes, then circled around some stacked bar stools. The sound grew louder now, and shriller. The terror in it was so intense, it seemed inhuman. Manny flashed back on her eight-year-old self hearing the squeals of a baby rabbit being carried off by the neighborhood tomcat. She'd been powerless to help then, but she wasn't now.

"Deanie, it's okay. We're coming to help you," she shouted. All thoughts of a trap had dissolved, replaced by determination to find a way through the room's piles of junk and rescue this poor girl.

Jake clipped a pyramid of bathroom tissue with his shoulder, toppling it. Manny stared at the resulting roadblock. There was no going over it; she'd have to go around it. Up ahead, Jake was moving forward on the main path. Manny chose a tributary that she hoped would lead her back to him and squeezed through.

A hand clapped down on her shoulder.

Manny's scream ricocheted through the building.

CHAPTER
TWENTY-EIGHT

"Calm down!"

"Sam! Where did you come from?"

"The PATH train stalled in the tunnel under the river. I've been stuck for over an hour. No cell service, so I couldn't even call you. When I got here, I saw the outer door propped open and this one broken down. How did you get in?"

"With me." Jake's voice floated over to them. "Now stop jabbering and come help me."

Sam and Manny heard the sound of something very heavy being dragged across the floor, then another high-pitched squeal. They scrambled toward it.

"Oh my God." Jake's voice, always so calm and clinical, carried a real edge of distress.

"Jake? Jake?" Manny flung aside a rolling coatrack. "What is it? Are you all right? Is Deanie okay?"

Manny saw an old video game machine

ahead. She realized this must be what Jake had pushed to make a small pass-through on the right. She wedged herself through the opening, with Sam right behind.

Deanie Slade sat precariously planted on a bar stool that had been lashed to a post, her knees and ankles bent cruelly backward and tied behind her and to the bar stool in an excruciating contortion. Spiked glass shards from a broken beer bottle were inserted under the ropes. With her arms and legs immobilized, any movement to try to undo the restraints caused pain and created the risk of dangerous cuts. It took extraordinary strength and concentration for her to remain still. Even the floor surrounding the stool had been liberally sprinkled with sharp shards of broken glassware. Deanie's eyes and mouth were bound shut with duct tape, but she seemed well aware of what lay beneath her. When Jake kicked some of the glass away so he could kneel beside her, she moaned and whimpered at the sound.

"It's all right, Deanie. I'm going to help you," Jake said gently as he pulled a pocket-knife from his jacket and prepared to free the girl. "I'm a doctor."

Manny watched with surprise as the girl cringed away from Jake at this news. She wore nothing but a halter top and a very short skirt. The ropes and glass around her bare legs and arms had chafed her pale skin raw. She trembled convulsively, both from fear and cold.

Jake continued to speak to Deanie soothingly, telling her exactly what he was going to do. Manny saw him then as a medical doctor, trained to save lives. First, he cut her arms free, and Manny could tell that the pain of being released from this unnatural position was almost as great as the pain of maintaining it.

Jake held the rope with his fingertips and jerked his head in Manny's direction. "Find some clean paper to put this on."

Manny accepted the command. Jake the doctor had been replaced by Jake the forensic scientist, eager to preserve evidence. She ripped open a carton of paper towels and gingerly took the rope from Jake.

Next, Jake cut the girl's legs free, carefully guiding each one to rest on the bottom rung of the stool to keep her bare feet away from the remaining glass. Then he turned his attention to the tape across her eyes and mouth.

"I have some hand lotion in my purse," Manny offered. "You can use it to loosen the glue."

Jake shook his head. "I'm afraid not. This

tape may contain traces of the assailant's DNA, fibers from his clothes. I can't risk destroying that." He slit the tape at her temples and removed it with one quick yank. Manny winced. Deanie made a gasping sound from beneath the tape on her mouth, but compared to her joint pain, the tape removal must have been a minor discomfort. She seemed more bothered by the effect of light on eyes that had been in darkness for a long time. Her eyes peeked open briefly before she scrunched them shut again. Jake repeated the process with the tape on her mouth, leaving two angry red weals across her face.

Deanie rubbed her face, then, shielding her eyes with her fingers, peeped at her rescuers. Recognizing Sam, she inhaled sharply, but she still did not speak.

"Do you see her shoes?" Jake asked. Manny and Sam looked, but the shoes were nowhere in sight.

"Well, let's get you out of here," Jake said. "I'll carry you over the glass." Putting his right hand under her arms and his left under her knees, he lifted her off the stool. As he did, a slip of paper fluttered to the floor. Manny stepped forward to retrieve it.

"Don't touch it," Jake commanded.

So she crouched over it and read aloud:

" 'The innocent suffer when the guilty are allowed to go unpunished.' "

"What does that mean? Who are you? How did you know I was here?"

Big hair flattened, long acrylic nails snapped off, eye makeup washed away by a river of tears, Deanie was no longer the jaunty Jersey girl who had given up secrets to Sam in a drunken night of dancing at Club E.

"I got a call from your cell phone at nine-thirty this morning asking me to meet you here at eleven," Sam said. They were all four sitting at the deserted bar, watching Deanie drink a big Diet Coke. "How long were you tied up back there?"

She clutched her glass as if it alone were keeping her from keeling over. "Since last night. I got grabbed coming home from work. Someone came up from behind me and put this bad-smelling cloth over my face. When I woke up, I was in that store-room."

Jake leaned toward her. "What can you tell us about your attacker?"

Deanie edged away, obviously disturbed by the urgency in his voice, and pressed her back against the bar. "Who *are* you people?" She glanced at Sam, then peered down into her drink, as if eye contact with him scared her. "You got me into this. You killed Boo, didn't you?"

"I know it looks bad that Boo died a few days after talking to me," Sam said, "but believe me, I didn't kill him. We think . . ." he paused, silenced by his brother's warning glance. "We think Boo was mixed up in something bigger than he realized."

"Well, whatta they want with me? I don't know nuthin about Boo's business." Deanie hugged herself and began to cry.

"Deanie, we don't want you to get hurt again," Jake said. "That's why it's important that you tell us everything you can remember about last night."

Deanie wasn't the brightest crayon in the box under the best of circumstances, and fear, exhaustion, and dehydration weren't helping her reasoning abilities.

"I don't know nuthin," she repeated sullenly. "I didn't see them. When I woke up, that tape was already over my eyes." Compulsively, her right hand stroked her left arm.

"Them? There was more than one?" Jake's eyes lighted up, but he was careful to keep the eagerness out of his voice.

"A man and a woman."

Manny and Jake exchanged glances. They

didn't have to speak to know they were thinking the same thought: Maybe this was Tracy, the woman at the nursing home who had recommended Manny to Maureen Heaton.

"Why did they torture you like this, Deanie?" Manny asked. "What were they trying to get you to tell them?"

"They didn't ask me nuthin." Deanie slammed her glass on the bar. "They told me not to try to get away, that there was broken glass all around me. They tied my legs back like that, and when I started to cry, the woman said something. So I thought the guy was going to loosen the rope, but instead he made it tighter and then put the sharp glass underneath the ropes on my skin. They told me not to try to escape, said if I was still and silent, someone would come for me. That's it."

Deanie continued rubbing her hands up and down her bare arms, trying either to stay warm or to massage away the pain of her bondage. Suddenly, she stopped and looked down at the crook of her right arm. "What the fuck? I must have cut myself after all. I'm bleeding!"

Jake reached out for her arm and saw it: the tiny puncture of a blood draw, now oozing some fresh blood. He found a clean napkin and applied pressure. "They drew your blood. Were you aware of that?"

"Drew blood? Why?"

Jake and Manny exchanged a glance. Could Deanie be the only person in the entire metro area unaware of the work of the Vampire? If so, she'd be happier staying in that state of ignorance.

"What did they say to each other?" Jake asked.

"I don't know. They spoke to each other in Spanish."

CHAPTER
TWENTY-NINE

"I gotta pee," Deanie announced after finishing off her second glass of soda.

"Manny, go with her," Jake instructed.

They had found Deanie's high-heeled mules on the way out of the storeroom, and Deanie now clumped down the hall to the restroom, with Manny following. Making small talk seemed ridiculous, so Manny kept her mouth shut.

She opened the door for her charge and followed her in. The Club E ladies' room was as big, dim, and uninviting as the rest of the place. A grimy-looking divan stood against one wall. Not caring to dwell on the types of activities that might take place on it in the course of the average evening, Manny stood guard by the sinks as Deanie went into the last stall. Catching a glimpse of herself in the mirror, Manny pulled out her brush and lipstick and began to repair the damage of the morning's excitement. In a few minutes, she heard the toilet flush. She put away her makeup and waited for Deanie's stall door to open.

It stayed shut.

"Deanie? Are you okay in there?"

No answer.

"Deanie?" Manny strode across the bathroom and rattled the stall door. "Open up!"

Only then did it strike Manny that the stall doors came all the way down to the floor and were at least six feet high, the better to protect their clubgoing occupants from prying eyes as they got high or got screwed.

Heart pounding, Manny went into the adjacent stall and jumped up on the toilet. Propping one leg on the toilet back, she pulled herself up far enough to look over the top of the stall divider.

Deanie's stall was empty. A small window facing the parking lot was open.

Jake patted Manny on the shoulder. "Don't beat yourself up. This may actually work to our advantage."

She eyed him suspiciously. It wasn't like Jake to humor her. She had screwed up and she fully expected to catch hell for it.

"How do you figure?" Manny asked.

"Sam and I were talking strategy while you were gone. There's no way we can avoid reporting this to the police and turning over the evidence, and we were both concerned about how this implicates Sam. But with Deanie temporarily out of the picture, we can bend the truth a little regarding how you and I came to be at Club E, and leave Sam out of the equation."

Manny nodded. "So we tell them what? That I got an anonymous call to come here and brought you along?"

"Yes," Jake said. "And that after we freed her, she immediately needed to use the bathroom. It never dawned on us to guard the victim, and she ran away. We called nine-one-one immediately. We don't know who the victim was."

"That'll work. But wait — they'll want to see my cell phone to trace the call. All it shows is a call from Sam at ten this morning."

Sam grinned. "A call I made from a pay phone at Penn Station. I couldn't get a cell signal in there today."

Jake clapped his brother on the back. "Man, you travel under a lucky star. Get rid of any signs that we were in this bar area. Wrap up the glass that Deanie used and take it with you, then disappear. Manny, give me five minutes, then call nine-one-one."

"Where are you going?" Manny asked.

"Back to the storeroom. I plan to borrow one small piece of evidence."

CHAPTER THIRTY

"You wanna know what?"

Pasquarelli's voice came through the phone line loudly enough to make Jake move the receiver away from his ear. He and the detective had spoken only briefly since Manny had reported the incident at Club E to the police in Hoboken. Jake knew his friend was frazzled, but he needed his help. "I want to know who published the cookbook I found hidden in Ms. Hogaarth's kitchen," Jake repeated.

"Cut me a break, will ya. I got my hands full here. I thought once we discovered the link between the Vampire and the Judge Brueninger bombing, the mayor would finally let the FBI have this case. But no, he still wants to keep a hand in it, even though the feds are the ones with a database full of information on Islamic terror groups that they won't let me see."

"Look, Vito, if the Vampire and the Preppy

Terrorist cases are really tied to Islamic terrorism, then you're right — you don't stand a chance of solving them," Jake said. "You might as well lie low, shuffle papers, and wait for the feds to clear it up. But if my hunch is correct, something entirely different is behind these cases. If you work on my leads, maybe you'll have a chance to score the coup the mayor's looking for."

"And if you're wrong?"

"Then you're screwed," Jake admitted cheerfully. "But you're screwed right now anyway. Seems to me you've got nothing to lose."

A long silence filled the phone line.

"Talk," Vito said finally.

"I want to find out where the Spanish-language cookbook we found in Ms. Hogaarth's apartment was published. I suspect it was Argentina. Argentina could be the link that ties all the victims together."

"Did I miss something here? There is no link between the victims — they're totally random. And none of them is Argentinean. Number three was Chilean, but that's as close to Spanish as we get."

"We may not see the link between the victims yet," Jake said. "But it's there. We have to keep digging."

"Nixon made a speech about the place

more than twenty-five years ago, and you think that's the key to our Vampire? C'mon, Jake, get real."

"Nixon's speech and the fact that the Sandovals are Argentinean. If it turns out that Hogaarth's Spanish-language cookbook was published in Argentina, that would be three links in the chain. Then we could ask the other vics if they have any connection in their lives to Argentina."

"You think these people are all withholding information from us?" Vito asked. "No way. I interviewed them. They're scared, freaked-out by the fact that they were randomly targeted by this nut. You can't fake that five times."

"No, I don't necessarily think they're hiding information. The victims themselves may not be aware of the significance. You didn't ask any of them if they had ties to Argentina."

"You can ask. As for Hogaarth's cookbook, the apartment's been released as a crime scene. We had no reason to keep the cookbook. It's all part of her estate. If you want access to it, you'll have to contact her lawyer yourself. Frankly, I think this case might be easier if the Vampire is a terrorist."

"The Vampire is a terrorist all right, but not an Islamic one," Jake said. "And just like Osama or the Taliban or the Palestinians, he's trying to get publicity for his cause. He's trying to lead us toward something. I'm sure of it. And somehow, Argentina is part of the puzzle."

Jake pressed against the eyepieces of his microscope and studied the pattern of the long, thin single hair with a central nonpigmented line, dye-stained for two-thirds its length. This long blond strand, which he'd retrieved from the tape used to bind Deanie's eyes, was almost certainly hers. Jake had found it on the end of the tape, near where it had touched her hairline. The tape was also filled with skin cells, but it showed no fingerprints. Deanie had never been able to touch it, as the tape had gone on after her hands were tied, and the Vampire had obviously worn gloves when applying it.

Jake had left the other piece of tape for the Hoboken police, so they, too, had bits of Deanie's DNA. Not that it would do them much good, as it was unlikely that the young woman's DNA would be on file in any criminal database. But the tape held one other tantalizing piece of DNA evidence. Jake changed slides under the microscope and looked at this prize: a very short dark curly hair with a prominent central medulla line. DNA could be extracted from the hair root. Jake knew this couldn't be Deanie's hair. Her skin was quite fair, her arm hair light and downy. He suspected that the highly sticky duct tape had brushed against the Vampire's arm as he bound his victim, pulling out an arm hair. Even the most careful criminal leaves behind traces of his presence.

So he probably had a piece of the Vampire's DNA. But what good would it do him in the short run? It would take days even for an expedited DNA analysis, and if the Vampire's DNA wasn't on file, the sample wouldn't bring him into their sights. In the meantime, Travis was out there somewhere under the control of this killer. More than a killer — someone who didn't hesitate to use torture to achieve his ends. Jake sighed and prepared the sample to be sent to the lab. They couldn't afford to sit back and wait for results or count on the feds to find Travis soon. After all, they hadn't been able to find a nearly seven-foot-man in a turban for years. Nor would the feds protect Travis. As far as they were concerned, he was another defendant who had violated house arrest. It was up to Manny and him to keep pursuing every possible lead.

Jake stared at the phone, commanding it

to ring. He'd called Ms. Hogaarth's attorney earlier that morning to see if he could get access to the cookbook, but when did any lawyer ever accept a call on the first try? Jake grabbed the phone and dialed again. If he made himself annoying enough, eventually the lawyer would have to answer.

CHAPTER
THIRTY-ONE

"Achoo!" Manny dabbed at her nose with the crumpled remains of her last tissue. "The cloud of mold spores hanging over this place is visible to the naked eye. Tell me again why we have to be here instead of out looking for Travis?"

"This *is* looking for Travis," Jake replied as he pawed through a box of decaying books.

"I had in mind something a little more action-oriented," Manny said. "I'm really worried. The Vampire could be doing something awful to that kid right now, and we're here poking through this mountain of crap." Manny shoved past an ancient department store mannequin and started in on the next table of books.

"We have no solid leads on Travis's whereabouts," Jake said. "Until we do, this is as good a use of our time as any." Before she could object, he continued. "Hey, look at this — *Principles of Modern Microbiology,* circa 1932. Can you believe this diagram of the swine flu bug?" Jake chuckled and shook his head. "That's what it looked like many generations ago in the swine population before it morphed into the influenza A subtypes that exist now."

"Oh, those wacky Depression-era biologists. Always good for a few laughs." Manny looked in disgust at her dust-blackened fingers and surveyed the tables and tables of books they still had to search through. "Put that down, Jake. We're looking for a cookbook, remember."

As executor of her estate, Amanda Hogaarth's lawyer had packed up the contents of her apartment and shipped them off to the St. Anselm's Altar Society Thrift Shop in Chelsea. Jake and Manny had followed the stuff here. The church-lady volunteers at the counter had informed them that the delivered items had been sorted and put out for sale just the day before, so Jake was positive the cookbook would still be here. Finding it, however, wasn't proving easy. Ms. Hogaarth had hidden the book in her apartment, but it was much more effectively concealed here, an old book among thousands of others just like it.

Manny moved down the crowded aisle,

starting on her third table of books. The smell of this place made her eager to find what they were looking for and get out. Forgotten lives, discarded objects, mementos that held no value for the people who'd inherited them — St. Anselm's was the last stop before the landfill and it smelled only marginally better. Manny's eyes scanned quickly, pausing to read titles only when the book met the physical description Jake had provided: thick, blue, no dust jacket.

Jake worked his way toward her from the other end of the book room, but he wasn't moving anywhere near as fast. When Manny paused and looked up, she saw Jake with a slender red book in his hands. "Asking you to search a used-book sale is like asking Emeril to search a farmers' market. Stop reading!"

"I can't help it — 'The Cask of Amontillado' and 'The Tell-Tale Heart' in a special illustrated edition. Look at the detail in this picture of the dungeon; it's like the artist was inside Poe's head."

"The cookbook, Jake. Look for the cookbook."

Jake tucked the Poe volume under his arm with the *Principles of Modern Microbiology* and resumed the search.

"You're buying those?" Manny asked.

"Yes. I thought you'd be pleased. You're always suggesting we go shopping together."

"For clothes, Jake. To replace the pants and shirts you bought during the Reagan administration."

"I tell you what: Once we find the cookbook, you can pick me out a new sports coat."

Manny brightened. Banishing the peat moss–colored tweed sack with the baggy elbows that passed for Jake's formal attire was her heart's desire. "Really? Barneys is not that far from here. We could choose something in half an hour flat."

"I'll give you ten minutes. Better find something here on that rack near the front door. There's a nice lime green one that caught my eye when we came in."

"Great motivation," Manny grumbled. "Seriously, what are we going to do if we find the cookbook and it really is Argentinean?"

"Then we start contacting victims," Jake said. "I want to start with Annabelle Fiore. You remember I visited her in the hospital after she was attacked."

"She was the opera singer who the Vampire used too much ether on, right?"

"Yes." Jake kept his head down and searched in earnest as he spoke. "At the time, I assumed it was unintentional — after all, it's hard to deliver an accurate dose of anesthesia on a rag. But in retrospect, Fiore may have been the first escalation. Before her, the victims weren't harmed. After her, Hogaarth and Fortes were murdered."

"You may be — ah!"

Jake's head snapped up. "What?"

Manny held a thick blue book aloft. "This is it! *Recetas Favoritas.*" Manny stood motionless with the heavy volume in her hands. She had started to feel like she was on a quest for a legendary object, and now she felt too stunned at holding the Holy Grail to open it.

Jake crossed to her side and took the book from her, turning quickly to the title page. He read aloud, " *'Publicado en 1967. Buenos Aires, Republica Argentina.'* "

CHAPTER
THIRTY-TWO

Jake studied his brother, trying to interpret the expression on his face. All their lives, he'd been able to tell when Sam had good news to share. He hoped to detect that gleam in Sam's eye now.

Finding the cookbook had convinced Jake that he was on the right path with the Argentine connection, but Vito Pasquarelli had been unimpressed. "Hogaarth liked Argentine food — so what? My wife's got *The Great Wall Cookbook,* but she doesn't know anyone in China."

Now Jake desperately needed his brother to have turned up something useful in his research on the attendees at Nixon's speech. Maybe then Pasquarelli would take his theory seriously. Without Vito's support, it would be hard to reinterview all the Vampire's early victims, looking for an Argentine connection. But hoping didn't make it so. His brother appeared disappointingly straight-faced.

"There's good news and there's bad news," Sam began. "The good news is, it was surprisingly easy to track down most of the people on this list with a simple Internet search. They're all fairly prominent in their respective fields, so they leave a public record that's easy to follow."

"So what's the bad news?" Manny asked. "You think that because these people are solid professionals, one of them can't possibly be our Vampire?"

"Not necessarily. I'll present the evidence; you be the judge." Sam picked up the list of attendees. Jake could see that each name on the list had a color-coded check mark.

"Three people have died since they attended Nixon's lecture. Of natural causes," he said, heading off Jake's question. "Thirty-four are journalists, most of them foreign correspondents posted overseas. Only one lives in the metro New York area — Phillip Reiser."

"That name sounds familiar," Jake said.

"Assistant managing editor of the *New York Times*," Manny said. "I've met him a few times. Very smart, very charming, insanely busy. I'm willing to concede he's not the Vampire."

"Next come the academics," Sam continued. "Sixty-two college professors, none of whom works at a school in the New York area."

"But professors are always going on sabbatical," Manny said. "Any of those people might have taken off a semester and come to New York to carry out these attacks."

"Gold star to Ms. Manfreda," Sam said. "It turns out three of them are on sabbatical right now. One's in Thailand, one's at Berkeley, and one is right here at Columbia. Wilford Munley. He's a sociologist, not an historian."

"Sociologists sometimes do laboratory experiments," Jake interjected. "He might have experience working with lab animals."

"I thought of that. When I spoke to him on the phone, he sounded so cagey and evasive that I headed up to campus to check him out."

"And . . ." Jake leaned forward in excitement.

"Paralyzed. Uses a motorized chair."

"He could have an able-bodied collaborator," Jake said.

Manny brushed him off. "So that leaves the ones who work for the government. If you ask me, they're the most likely suspects anyway."

Sam smiled. "Yes, Manny, I know you'd

find that convenient, but I checked out these remaining twenty-one names, and I don't think any of them could be our man . . . or woman. First, they all live and work in D.C."

"Two hours by Metroliner — it can take that long to commute to Jersey some days."

"Train travel isn't as anonymous as it used to be. The Metroliner requires a reservation, and none of these people shows up as a regular passenger around the dates of the attacks."

"You can drive the distance in four hours," Manny insisted.

"Yes, but some of the attacks occurred during the workday, and Fortes was tortured over a period of days. None of the remaining people on the list was away from his or her office on all of the days in question. So, unless there's a conspiracy among the attendees at Nixon's speech, I don't think your killer is anyone on this list."

Jake jumped up and paced around the room. "And yet the mug had to have come from that conference. No other fingerprints were on it. Almost certainly, someone picked it up and preserved it as a souvenir."

"eBay."

Jake and Sam turned to Manny. "Huh?" they said simultaneously.

"eBay is the single best place to buy and sell collectibles." Manny turned to Jake. "You've seen my collection of porcelain shoes. I used to have to dig through flea markets and garage sales looking for that stuff. Now I do all my collecting online."

"Have I entered into some sort of parallel universe?" Jake asked. "I thought we were talking about the Vampire and Nixon's coffee mug, not your latest shopping addiction."

"One and the same." Manny dragged Jake's laptop across the table and started typing. "Let's just do a little search. Presidential collectibles. You see — that brings it right up."

Sam looked over her shoulder. "Herbert Hoover campaign buttons, Eisenhower cuff links. Three hundred and ninety-five dollars for a blanket from *Air Force One*? You gotta be kidding me."

"The bidding has just started on that one; it'll go much higher." Manny continued to scroll through the pages. "Most of this is souvenir stuff given away by candidates or the White House. What we're looking for is stuff owned by the presidents. Ah, see — here's one. Gerald Ford's nine iron."

"Only three hundred dollars," Jake said. "I bet his ski poles would be more valuable than his golf clubs."

"I don't get it," Sam said. "This could be anyone's golf club. How can you know it's Ford's?"

"Provenance?" Manny clicked a few more keys. "See, the dealer selling it says 'Documentation authenticates the ownership.' That means he has some letter or photo that proves it belonged to President Ford. And you see, this dealer receives the highest ranking by eBay shoppers. That indicates he's legit."

"So you think whoever saved the coffee mug at the lecture might have sold it on eBay to the killer," Jake said.

"Now you're catching on."

"It makes sense, but I don't see how it gets us any closer to finding the Vampire. Anyone can sell on eBay, and anyone can buy. If you register to bid under a false name and pay your bill, no one would be wiser."

Manny's fingers continued to fly across the keyboard. "True. You can certainly make it psuedo-anonymous. But what if you saw no reason to cover your tracks?" She stopped typing and leaned back. "When I wanted to sell some of my porcelain shoes, I didn't set up my own eBay account to do it. I contacted one of the dealers that I'd bought from and consigned them for sale through him. He got a cut of the sale price, but it was less hassle for me; plus, I got a better price because he was a reputable eBay dealer. So it's quite possible that whoever originally owned Nixon's mug sold it through a dealer that sells on eBay. Let's contact the most highly ranked dealers in presidential collectibles, describe the mug, and see if any of them handled the transaction."

Jake shrugged. "Seems like a stretch. But give it a shot." He glanced at his watch. "I've gotta run. I have an appointment with Annabelle Fiore."

CHAPTER THIRTY-THREE

Jake sat on Annabelle Fiore's sofa and stared at the great singer's chest. Her mighty bosom rose from her pale green sweater like twin volcanic peaks emerging from the Pacific. What man, even a cultured, politically correct, genuinely feminist man, could keep his eyes focused exclusively above Annabelle's neck? Jake was no saint. He couldn't help the thought that popped into his head: *Wow, would I love to do an autopsy of those lungs!*

Not that he wished the opera star dead — far from it. She must have been pushing fifty, but she had a lot of good performances left in her. He admitted he'd love to discover some scientific explanation for the fact that opera singers all had huge mammary glands. There was no anatomical reason for it, Jake was sure. A singer needed exceptional lung capacity, certainly, but what resided inside the chest cavity should have no correlation to what rested on top of it. Annabelle's mammary glands definitely were well developed. But what did her bronchi look like? That's what Jake really wanted to set his eyes on. But today he had a different agenda.

"Thank you for agreeing to see me, Ms. Fiore," Jake said. "I know you must be very busy."

Annabelle threw her hands up. "No, no! The pleasure is all mine! I am so grateful you are working hard to capture this terrible man. I tell you, I haven't slept a wink since the attack." She shook her head forlornly. "The stress, it is taking a toll on my voice."

Jake murmured sympathetically. In truth, Annabelle had looked well rested, the picture of health, when she'd opened the door to him. Now, however, she slumped back in her seat and let her eyelids droop to half-mast. Jake was glad he had come. Annabelle had offered to answer his questions on the phone, but he'd been eager to assess her physical response to everything he asked. Annabelle was an actress, but he could see she was also the kind of woman who wore every emotion on her sleeve. If she was frightened, or unnerved, or evasive because of his questions, he would know it instantly by watching her face and gestures.

"Ms. Fiore —"

"Annabelle, please."

"Annabelle. Let's go over again the night of the attack." Jake leaned forward in the overstuffed peacock blue chair. She had already told Vito Pasquarelli when he'd spoken to her in the hospital that she could not recall her attacker's face. But sometimes memory revives after the initial shock passes. "When you opened the door, what was your initial impression of the person standing there?"

"You see, I didn't even look through the peephole because I was expecting my friends. I just threw open the door." She flung her arm out to the side, narrowly missing a delicate lamp on the end table. "And in a split second, this maniac was in my home."

"There was one person at the door, not two," Jake confirmed.

"Yes. Now that you mention it, I remember a moment when I thought, *Well, David must still be parking the car.*"

Jake's eyebrows arched. "You thought David was parking the car and the person on your doorstep was his wife? A woman?"

Annabelle propped her chin in her hand. "I'm not sure that it was a woman. I just remember being aware that the person standing there was too small to be David. He's a big fellow, six three, two hundred and fifty pounds.

"I have this thought only like that" — Annabelle snapped her fingers — "before the person is putting a rag over my face and I am dizzy and falling down." She shuddered as she relived the moment, then fell silent.

Jake waited.

Annabelle looked up and wagged her finger. "I remember seeing the needle before I passed out. Yes, I remember thinking, *This must be that Vampire they talk about in the newspaper.* And I said to myself, *Why me, dear God, why me?*"

"That's just it, Annabelle," Jake said. "I want to determine why you were targeted."

Her strong, dark brows drew down. "But surely it was random, no? I thought the newspapers have said there is no connection between the people he attacked. Certainly I don't know any of the others."

"No, I don't think you all know one another. But I do think there's a connection." Jake watched Annabelle closely. "Tell me: Have you ever visited Argentina?"

She blinked three times, quickly. "I have performed there, yes. Teatro Colón, the opera house in Buenos Aires, is quite fine."

"And do you know anyone there? Have friends who are Argentine?"

Annabelle cleared her throat. "Uh, friends, no. No friends there."

Jake studied her. He could tell she was uncomfortable. Maybe not lying, but holding something back. "Did you meet anyone . . . memorable . . . during your visit there?"

Annabelle tossed her hair away from her face. "There was — Oh, really, I don't see how this could be relevant. What's the significance of Argentina, anyway?"

"Three pieces of evidence in this case are linked to Argentina. I'm looking for more."

Annabelle's eyes widened. She turned away from Jake as she spoke. "This is a little embarrassing. I'm sure it's not important, but just in case. . . ."

"I'd appreciate your candor, Annabelle. I won't share the information publicly if I can avoid it."

Annabelle took a deep breath. "A few years ago, I found myself in a bit of a jam financially. When I was performing in Argentina, a man approached me and said his boss, General Rafael Cintron, would pay me ten thousand U.S. dollars to sing at his birthday party. Now, this is something I would never do! I am a star! I don't sing for my supper. So I say no, and he raises the price to fifteen thousand dollars." Annabelle threw her hands up in the air. "I would never do such a thing in Europe, or here in New York, but an Italian diva performing arias for a private party in Argentina . . . well, it's generally off the paparazzi radar. No one outside of native Argentineans pay much attention to me there. I figure no one will find out. And I really needed the money."

"So you sang. What happened?"

Annabelle grimaced. "Horrible, boorish evening! The general, he sits there with a big grin on his face, like I am stripping, not singing 'Un Bel Di.' And the others at the party" — she mimicked talking with her hands — "yak, yak, yak, the whole time I'm singing. Disgraceful!"

Jake made an effort to look suitably appalled. "Thank you for telling me this, Annabelle. You've been very helpful."

"Really? Surely this general is not the Vampire? He was old and fat."

"No, he's not the Vampire. I think Cintron may be someone the Vampire despises even more than you do."

CHAPTER
THIRTY-FOUR

"How did it go?" Manny eyed Kenneth, who was balancing his own eye-popping sequined and velveteen man bag on his left arm against Mycroft's initialed white Goyard carrier on his right.

"Great! That new vet is adorable. What gorgeous brown eyes."

"You're looking for the scientific type now?"

"Just thought I might ask him to the club to hear me — Kenneth Medianos Boyd — performing as Princess K. Calypso."

"Forget it. He's married."

Kenneth adjusted his pose, put his hands on his hips, and gave his hips a wiggle. "Like that matters? Think Jim McGreevey and Rock Hudson." Kenneth's eyebrows were knowingly raised. "I even heard a delicious rumor the other day that Cary Grant was bi."

Manny declined to make eye contact, for

fear of setting Kenneth off on one of his favorite discourses — that every man on the planet was in the closet, just waiting for the right guy to open his door. "I'm not going there with you. How is Mycroft? Is his wound healed?"

"Oh, yeah — he's fine. Aren't you, punkin?" Kenneth bent over and released Mycroft from his carrier. The little dog bounded across the office and leaped into Manny's lap. "The doctor seemed disappointed that you didn't bring him to his appointment. I told you, the wife's irrelevant."

"He must think I'm a terrible mother." Manny stroked Mycroft's curly head and scratched behind his ears. "I totally forgot the first appointment, and I would've missed this one, too, if I hadn't been able to send you." Manny looked at the pile of file folders on her desk. "I'm just swamped. I can't leave my desk until I finish answering these three hundred burdensome interrogatories that asshole law firm sent over on the Greenfield case. Just like a large law firm. They get paid thousands of dollars by the letter. Try to bury justice in paperwork."

"I'm sure Dr. Costello understands. He asked how you were doing, said to tell you not to work too hard." Kenneth picked up a stack of paper. "Is this complaint on the

Conceicao employment discrimination case ready to go?"

"Yes," Manny said. "But you're going to have to scan the appendix into a portable file format so that we can electronically file the matter with the clerk of the federal court."

"You wanna check out the sale at that new shoe boutique on Madison?" Kenneth asked.

"Casa Bene del Sole? That's cruel! Don't tempt me when you know I can't possibly go."

Kenneth reached over and popped up the to-do list Manny had minimized on her computer toolbar. "Oh, come on. What if I take care of a few more things on this list?"

"I appreciate it, Kenneth, but I don't think —"

Kenneth interrupted her with a thrust of his right hand, looking for all the world like Diana Ross doing "Stop! In the Name of Love." "Delegation is the soul of good management. What about this number four — talk to InTerVex? I'm great at talking."

"Well, maybe you could do that," Manny admitted. "It's the pharmaceutical company where one of the Vampire's victims, Raymond Fortes, worked."

Kenneth wrinkled his nose. "The rat-bite guy?"

"Yes. Jake and I want to know if Dr. Fortes had any connection with Argentina. Apparently, he was a lonely workaholic, so his business seems the best place to start looking."

"No problem. I can do that." Kenneth headed out to his desk.

"But, Kenneth, remember, don't just come right out and ask —"

Kenneth pivoted, the ends of his metallic silver scarf fluttering, his Vamp fingernails adorned by crystal faux diamonds flashing. "Come on, Manny — give me a little credit. No one's better than me at being subtle."

Manny went back to answering interrogatory 221: "Describe how the alleged actions of the defendant in failing to treat the prostate interfered with the future income stream of the plaintiff." Some days Manny felt that she wanted to represent a stream of urologists, just so they could all pee together on the justice system.

She jumped, startled from her concentration by Kenneth tapping his size-twelve Manolos. "Grab your bag. We're going to Casa Bene del Sole. Have to hurry to get there before it closes."

"Already? Did you —"

"Dr. Raymond Fortes graduated from the Universidad Nacional de Córdoba, Argentina's second-oldest medical school. He worked as a doctor in Córdoba for fifteen years before moving to New York in 1990 to work for InTerVex. He's a naturalized citizen."

"Great work, Kenneth. I don't suppose you found out what kind of drugs Dr. Fortes was developing at InTerVex?"

Kenneth tossed his scarf over his shoulder. "Of course I did. Fertility drugs. Fortes was an OB-GYN in Argentina at the Hospital Universitario de Maternidad y Neonatología."

CHAPTER
THIRTY-FIVE

"Google him," Jake commanded.

Manny and Jake sat hunched over Jake's office computer. Two half-eaten calzones leached tomato sauce onto the papers strewn across his desk. Manny, lightning fast on the keyboard, was at the controls.

"Twenty-four thousand hits on General Rafael Cintron," Manny reported. "It would be nice to have some idea of what it is about him that's of interest to us."

"Start reading," Jake said through a mouthful of meatballs and dough. "We'll know it when we see it."

Manny doubled-clicked. "Here's his official biography. You read. My eyes are burning."

Jake scanned the screen. "He's sixty-three years old. Been in the army since he was eighteen. Worked his way up through the ranks. Seems to have successfully weathered several regime changes. That says a lot about him."

"If you're looking for something contro-versial, we need to go to some of the news reports about him," Manny advised. She scrolled through the top entries brought up by the search engine. "These four are all in Spanish. I'll use Google to translate them.

" 'General Announces Plans for New Training Procedures,' " Manny read. "Snore. Here, this looks more promising."

" 'Grandmothers Protest General's Link to Dirty War.' " Jake read the headline aloud, then moved over to give Manny a chance to read the rest of the article silently with him.

"Sounds like these grandmothers claim General Cintron was implicated in the disappearances of their adult children dur-ing the military dictatorship of the late seventies, early eighties," Jake said. "Los De-saparecidos — the disappeared ones — that's what they call the victims. The grand-mothers are still protesting, all these years later."

"But Argentina is a democracy now," Manny said. "What's Cintron still doing in their army?"

"I'm no expert on Argentine history, but I think there's been a lot of controversy over amnesty for those who participated in the junta. They weren't all arrested and imprisoned. A lot of them are still actively part of Argentine society. I guess Cintron must be one of those clever survivors who plays on whatever team is at bat."

"I was still only a babe in arms when all this was going on," Manny said, "but doesn't this tie in with our Nixon lecture? Wouldn't Nixon have been a supporter of that regime?"

Jake sighed. Reminders of Manny's youth always depressed him. "Yes, my little peep, you must have been paying attention in college history class. The junta was rabidly anti-Communist, which automatically made them allies of Nixon and Kissinger. Nixon was out of office by then, of course, but this was the period when he was casting himself as elder statesman and foreign policy guru. Hence the lecture at the Scanlon Center on the necessity of supporting a regime that he knew committed atrocities against its own people."

Manny bit off a chunk of calzone and chewed thoughtfully. "I don't get it, Jake. Why would the Vampire be killing people in New York because of something that happened in Argentina decades ago?"

Jake shook his head. "I'm not sure. But a possible link between Cintron and Nixon seems to lead in that direction. And then there's the instances of torture: Hogaarth, Fortes, and Deanie Slade. Torture was one of the hallmarks of the Dirty War. People who opposed the regime would suddenly disappear. Most were held in secret government prisons, tortured for information on their comrades, and then killed."

Manny rubbed her temples, leaving a small smear of tomato sauce. "You're making me more confused. We know Dr. Fortes was Argentinean; we suspect that Ms. Hogaarth was, too. Why were they tortured before their deaths — because they were once part of the military junta, or because they once opposed it?"

Gently, Jake wiped the tomato sauce off Manny's face. "Don't demand so many answers. We're just laying out the facts."

"Well, what do you make of this fact? Deanie Slade was tortured, and she's New Jersey through and through. No connection to Argentina there."

"It's another data point."

"This isn't an academic exercise, Jake!" Manny balled up the remains of her dinner and stalked across the room to throw it in the trash. "In all this calm analysis of data points, let's not lose sight of the fact that Travis Heaton is under the control of people who not only kill but torture. We need to find him, fast."

"Drama has its uses in the courtroom, Manny, but investigations succeed on the steady accumulation of evidence. The process can be maddeningly slow, but no one's invented an alternative."

Jake patted the chair beside him. "There's more data to be dug. Are you in, or out?"

Manny returned and dropped into the chair. "Of course I'm in. I'm sorry I snapped at you, but I'm just so damn worried about Travis. And it infuriates me that the Sandovals are allowed to hide behind diplomatic immunity. They must know what's going on here, but somehow it's against their personal best interest to cooperate with the investigation."

"Let's see if we can turn up any link between Ambassador Sandoval and the Dirty War," Jake said, turning back to the computer. He could feel Manny's barely suppressed impatience as he typed. He wondered, not for the first time, how she'd ever managed to sit through Civil Procedure and Contracts in law school.

"Here's Sandoval's official UN biography. It doesn't mention that he ever served in the military. He's only fifty-one years old. He probably would have been in college and law school during the Dirty War years."

"So maybe he and his wife were part of the opposition," Manny suggested. "Wasn't it mostly young people — students — who were disappeared by the government?" She leaned forward, gesturing, as her mind raced ahead of her ability to form sentences. "Paco seemed frightened by the letter I found in his room. Maybe someone from his parents' past has come back to haunt them. Maybe they're manipulating Paco to get what they want." Manny flung her pen onto the desk. "Damn, I wish I still had that document!"

Jake said nothing, only pursed his lips and kept scrolling through information brought up by the search engine.

"I know what's going through your head." Manny knocked her knuckles against the wild tangle of Jake's hair. "You think I should focus on this research instead of obsessing about what's out of reach. But I tell you, if we could just find out what the Sandovals are hiding, we wouldn't need to be piecing together all these scraps of information."

Jake paused, his hands suspended above the keyboard. "This is the best way to find out, Manny. We're not breaking into their home again."

Manny shook her head slightly, as if she'd already considered this but rejected it. "No, no more clandestine operations now that our cover's been blown. But I feel that if I could just get Paco alone and talk to him, really talk to him, he'd tell me something valuable."

"Why should he?" Jake demanded. "If it would endanger his family?"

"Because now it has to be clear to Paco that he's put Travis in danger. Paco's not a bad kid — he must feel guilty about what he's done to his friend."

"What do you know about Paco's character? You've spent all of five minutes with the kid, and half of that time you were on his back, literally."

"You'd be surprised the insights gained by jumping on a person." Manny grinned, poised to pounce. "Want me to demonstrate?"

Jake squirmed in his seat. Why did working with Manny always give him this precarious feeling, like he was riding in a ski lift without the safety bar down?

It was only nine-fifteen — too early to succumb to temptation. Jake knew he could easily put in three or four more hours here, digging for clues, reviewing the case files to look for significant details. He met Manny's teasing glance cautiously. "Hold that thought," he said, and waited for a storm or a sulk.

But Manny merely laughed. "Don't worry — I won't forget." She pivoted and looked around the office. "Say, as much as I love bonding with you by sharing this computer, don't you think we'd get to our reward a little faster if we were to divide and conquer? Isn't there another computer here I can use so we can both look things up?"

"Sure. You can use Dave's." He pointed to a desk just outside his office door.

"All right. Yell if you find anything interesting. I'm going to dig up more information on this grandmother's organization that does the protests, Asociación Civil Abuelas de Plaza de Mayo."

Regret mingled with relief as Jake watched her retreating figure. He could certainly focus better when he wasn't breathing in Manny's perfume or brushing against her soft skin. But he liked knowing she was nearby, close enough to shout out an idea or ask an opinion.

He turned back to his own work. Forsaking the computer for the time being, Jake again pulled out the case files on the Vampire's victims. He'd already gone over them countless times, but it wouldn't hurt to look at them once more, bearing in mind his new knowledge of General Cintron and the Dirty War.

He had already tried to recontact each of the first four victims — the ones before Annabelle Fiore, whose blood had been taken but who had not been injured — to ask about a connection to Argentina in their lives. Victim number four, Jorge Arguelles, a tourist from Chile, seemed to have the closest connection, but he had already returned home, and Jake had not yet been able to reach him to ask if he had recently visited neighboring Argentina or had friends there.

Jake had not had the time to visit each victim personally, as he had with Annabelle. In his telephone conversations with the first three victims, each one had claimed to have no connection to Argentina. Now he wished he had made the effort to interview them in person, so he could have observed their eyes and hands as they spoke, listened to their breathing and vocal pitch, tracking any signs of deception.

Jake reread his notes. Victim number one, Lucinda Bettis, stood out. The other victims had thoughtfully considered his question about Argentina but had ultimately claimed no connection. Mrs. Bettis had replied in the negative almost before the question about Argentina had left Jake's mouth. Then she had rushed to get off the phone, saying she needed to get back to her children. Given that the other victims he had reached had answered in the negative, her response hadn't raised a red flag at the time, but now Jake studied her file more closely.

Born in 1977, married, mother of two. She had been attacked in her Upper West Side apartment in the middle of the day while the kids were at nursery school. No sign of forced entry; she said she'd answered the knock at the door because she was expecting her neighbor, who had agreed to pick up a dozen eggs for her at the market.

Again, he compared her file with the others, searching for some significant detail, something that either set her apart from the others or joined them all together. It eluded him.

From the other room came the sound of Manny's outrage. "Oh my God! This is horrible!"

Manny pulled two sheets of paper from the printer and entered Jake's office, reading aloud. "Listen to this: 'The junta led by Videla until 1981, then by Roberto Viola and Leopoldo Galtieri, was responsible for the illegal arrest, torturing, killing, or forced disappearance of citizens who voiced opposition to the government. Critics claim there are documents showing Argentina's brutal policies were known by the U.S. State Department, led by Henry Kissinger under both the Nixon and Gerald Ford presidencies.' "

Manny looked up. "Isn't that outrageous? Nixon and Kissinger's foreign policy extended long after the impeachment. And there's more." Manny continued reading aloud, her voice rising with indignation at every ghastly detail — secret imprisonment, torture, mutilation, murder — of the Argentine government's brutality.

"Say that again." Jake suddenly cut her off in mid-sentence.

" 'Some of the bodies were never found because they were taken far offshore and disposed of in the ocean,' " Manny repeated.

"No, not that. What you said before."

Manny flipped back to the first page she'd printed out. " 'The government claims that about nine thousand people were victims of forced disappearances, but the grandmothers of the Plaza de Mayo estimate that nearly thirty thousand dissidents, students, and ordinary citizens disappeared between 1976 and 1983. The higher number includes children who disappeared with their parents, and pregnant women who may have given birth while in captivity.' "

Jake lowered his head and scrambled through the file folders on his desk, checking each one quickly and moving on to the next.

"What? What is it?"

Jake looked up and met Manny's eyes. "Victims one, three, and four were all born during the Dirty War. Victim two was born two years earlier. That's it. That's the connection. These victims — they're all children of the Desaparecidos."

CHAPTER
THIRTY-SIX

"What are you thinking?" Manny asked. She and Jake were lying in her Murphy bed, with Mycroft curled at their feet. They didn't often spend the night at her place, even though Jake praised the coziness of her five-hundred-square-foot apartment: "Makes me feel like I'm sleeping in a casket."

Manny rolled over on the six-hundred-thread-count sheets and ran her finger down Jake's sinewy arm. *Turning corpses over on a daily basis is good for the muscles*, Manny thought. She read the deep recessed lines documenting Jake's thoughts. "I'm sure you're only thinking about how fabulous it is to be here with me, naked and alone."

"I was thinking about the blood." It never occurred to Jake to utter a judicious lie.

Manny flopped onto her back and looked up at the ceiling. "I love it when you ply me with romantic pillow talk. What blood?"

"The blood the Vampire takes. He went to

all the trouble of collecting those samples, then abandoned them in that apartment in Brooklyn."

"He must be done with them," Manny said. "Because if he still needed them, it wouldn't have been hard to take them along when he left that place."

"Exactly. So if he was testing the blood samples, as I've always suspected, he now has his results. What's his next move? What's he going to do with this information?"

"I don't know. The note he left with Deanie told us to await instructions. He must be planning something."

Jake unexpectedly sat up and slammed his fist so hard onto the down comforter that three feathers shot into the air. "Well, I'm not waiting for him to act. I want to be one jump ahead, anticipating him."

Manny had been about ready to drift into blissful and much-needed sleep, but being in the presence of Jake when he was so excited was the equivalent of drinking three cups of double espresso — and infectious.

She sat up, too, and faced him across the rumpled covers. "But even with what we know now, or what we suspect, we still aren't any closer to understanding the Vampire's motivation. And without that, how can we anticipate his next move?"

Jake said nothing, eyes focused on the seemingly nondescript pattern of her new white-on-white silk comforter.

"Jake?"

No answer.

"Jake! You know something that you haven't told me."

He started, as if he just noticed that he wasn't alone in the bed. "Not that I haven't told you. It's something that just clicked." He grabbed Manny's hands. "If victims one through four are children of Los Desaparecidos, but the ones I talked to claimed no connection with Argentina, then how did three of them get here to New York? Even the businessman tourist from Chile claimed he was born in Chile. So, who took them out of their country? Who raised them?"

"They're all adopted," Manny said, catching his excitement and building on it. "But they don't know one another. . . . They probably don't even know that they're adopted. Their adoptive parents concealed their true heritage — didn't want them to know their biological parents had been murdered."

"Maybe because —" Jake's grip on Manny's hands tightened.

Her eyes widened. "Because the people who adopted them were responsible for the parents' deaths. Were part of the junta. Why else keep the adoptions secret, when today everyone's so open about the process?"

"Adoption," Jake said. "We've just found where another of our puzzle pieces fits."

"The Family Builders adoption agency. They must have facilitated these adoptions. That's why Ms. Hogaarth left them money in her will."

"We have to talk to the director." Jake glanced around for Manny's phone.

She reached out and pulled him back. "It's three-thirty in the morning, Jake. We have to wait a few hours."

He flung himself back on the pillows and yanked the covers up to his chin. "I hate waiting."

Manny snuggled up beside him. "So do I."

Ten minutes passed in silence. The only light in the room came from the reflected glow of streetlamps far below. Mycroft snored gently.

"Are you asleep?" Manny asked.

"No."

"My mind's racing."

"Mine, too."

"There's really only one cure for this," Manny said.

Jake slid one leg over the edge of the bed.

"You're right. I may as well get up and go to the office."

Manny twined her arms around his neck and yanked him back. "No! Not that!"

"Oh," he said, catching on. "Yeah, that works, too."

"Isn't that what you're always telling me?" Manny murmured. "Keep your mind open to all the possibilities."

CHAPTER
THIRTY-SEVEN

"We have never handled international adoptions," Lydia Martinette said.

Jake sat across from the director of the Family Builders adoption agency, surrounded by the relentless good cheer of her office's happy family photos and precious children's drawings. Not liking the answer he'd received, he posed his question again. "This would have been late 1970s, early 1980s. Argentina." He was certain that Family Builders had brought the children of the Desaparecidos to New York. All he needed to do was make Mrs. Martinette comprehend.

"I understand the time frame, Dr. Rosen. You mentioned it before. But I'm telling you, this agency has never handled international adoptions. In fact, bringing foreign-born babies to the United States for adoption is antithetical to everything we stand for." When Jake had called the director at home at 8:55 that morning, demanding an interview at her office, Mrs. Martinette had been polite and helpful, but now her voice took on an edge.

But Jake was not deterred. "These names, Mrs. Martinette." He read the list of victims one through four. "Do they sound familiar? Did you place any of these children?"

"I'm sure we didn't, but if it will set your mind at rest, I'll look them up." She took the list from him and tapped the names into a database on her computer. After each search, she shook her head. "Not here."

Jake felt a rising tide of desperation. There just had to be a connection. Yet he believed Mrs. Martinette. He looked at a photo of a kid with stumps for arms surrounded by his new family. She found homes for kids like that. Her agency's reputation was stellar. He couldn't doubt her sincerity or her honesty. Still, he persisted. "How about Dr. Raymond Fortes. He's an OB-GYN specializing in fertility. Have you ever worked with him?"

"No." Seeing his distress, Mrs. Martinette's attitude softened a bit. "Look, I can give you the names of agencies that do handle foreign adoptions, but honestly, Argentina isn't a common source of infants. Guatemala, Colombia, Peru — those are the Central and South American countries that American couples most frequently turn to when they're looking to adopt." Her usually smiling mouth turned down in disapproval.

He'd been so focused on his own agenda that he hadn't been paying attention to the signals Mrs. Martinette was sending. He stopped trying to drag her where she didn't want to go and allowed her to give him the information she wanted to share. "Why don't you approve of international adoptions, Mrs. Martinette?"

She came out from behind her desk and sat next to Jake. "I don't disapprove in all cases. People want the experience of raising an infant from birth, I understand that. It can be difficult for some to adopt an infant in this country. But I resent all these celebrities traipsing off to Africa and India and Cambodia to 'rescue' children when there are thousands, tens of thousands, of children in America who need good adoptive homes. And the ramifications of culture shock for older children taken away from their countries of origin can be considerable."

Jake watched Mrs. Martinette as she spoke, noting the way she leaned forward, the way she looked into his eyes, the way her voice shook with intensity. In her he saw a kindred spirit, a woman who cared as deeply about her work as he cared about his own. She didn't happen to have the information that he had come here seeking, but he thought she could be useful to him anyway.

"Tell me, Mrs. Martinette," he said. "Is it ever justifiable to conceal a child's origins from him, to never tell him he's adopted because of the circumstances of his birth?"

"We often place children who are the products of rape, and we don't recommend telling the child that detail, but we never say that a child shouldn't know he's adopted."

"What about reuniting children with their birth parents? If an adult child comes here wanting to know the identity of his or her birth parents, do you tell that person?"

Mrs. Martinette brushed a strand of glistening white hair away from her face. "Magazines and TV are filled with heartwarming stories of birth parents and children being joyfully reunited, but the truth is more complicated than that. Both parties have to want the reunification. Many times, the birth parents don't want to be found; they've separated from the baby they gave up and they don't want to reopen that wound."

She spread her hands out on her lap. "And many children have no interest in meeting the parents who surrendered them. Their adoptive parents are the only parents they want in their lives. We have to respect that, although it's very distressing when one party wants the reunification and the other doesn't."

"So what do you do in those cases?" Jake asked.

"We have to honor the wishes of the party who wants privacy. We provide any information on health and well-being that would be reassuring, but we don't reveal the identity."

"And do people ever have . . . er . . . violent reactions to that decision?"

Mrs. Martinette cocked her head. "What an odd question. Sometimes there are tears and pleading. If I feel the person is having serious trouble adjusting to the idea that he'll never be reunited, I have a few therapists I can recommend."

"Hmm." Jake stared down at the pale blue carpet beneath his tattered loafers.

"Dr. Rosen? Is that all?"

"Huh?" Jake pushed himself out of his chair with a jolt. "Yes. Yes, I suppose it is. Thank you for your time, Mrs. Martinette." He shook her hand and walked toward the door.

With his hand on the knob, Jake paused and looked back. "Ma'am, aren't you at all curious about why Ms. Hogaarth left Family Builders all that money?"

The older woman fingered a strand of beads around her neck before she spoke. "I gave up looking for reasons years ago, Doctor. I used to want to know why a father would beat his crying infant so hard that the child would never be able to form words again. I used to want to know why a mother would drop her toddler in a scalding bath because she wet the bed. I don't ask why about those things anymore, so I sure don't ask why when something good comes my way."

CHAPTER
THIRTY-EIGHT

Manny sat on a park bench a few blocks south of the Central Park Zoo, Mycroft curled at her side. A jaded New Yorker, Mycroft found little of interest in the passing tide. Squirrels and pigeons were beneath his contempt; joggers, bladers, and skateboarders didn't merit a second glance. A four-foot-tall Afghan hound provoked a low growl; a strolling incense vendor prompted a sneeze. Only a toddler with a tenuous grip on a hot dog got the poodle to sit up and tense for a spring into action.

Manny tugged his leash. "Don't even think about it. I've got something better." She glanced at her watch. "You don't have much longer to wait." Her other hand rested inside her purse, fingers already curled around a tin of bacon and liver strips. Mycroft wouldn't perform for just any treat. He scoffed at Milk Bones, ignored Snausages. While he wouldn't eat Fortune

Snookies, he'd do just about anything for fusion cuisine from the China Grill, but it really wouldn't be practical to toss a handful of lobster pancakes onto the path when her prey came into sight. But like his mother, Mycroft could be a bundle of contradictions. He'd also kill for a dirty-water hot dog from any street vendor in New York.

So Manny watched for Paco, armed with organic bacon-and-liver-infused dog snacks ordered from Canine Gourmet and a hungry, bored pet. Although the sun was long past its peak, she wore large dark glasses and had stuffed her red hair under a bucket hat.

She knew the Ultimate Frisbee game Paco played with his friends every Sunday afternoon in the park must have ended by now. Paco lived farthest downtown, so the other friends would have peeled off for their homes by the time he reached this point on the path.

Manny watched the bend in the path to see who would come along next. Two black women pushing white babies in strollers — Haitian nannies taking their charges home; a middle-aged man talking on his cell phone; three old biddies clutching one another's arms for support.

Then she saw what she was waiting for. A long, casual stride, a familiar toss of dark hair. Paco Sandoval emerged from the shadows of some maple trees and headed toward her. When he was ten feet away, Manny opened the container in her purse. Mycroft sat up and sniffed.

When Paco was seven feet away, Manny tossed two gourmet strips across the trail. Mycroft shot after them, a blur of red trailing his bright green leash.

"Oh, my dog! He's loose! Get him!" Manny rose from the bench but made no effort to chase Mycroft. Paco glanced her way, questioning.

"I can't chase him. I sprained my ankle. Please grab his leash for me," Manny said, averting her face by looking down at her Ace bandage–wrapped ankle.

Dutifully, Paco sprinted after Mycroft, who wasn't terribly hard to catch. Having downed two bacon and liver strips, he was busy sniffing the grass on the off chance he might have missed a third.

Manny limped across the path, holding her hand out for the leash. When Paco extended it to her, Manny took it with her left hand and linked her right arm firmly through Paco's. "Thank you, Paco. You're very good with animals."

He looked down at her in surprise, still not recognizing her.

"Let's walk a bit, shall we? We have a little talking to do."

Her voice triggered Paco's memory and he tugged to release his arm.

"Don't run, Paco," Manny said, her voice quiet and firm. "If you do, I'll start screaming that you stole my wallet. You know I'll do it."

She felt his arm, which was still hard with tension as he continued trying to pull away. No time for an opening argument; just move straight to the cross-examination.

"The mailbox explosion, the Vampire — it's all related, and it all goes back to your family's past in Argentina, isn't that right?"

Paco's glowing olive complexion seemed a little grayish now, his lips pale and pressed to a thin linc. His head swiveled left, then right. "We can't be seen together," Paco said, his voice low and urgent. "Don't you understand? If they see me talking to you, they'll kill Travis."

"Who will? Who has Travis?"

Paco stopped on the path. The old ladies who had passed Manny earlier were now sitting on a bench, taking a breather. Two joggers passed in iPod-induced oblivion. The only place for anyone to hide was in the trees overhead. They were near Fifty-ninth Street and Manny spotted a red-and-black carriage pulled by a dappled mare clopping along.

"C'mon, Paco." Manny tugged his arm. "Let's see the park like the tourists do." Mycroft looked at her as if to say I was just there this morning. Boooring . . .

After finally settling Mycroft at their feet, Manny leaned forward and spoke to their driver, who only seemed interested in stating the duration and price of the ride.

Manny turned to look directly at Paco. "Tell me where Travis is now."

Paco shook his head. "I don't know, honestly. But I'm worried. I haven't heard from him in two days." He leaned forward and dropped his head into his hands.

"Travis contacts you regularly?"

"No." Manny had to strain to hear him. "They do."

"Who?"

"The Vampire. Sometimes it's a man, sometimes a woman."

Paco straightened and faced Manny. His dark eyes glistened with tears. "I got Travis into this mess. I was supposed to be the one to get arrested."

"What do you mean?"

"The first contact came about two weeks

ago." Paco closed his eyes as he spoke, as if he couldn't bear to see his confessor. "A text message saying I needed to call this number to get important news that would affect my family."

"Who answered?"

"It was a recorded message directed to me. The voice said they had information that would destroy my father's career, put him in prison. They told me to go to that club in Hoboken, said that someone would make contact with me there. I wanted to go because I needed to protect my mother from any harm, but I was nervous, so I asked Travis —"

"If he wanted to go clubbing." Manny sighed. Her poor client. He wasn't even supposed to have been there. The Vampire had set up the mailbox bombing as a trap for Paco, but the wrong little mouse had stumbled into it. And Paco had stood by and watched his friend go down and did nothing to help.

"Let me get this straight," Manny said in the tone she reserved for liars on the witness stand. "You let your friend be arrested on a charge of terrorism and you said nothing to the police about the strange phone call that brought you two to Club Epoch?"

Paco bit his lip, but to give him credit, he

didn't look away from her. He met her gaze and held it. "By that time, I knew what they had called me there to tell me."

"Which was?"

Paco held his hand up to deflect her question. "I couldn't speak up on that night. I had to have time to think. Travis and I were separated by the police. They let me go, so I assumed they'd let him go, too."

"But they didn't. And you still didn't speak up. So do the right thing now. Come forward and tell everything you know to the police."

"No!"

Paco's shout made the carriage driver glance back over his shoulder. Then he turned discreetly away. Manny guessed he'd probably witnessed plenty of lovers' quarrels in his career.

"The next day, the Vampire contacted me again. He told me they would kill Travis and his mother if I went to the police. After Travis got out of jail, he told me the same thing. Every time I speak to him, he begs me not to tell the authorities. He says if we wait it out, everything will be okay."

The gentle sway of the carriage should have been relaxing, but Manny had never felt more tense. "And you believe that? Paco, these people have attacked six people and tortured and killed two more. You can't possibly trust anything they say."

"I don't trust them, but I trust Travis. He says the FBI won't believe anything he says. They're convinced he's a terrorist."

Manny took a deep breath. She could hear an edge of hysteria building in Paco's voice. She needed to calm him down and get his story straight from the beginning. Then she could talk some sense into him.

"We need to talk about the past, Paco," she began. "What were your parents doing during the Dirty War?"

Her sudden about-face startled Paco. "Nothing," he said loudly. "My parents are good people."

"The Vampire knows something about your father's past, doesn't he?" Manny continued. "Something that would destroy your dad's diplomatic career. This killer is using you, Paco. He's taking advantage of your desire to protect your family. I understand you don't want anything to happen to them, but this has gone on long enough. Innocent people are getting hurt."

"Innocent?" Paco spat the word out like a piece of bad meat. "Amanda Hogaarth wasn't innocent. Raymond Fortes wasn't innocent. They got what they deserved."

Surprised by his intensity, Manny considered her next move. Clearly, she was on to something here, but she had to tread carefully to keep him talking. She had no idea why Paco claimed Ms. Hogaarth deserved to die, but she could guess why Dr. Fortes had met his grisly end.

"Dr. Fortes was tortured because he was a torturer himself during the Dirty War, right?"

"The worst kind." Suddenly, Paco wanted to tell her more. He glanced around, but no one was near but another carriage ten feet behind them. Paco's face shined with recently awakened idealism. "He supervised the torture. Told the soldiers just how far to go so the person wouldn't die. So that he would live to be tortured some more the next day. This is how he used his medical training."

Manny shivered. She had seen the autopsy photos of Fortes's rat-gnawed body, imagined his slow, agonizing death. At the time, she couldn't fathom how one human being could do such a thing to another. But Paco's claim, if it was true, made Fortes's death seem, if not justifiable, maybe understandable. How chilling to think that Fortes had coolly directed the torture of young people for maximum effectiveness, then left that life behind and came to New York to take up legitimate work as a researcher. Imagine developing fertility drugs to create new life when you were a cold-blooded killer.

She began to think out loud. "Back in Argentina, Fortes was an obstetrician. He delivered babies."

Paco stiffened. Manny sensed he might be about to leap out of the slow-moving carriage, so she shamelessly threw her arms around his neck, locking her fingers tightly, yanking up poor Mycroft on his leash. To anyone passing by, they were lovers engaged in a flagrant public display of affection.

Their faces were inches apart. "Raymond Fortes delivered the babies of the Desaparecidos," Manny said, her eyes locked on Paco's. "Then he took them away to be adopted by strangers."

Paco's eyes filled with tears. He squirmed away from Manny's embrace.

"You know someone whose baby was taken," Manny said. "Your parents . . . long before you were born . . ." But then she thought of the photo she'd seen in Paco's room. That photo, a recent photo, showed him with a man old enough to have been born during the Dirty War. Who was that?

Manny released her grip. Paco slumped on the carriage seat. He looked young now, much younger than the sophisticated eighteen-year-old she had waylaid fifteen minutes ago. He had seen the world, more of it than most people his age, but he didn't know the world. He was a child, a frightened child.

Manny took his hand. "Paco, in your room there's a photo of you and another man, a man about thirty. Who is that?"

"Esteban," he whispered. "My brother, Esteban."

"He was adopted?"

Paco nodded. "I never knew. Until —"

Paco stopped talking.

"Until the Vampire told you," Manny said. "He knows your family's secret."

Paco nodded. "That night at Club Epoch, one of the guys took me into a back room and gave me an iPod to listen to. A voice just started talking. He spoke in Spanish, and it was like listening to my father read me a scary story when I was a kid, except the characters in this story were my own family.

"The voice said Esteban's birth parents were a young couple in graduate school named Estrella and Hector, who opposed the dictatorship and participated in protests. They were kidnapped when Estrella was seven months pregnant, and Hector was killed before her eyes."

Paco's voice trembled and his dark eyes blinked furiously. "Then Estrella was tortured for weeks in terrible ways, until the torture finally brought the baby's birth early. They took the baby away from her and she died a few days later. They dumped her body in the ocean."

Paco paused, his face pale and clammy, his breath coming in shuddering gasps. "What else did the man tell you, Paco?" Manny whispered.

"The soldiers gave the baby boy to my father. They wanted that baby to be raised by someone with the right politics."

Paco stopped, too exhausted to continue.

"But, Paco, how can you be sure that this baby of the disappeared young couple was really your brother, Esteban? I mean, this crazy person calls you up with this story and you believe him? What did your father say?"

"He doesn't know that I know. He's kept this secret from all of us. He's still controlled by those terrible people. Telling lies, lies, lies. My whole childhood was full of things that didn't make sense, things that I wasn't allowed to ask about. Now everything makes sense."

"Like what?"

"I was always my grandparents' favorite. They were cold to Esteban, and I never could figure out why. And my father . . . well, my father is harsh to everyone, but he was particularly hard on my brother."

"The biological child favored over the adopted one," Manny said.

"Yes. And there are no photos of Esteban as a baby, and none of my mother pregnant with him, but there are tons of me. And Esteban was small and sickly as a child."

"Because of the premature birth," Manny said. "The nurse must have been Amanda Hogaarth. She worked with Dr. Fortes on the side, helping deliver the babies."

Paco nodded. "That's why I said I don't care that the Vampire killed those two people. But I don't want Travis to be hurt, and I don't want my mother ever to learn any of this."

"But, Paco, your mother knows Esteban is adopted."

"Yes, but she doesn't know how my father got the baby. I'm sure of that. He had to have lied to her, told her Esteban was simply an orphan who needed a home. She must have wanted a baby desperately. But my mother would never have agreed to take the baby of a murdered girl, take him away from the rest of his biological family. You see how kindhearted she is. She had no trouble raising Esteban as her own, because she thought he was abandoned. She loves him, always has. Not like my father."

A dark scowl settled over Paco's face. The dour expression brought out a resemblance to his father. "Paco," Manny said, "you've got to talk to your father about this. Find out what's true. He may know who the Vampire is, what motivates him."

"No way! He'll just lie — he's a master at that. He'll do anything to protect his reputation, his position." Paco's voice rose, and again the driver turned to look at his mercurial passengers. "He'll have me sent away, and then there will be no one to protect my mother. I'm all she has. I can't let that happen."

"What about your brother? Does he know?"

"Esteban is a doctor. He took a year off after his residency to work for Doctors Without Borders. He's in Sudan now — completely out of touch. Sometimes he's able to get an e-mail through. But I can't send him an e-mail with news like this. He'll be knocked flat by it. And he's in a very dangerous place. He needs to stay sharp, alert. I can't endanger him. I'll tell him when he gets back in six months."

Manny stared down at Mycroft, who was blissfully napping at her feet. Rarely had she felt so completely stymied. She simply couldn't relate to a family like Paco's, where everyone presented a cheerful face to the world while tiptoeing around land mines in private. In the Manfreda family, everything was out in the open. You were happy — everyone shared it; sad — everyone knew why; mad — you screamed at the offender and two minutes later you kissed and made up. Impossible to keep a secret, no matter how you tried. Uncle Bobby's gambling problem, cousin Kay's extra-marital fling, Aunt Joan's colonoscopy — all fair game, reviewed in excruciating detail at family gatherings. Manny simply had no expertise in the kind of evasion practiced by the San- dovals. How could she get Paco to confront his father with what he knew? She couldn't unravel eighteen years of twisted family dynamics in one carriage ride around Cen- tral Park.

Would it be any easier to get Paco to tell his story to the police? Because as tantaliz- ing as this new information was, it really didn't help the Vampire investigation if she was the only person who knew it. Sure, she could take it to Pasquarelli and he would most likely believe her, based on his friendship with Jake. But how could he move forward with it?

There were instances in which diplomatic immunity could be breached, in which the police could force a diplomat to cooperate in an investigation, but hearsay evidence from the defense lawyer of an escaped federal prisoner charged with terrorism wasn't one of them. Not even close. For Pasquarelli to be able to act on this information, he needed to hear it directly from Paco.

Chapter
Thirty-Nine

Manny didn't hesitate to play the guilt card.

Sure, Jewish mothers grabbed all the headlines for inspiring guilt, but Italian mothers were no slouches, and Manny had learned at the knee of the best.

"Do I have to remind you that your friend is in the hands of a multiple murderer, a torturer, because of your actions?"

Paco grew petulant now, just as she had always done when her mother pulled the old "After all I've done for you, can't you do this one little thing for me?"

"Travis is the one who told me not to tell," Paco said.

"He's terrified, Paco!" Manny reminded him. "And now he's being held captive by people who haven't hesitated to kill and torture. Of course he's going to say whatever they tell him to say."

She took both of Paco's hands in hers and spoke slowly and patiently, as she would to a child. "This has gone on long enough. You need to do the right thing. Come with me now to talk to Detective Pasquarelli. He's a good man. He can help."

Paco wrenched his hands away. "It's not that easy! They won't be able to talk to me and my father without my mother finding out. Since the bombing, she's been a nervous wreck. She doesn't like me going anywhere. In fact" — he checked his watch — "I'm late getting home now. She's going to start calling me."

Manny made a concerted effort not to roll her eyes. She suspected that Mrs. Sandoval was a lot tougher than her son gave her credit for. "Paco, your mother's going to find out about this sooner or later. The adoption doesn't reflect badly on her. In fact, she's done a great job raising Esteban. A doctor, and one who does volunteer work — she must be very proud of him." Manny let out all the stops. "Now, make her proud of you. You know she would never want more people to get hurt. Come and talk to the police and put an end to all these attacks."

"No!"

And before Manny could even snatch at his sleeve, Paco leaped from the slow-moving carriage and dashed nimbly into the trees, heading east. Manny watched him go. She wasn't crazy enough to try the same stunt, wearing high heels and dragging a poodle.

The driver soon exited onto Central Park South and pulled up at the curb. He held out his hand to Manny. "Ride's over. Forty dollars, please."

CHAPTER FORTY

BLOOD.

Jake had printed the word in block letters on the whiteboard in his office, retraced cach letter with bold strokes of his red marker, drawn a box around it, sketched arrows radiating out from it. Still, the word refused to cooperate.

It was like a "Down" answer in a crossword puzzle that fit neatly into the allocated spaces but wouldn't mesh with the "Across" clues.

He tried again. "Just listen to me, Vito. Give me the benefit of the doubt while I work through the evidence." He hadn't seen or spoken to Manny all day. She was his preferred sounding board, but in her absence, Vito would have to do.

Vito Pasquarelli had pushed himself halfway out of the chair in Jake's office, but the plea in his friend's voice made him fall back into his seat. "You've been over it twenty times already. Be careful not to twist the facts to fit the theory."

Jake finished a Coke, which kept him from passing out at his desk, then crushed the can and flung it into the trash. He'd seen plenty of scientists, and plenty of cops, come to grief trying to make evidence support a theory they'd grown too fond of. Is that what he was doing here? he wondered. He started once more to run through the evidence, looking for the one fact that would make all the others come together coherently. *Make no judgments; let the facts do the work.*

"Victims one, two, and three, and possibly victim four, were children of the Desaparecidos." Of this, Jake was now positive. He'd spoken again to three of the early victims. Numbers two and three had readily admitted to being adopted. Both said they had no knowledge of their birth parents and had never tried to contact them. They assumed their birth parents were American, but when pressed, they admitted they really didn't know.

Victim number one, Lucinda Bettis, had once again reacted differently from the others, shouting "No" and slamming down the phone when Jake asked her if she had been adopted. To him, that was as good as a yes.

It was this discovery, at least three of the four early victims linked through adoption, that had reluctantly brought Vito around to discuss the case with Jake again.

Jake stood and made notes on the whiteboard in the corner as he spoke. "Fiore, Hogaarth, Fortes, and Slade, by virtue of their ages, are not children of the Desaparecidos. The first three are too old; Deanie Slade is too young. But three of the four have definite connections to Argentina."

Pasquarelli's only response was to purse his lips into a tight line. He refused to make the leap from adoption to Argentina. He still hadn't completely let go of Islamic terrorists.

"The Vampire takes blood from all of them but tortures only the last three, and kills only Hogaarth and Fortes," Jake said. "Why?"

"Because he's a fuckin' terrorist nut!" Pasquarelli shouted. "Why do they strap bombs to themselves and blow themselves up in buses full of innocent people? They're nuts!"

Jake shook his head. "Not a nut. The Vampire's escalating violence may be a sign of increasing mental instability, but when he began this series of attacks, I'm sure he had a very specific purpose in mind."

The pained look returned to Pasquarelli's

face, as if he were humoring a temperamental child. "Which is . . ."

Jake stopped writing on the whiteboard and chewed the end of the marker. "Identification. To be able to match the children of the Desaparecidos with their biological families."

"You just said the last four victims weren't des . . . des . . . des . . . peradoes. Why take their blood?"

"I've gone around and around on this point in my mind. That's the inconsistency I can't resolve. But identification still seems the most likely scenario," Jake said.

"Wait a minute," Vito objected. "Why go to all the trouble to knock them out and draw their blood if all he wants is to prove they're related to someone? He could've just broken into their homes and taken their hairbrushes or toothbrushes. Or followed them until they dropped a Starbucks cup in the trash and then fished it out. Those are much easier ways to get a little DNA."

"That had me puzzled, too," Jake said. "But remember, DNA analysis has only been in use since 1989. Before that, blood-group factors were used to establish paternity. Of course, it wasn't conclusive, but it was the best technology available. Right before I called you, I stumbled across this in all the research I've been gathering about the Dirty War. Take a look."

Jake tossed a journal article into Vito's lap. The detective's eyes glazed over as he scanned the dense columns of type. "Give me the highlights."

"After the right-wing dictatorship collapsed in 1983, parents who suspected their daughters had given birth while in custody, or whose baby grandchildren had been kidnapped along with their parents, began to mobilize to seek reunification between the children of the Desaparecidos and their biological families. They knew it might take years, so they established something in Argentina called the National Genetic Data Bank to collect evidence from the biological families. Nowadays, they preserve dried blood spots for DNA, but when they first began the project in the early eighties, all they could save were meticulous records of the blood-group factors of the grandmothers and grandfathers. ABO, Rh . . ."

Vito sat staring at a scratch on the front of Jake's desk. Jake could tell he was beginning to pry open a door in his friend's mind. "If any of these grandparents died before 1989, all that would be left as evidence would be their blood-group factors," Vito said. "So you're telling me DNA wouldn't be of any use in that case?"

"Exactly! DNA doesn't show blood-group factors. You'd need actual blood from the grandkids to try to make a match."

Vito held up a restraining hand. "Don't get too excited. Why does the Vampire have to knock them unconscious, steal their blood if he's trying to reunite them with their own grandparents?"

Jake scribbled on the whiteboard, his back to Vito. "Mrs. Martinette and Family Builders helped me understand." He stood aside to reveal the sentence on the board: BOTH PARTIES MUST WANT TO BE REUNITED. "The grandparents want to find the kids, but the kids might not want to be found. They have their lives here; they don't want to know about some awful past in Argentina."

Vito rubbed his eyes. "But that implies the victims were all contacted by this grandparents group and declined to be tested. Don't you think that would have come out when we first interviewed them, searching for connections? Like, wouldn't someone have said, 'Yo, here's something weird — some guy called me last week to tell me my biological mother was an Argentine political prisoner'?"

Jake grinned. God bless Vito. He was such

a New Yorker. No chance he'd ever let you get too full of your own brilliance. "Of course you're right. If the victims had all been approached, we would have seen the pattern before now. But here's what I'm speculating. As far as we know, only victim number one, Lucinda Bettis, was openly approached about establishing her biological identity. And she didn't respond positively. And that's what set the Vampire into action."

Vito gnawed his lower lip. "When you talked to this chick, she was really cagey, right?"

"I think she might be more forthcoming in the presence of a New York City police detective."

Vito stood up. "All right, all right. I'll go talk to her."

Jake beamed. Finally, Vito was back in his corner. "I think you'll be glad you did."

"Humpf." Vito paused with his hand on Jake's office door. "Wait a minute — what about the other vics? The Vampire doesn't need their blood to match with grandma's. How do you explain that?"

The smile faded from Jake's face. The word BLOOD pulsated again from the whiteboard. "I'm working on it."

CHAPTER
FORTY-ONE

Jake's house, never tidy under the best of circumstances, had degenerated over the course of the Vampire investigation to something between chaos and biohazard. Plates of Chinese and Indian carryout lay around the first floor in varying degrees of petrifaction. The tower of unopened mail, some envelopes emblazoned with "Second Notice" imprints, threatened to consume the hall table. A battered cardboard box with a Romanian return address disgorged a suspicious ashlike substance.

Manny surveyed the scene with disgust. "You and Jake are going to supplant the Collyer brothers for the pack rat of the century title." She kicked aside some forensic journals. "At least they left little paths to navigate from room to room."

"How conventional." Sam finished a section of the *Times* and tossed it over his shoulder.

Manny reached to pick it up, then stopped herself. "You're trying to provoke me."

"Not so, dear woman. We simply represent different approaches to housework." Sam stretched out his legs on the couch and reached for another section of the newspaper. "I'll never be a clean-as-you-goer. Too Sisyphean — you push the rock up the hill every day, only to watch it roll back down again. I prefer the tactic Hercules used to clean the Augean stables. Let things get really bad, then divert a nearby river and wash it all away at once."

"When do you plan to work that wonder, Herc?" Jake emerged from the kitchen bearing paper plates of Vietnamese spring rolls. "With all the china plates out of commission, we're limited to nonsaucy food."

"Food. The great motivator." Taking her spring roll, Manny plopped into an overstuffed chair. "Tell me again what Detective Pasquarelli said after he talked to the FBI."

Manny had reported her entire conversation with Paco to the police. Detective Pasquarelli had been very excited about the information and naturally wanted to interview Paco himself. But the FBI's involvement in the case had compromised his autonomy. Because of the Sandovals' diplomatic immunity, he had to get FBI clearance to proceed. As Manny had feared, it hadn't been forthcoming.

"Vito said the agent he works with directly seemed just as excited about this break as he is. But that guy's low on the totem pole. He had to kick it upstairs for permission. They're still waiting."

"That's preposterous!" Manny said. "Diplomatic immunity is a courtesy; it should not be absolutely inviolable. In a case this serious, there should be no question about pressuring the Sandovals to cooperate."

"Maybe tomorrow they'll catch a break," Jake said.

"Don't count on it." Manny leaned back in her chair and promptly shot back out again. "Ow! It's booby-trapped." She pulled the cushions away. "My God, there's a scalpel in there!"

"Sorry, dear. I was doing an experiment to see if a scalpel could make accidental incised wounds if you lean back on it in a chair. Guess the defense attorney will have to try harder because you just proved that his client intentionally killed her husband." Jake then patted a space beside him on the love seat. "Come sit with me."

Manny eyed the cobweb stretching from the floor lamp to the arm of the love seat. "No thanks, I'll just clear a space over here."

She pushed a box of old slides into the corner. "This is the problem with having a big house. The more space you have, the more junk you accumulate. You know, when I drove over to Club Epoch in Hoboken, I was seriously considering moving to one of those big loft apartments in a converted factory. Now I'm afraid if I lived there, I'd wind up hoarding like you two."

"I think you should consider it, Manny," Sam said. "Think of how you could expand your shoe portfolio. But the time to buy is now. There are only a few factories left to be converted."

"The ones that are left all have hazardous-waste issues," Jake said. "You wouldn't want to expose your footwear to radiation. A Manhattan studio is much more salubrious."

"Your concern for my health is touching." Manny began heaving newspapers off the window seat. "Couldn't we at least get rid of some of these copies of the *Times*? They're weeks old."

She paused to read a headline. " 'Vampire Suspected in Death of Prominent Physician' — this one's from when Dr. Fortes was killed. 'Vampire's Lair Found in Brooklyn,' 'Vampire Tied to Bombing in Hoboken,' 'Mysterious Attacker Targets Opera Star.'

Geez, the Vampire's been on the front page of the paper just about every day since this case started. This pile is an archaeological record."

Jake stopped chewing and stared at her, a crumb of spring roll stuck to his lip. He dumped the half-full plate onto the floor. Mycroft shot across the room and immediately tucked into the delicate mélange of shrimp and vegetables.

"I hope you were done with that," Manny said as Jake crossed the room to the window seat.

Jake didn't appear to hear her. He fell to his knees and began digging through the newspapers, scattering them left and right.

"Jake, come on. I just stacked those for recycling," Manny protested.

"Help me find April fifth," Jake demanded.

"What's April fifth?" Manny asked.

"The day after the first Vampire attack. Lucinda Bettis, victim number one."

"Here it is."

Jake snatched the paper from her, quickly scanned the front page, then flipped to the Metro section. "Nothing," he said, checking the inside pages. "Not even a little blurb." He tossed the paper aside. "Now look for April eleventh."

"What are you —"

"Here!" Jake held it up and immediately began paging through the issue. "Nothing on page one, nothing on the front page of Metro, but here on page B-four we see it. 'Police Curious about Strange Similarities in Attacks.' A six-paragraph story comparing the MO of the attack on victim two with that of Lucinda Bettis. Now, find April twenty-third."

Manny handed it to him.

"By victim three, the story's moved to the front page. Prominent mention of the blood draw and the needle mark left on the victim. As I recall, this is when the *Post* first dubbed him 'the Vampire.' " Jake sat back on his haunches. "From then on, it's been headline news every day in every local paper. That must be it."

"What must be it?" Sam and Manny said almost simultaneously.

Jakes pointed to the sea of newsprint surrounding him and Manny on the floor. "This is why the Vampire drew blood from Fiore, Hogaarth, Fortes, and Slade even though they aren't children of the Desaparecidos. He must crave publicity for his cause. When he realized what a stir his weird blood draws were causing, he decided to use that as his signature, even on victims he intended to torture and/or kill. The blood draw itself was unnecessary, just done as a flourish."

"A signature," Manny whispered.

"For someone who seeks publicity, he's done an awfully good job of covering his tracks," Sam said. "He's got the police chasing after imaginary Islamic terrorists. You and Manny are the only ones who seem to know this is about the Desaparecidos."

Jake's and Manny's eyes met; then they both turned slowly to look at Sam. "He's planning something," Manny said. "Or, I should say, *they're* planning something, because we know there's a woman involved in this, too. She's the one who posed as Tracy and recommended me to Maureen Heaton. She intentionally drew me into this case" — Manny reached for Jake's hand — "and I bet, by extension, drew *you* into this case. They wanted us because of who we are, because of the results we achieved on the Lyons case."

"I think that must be it," Jake agreed. "The story of the Desaparecidos has been around for about thirty years. The mothers and grandmothers keep up their protests, but the outrage has faded. There are still victims who've never been accounted for, kids who don't know their true heritage.

But people aren't listening anymore. They want to forget about the Dirty War."

"And there are still perpetrators who've never been brought to justice," Manny said. "I sympathize, but I don't want to be part of the Vampire's vigilante scheme. I won't allow myself to be used this way!"

"We may not have a choice," Jake said. "There's no doubt in my mind that Travis plays into their plan for a grand finale. I'd like nothing better than to deprive the Vampire of his big bang, but we can't endanger Travis. If we can't anticipate the Vampire's next move, we may have to play out the game according to his rules."

CHAPTER FORTY-TWO

Manny rolled over in her bed and squinted across the room. The numbers 5:09 glowed greenly from her programmable coffeemaker. Given how exhausted she'd been the night before after coming home from Jake's, she was surprised to find herself awake before the deafening sound of the built-in grinder pulverizing French-roast beans was due to kick in at 6:00 a.m.

She'd been tempted to spend the night at Jake's. The growing suspicion that she was just a pawn in some unpredictable scheme of the Vampire's had made her jumpy and grateful for company. But she had an eight-thirty deposition in the Greenfield case and she didn't intend to arrive for it wearing yesterday's clothes. When she stayed at Jake's, she lived out of her handbag, slept in his WELCOME TO THE BOWELS OF FOREN-SIC PATHOLOGY T-shirt, and returned to her apartment in the morning to change.

She had no intention of moving parts of her wardrobe into his house. She didn't want her cashmere and silk absorbing the smell of formaldehyde, and besides, it wasn't that kind of relationship. She'd gone so far as to buy some French hand-milled rose petal and jasmine soap for his bathroom, strictly as a defense against the red bumps she'd developed from showering with his ghastly little bars of hotel-room freebies, but that was as domestic as she intended to get.

Manny stretched out and closed her eyes. She wouldn't fall back asleep, but she could rest in bed for a while until the coffeepot started its routine. The light lavender scent of her bedding lulled her, and she drifted, blissfully unconnected to the problems of the day to come.

Somewhere in the apartment, a sound.

Manny bolted straight up. There it was again: the unmistakable sound of a poodle retching. She realized that must have been what had awakened her early.

She clicked on the light. No Mycroft at the foot of the bed. A bad sign. Whenever he was sick, he slunk off to the corner of her closet. The last time he'd had an upset stomach, a six-hundred-dollar pair of Jimmy Choos had taken a one-way ride on a Department of Sanitation truck.

"Mycroft, sweetie, what's wrong?" Manny opened the closet door and peered under the racks of neatly hanging suits and blouses. Sure enough, she spied a little mound of red fur in the far corner, behind last year's handbags and her Uggs. Falling to her knees, Manny crawled forward and extended her hand. "C'mere, baby. Let Mom take a look."

Mycroft yelped as she slipped one hand under his trembling body and slid him toward her. When she got him into the light, Manny's heart constricted. This was no "I shouldn't have eaten all that mozzarella." Mycroft's eyes were glazed, his belly was distended, and he was breathing in short, sharp pants.

My God, what had he eaten yesterday? Had he stumbled into rat poison in the park when she had tossed those gourmet treats to waylay Paco? Or was it that spring roll he'd devoured at Jake's? Was there some herb in Vietnamese food fatal to dogs? Lemongrass? Cilantro?

Whatever the cause, Mycroft was in a serious crisis. As her panic rose, Manny's mind went blank. What should she do, call 911? Pound on the door of her neighbor, the cardiologist?

She took a deep breath. Getting hysterical

wasn't going to help Mycroft. Dr. Costello was on her speed dial. The vet could tell her what immediate action to take until she could get Mycroft over to him.

She lunged for her BlackBerry, then waited impatiently as the vet's office voice-mail system droned through its options. "Our office is closed now. To schedule an appointment, press one. To leave a message . . ." Manny's heart was pounding so hard, she could barely hear. *Hurry, hurry.* Finally, ". . . If this is a true medical emergency, please dial 212-555-3680. The doctor will respond to your page within ten minutes."

Manny dialed the pager number with trembling fingers. Ten minutes! Mycroft could be dead by then. She felt as if she were having an out-of-body experience, listening to a voice describing Mycroft's symptoms, begging for help, a voice much higher-pitched and rapid than her own.

Ending the call, she sat next to Mycroft to wait, stroking his silky head. The little dog's trusting brown eyes gazed up at her, begging silently for her to ease his pain. Why had she used him as a decoy? Why had she let him eat all that people food? *Please, God, let him live and I promise I'll give him nothing but Science Diet for the rest of his days.*

The phone rang. Manny snatched it up eagerly. "Dr. Costello? That was quick! Thank you so much for calling." Manny described Mycroft's symptoms and answered the doctor's questions.

"It sounds like he's gotten everything out of his system," Dr. Costello said. "But I'm concerned about the labored breathing. Keep him warm and get him over to my office." Then he gave a little grunt of displeasure. "No, that won't work."

"Yes! Yes it will!" Manny's voice was shrill and insistent.

"It's on the other side of town. If he is in true respiratory distress, time is of the essence," Dr. Costello explained. "My wife says you better bring him here, to our home. I have everything I'll need here."

"Oh thank God! I'll leave right away. What's the address?"

Manny scribbled on the only piece of paper she could find — page two of her Saks bill. She had no idea Dr. Costello lived so close to her. She could walk to his apartment; it would be faster than trying to find a cab before dawn. She threw on a pair of jeans and a T-shirt, and clipped on Mycroft's leash. The poor dog was too sick to walk. She'd have to carry him, but she preferred to have him in her arms, where she could see how he was doing, rather than in his carrier.

In the elevator, she pressed the B button. If she went down to the building's basement and exited out the rear service door, she could cut one block off her walk.

As she walked out into the gray dawn, the scents and sounds of the city greeted her, but the street and sidewalks were empty. At the end of the block, a trash truck beeped insistently as it backed toward a Dumpster. The smell of urine drifted up from the gutter. Tucking Mycroft under her arm, Manny trotted across the street in mid-block. A drunk sprawled on a sheet of cardboard, his dirty fingers still clutching a bottle of cheap wine, even in sleep. Manny averted her eyes as she passed him.

Something caught at her ankle. Manny looked down in surprise and saw the drunk's grinning face. She tried to shake him off, more in annoyance than fear. She had no time to be mugged this morning. She could hear other footsteps approaching from behind, and she took a deep breath to scream for help.

An unwise choice. As her lungs expanded, they filled with the cloying scent of ether.

The buildings dipped and spun. The side-walk came up to meet her. Mycroft fell from her arms.

"My dog! My dog!" Maybe Manny only thought those words, or maybe she spoke them aloud.

Either way, no one heard.

CHAPTER
FORTY-THREE

Jake extended his right arm, groping for Manny in the darkness of his bed. Pillows, blankets, sheets, but no soft curves, no tumble of hair. Then he remembered: Manny hadn't stayed last night, something about an early-morning deposition. He was surprised by the depth of his disappointment.

Oh well, I might as well get out of bed and catch up on a few things before going to the office. Jake headed downstairs for coffee and his laptop, nearly pitching headfirst off the second landing when he stumbled over a banker's box containing the evidence in a police-restraint death that had arrived two days ago from Los Angeles. Manny was right: This place really was careening toward Health Department condemnation.

Once the coffee was on, Jake popped open his laptop and logged on to his e-mail. The screen beamed at him, showing he had eighty-three new messages. He rubbed his eyes — could that be right? E-mail, a blessing and a curse.

Cutting the green spot off a bagel he found in a bag on the counter, Jake poured his coffee and settled down to tackle his inbox. Yes, he'd be happy to speak at Quantico on the subject of bioterrorism; no, he regretted he would not be able to travel to Latvia to address a conference on investigating civilian explosions. Would he come to Athens in September for a week of in-service training? Damn! That sounded good, but Pederson would never give him the time off. These days, it seemed that keeping Jake's light under a bushel was Pederson's top priority.

Fifteen e-mails answered, twenty, twenty-five. Jake glanced at his watch. It read eight-forty-five. *How did it get so late? I better get a move on.* Somehow, Pederson was always standing by the receptionist's desk when Jake rolled in at nine-fifteen, but never when he left at midnight. He scanned the list of remaining e-mails. Nothing urgent, except —

What was this from Roger@mycollect .com? Could it be a response from one of those eBay collectibles dealers Manny had contacted about Nixon's mug? He clicked and read the message. The dealer remembered the transaction. Jake stared at the screen. The buyer's name sounded awfully familiar. He trolled through the many dusty file drawers of his memory. Sometimes his brain felt as cluttered as his house.

Jake slammed the laptop shut. He knew that name! But from what part of this sprawling investigation? He'd have to wait until he got to the office and started searching the files. He headed for the door, then stopped and reached for the phone. Manny would know. She had the most amazing memory, able to recall the tiniest details instantly. He claimed it was because of her youth. Her brain filled her cranial cavity with the sulci and gyri of a virginal youngster. Not like his brain, shrunken and flattened.

He dialed, but the call rolled immediately to voice mail. *Of course — look at the time. She must be in her deposition now.* Even Manny turned off her cell phone during depositions. He left a message and continued on to the office.

Manny's head throbbed and her throat, parched and raw, protested every swallow. She opened her eyes a slit but quickly shut them when the room started to roll. She must be hungover. Odd, because she really wasn't much of a drinker.

Had she been celebrating, or drowning her sorrows? She couldn't recall. Something scratched at her wrists. She tried to brush it away but found she couldn't move her arms. That was odd, too.

Nearby, a dog barked — very loudly. How could Mycroft be barking so ferociously? Maybe someone was outside. She should check on that. She certainly should. But she was tired, so tired.

The barking continued.

In a minute, Mycroft. In a minute . . .

Jake's cell phone vibrated in the middle of the weekly staff meeting. He ignored it. A few seconds later, it started again. As Charles Pederson paced across the front of the room, pontificating, Jake discreetly looked down at the phone. The display said LITTLE PAWS.

He frowned. Why would Mycroft's silly doggy day care be calling him? Then he remembered he had given Manny permission to list him as one of three emergency backup numbers. If they were calling him, it must be because they couldn't reach Manny, or Kenneth, or Manny's mother,

Rose. Well, Manny and Kenneth were together at the deposition, and Rose was probably out somewhere having fun. She kept her cell phone turned off, using it only for emergencies, which she defined as times when she needed to reach others, not times when they needed to reach her. Jake turned his attention back to the meeting. Little Paws could wait.

Again, the cell phone vibrated. Annoyed, Jake reached down to turn it off. This time the display read KENNETH BOYD.

His heart rate quickened. If Kenneth was calling him, where the hell was Manny? Jake glanced at the clock on the wall. The meeting had been going for half an hour and Pederson showed no sign of wrapping it up.

"And now, I'd like to share this Power-Point presentation with you," Pederson said. "Lights, please."

The lights went down and Pederson began fiddling with his laptop. Nothing appeared on the screen. Finally, one of the secretaries took pity and got up to help the chief. As they huddled together over the computer, Jake slipped out the rear door of the conference room.

Back in his office, Jake dialed Kenneth. "Where's Manny?" he asked without a greeting.

"That's what I'd like to know. She never showed up for the Greenfield deposition."

Jake could practically see his adrenal gland preparing for fight or flight. "Little Paws also called me. Do you know why?"

"Because when they opened up this morning, they found Mycroft sitting at the door all by himself, dragging his leash behind him."

CHAPTER
FORTY-FOUR

"Let's get her up," a woman's voice said.

"I don't think she's —"

"I said it's time." A door clicked.

Manny opened her eyes and found herself looking into a very beautiful face: shiny black hair, almond eyes, high cheekbones. Human beings are hardwired to respond positively to beauty, but Manny did not smile. Neither did the other woman.

The room she was in had a very high ceiling, dingy green walls, and no furniture other than the bed she lay on and a small table. None of it meant anything to Manny. She hadn't recovered the ability to reason; she could focus only on her physical needs — to drink, to eat, and to stop the incessant pounding in her head.

"Can I have some water?" Manny's voice came out as a harsh croak, unrecognizable to her own ears.

The woman moved to the table and

poured water from a bottle into a plastic cup. Manny watched, her mind grinding slowly into gear. The woman looked vaguely familiar to her, but she didn't know why. Mostly, Manny was interested in the water. She propped herself up on one elbow, took the cup, and drank the water straight down. The fluids primed her brain and she looked around. The room was so dusty and dim, it couldn't possibly be someone's home.

"Where am I? Who are you?" Snippets of memory returned to her. A dirty man. A smell. A fall onto the sidewalk. A slight jingling sound . . .

Manny sat straight up. "My dog! Where's my dog?" The sound she remembered was the tinkle of Mycroft's tags as he ran. "Where's Mycroft? He was sick. I was taking him to the vet."

The woman observed her coolly but said nothing. Where had Manny seen her before? She was beautiful enough to be an actress or a model, but Manny didn't think she'd seen her on TV or in a magazine. Besides, what would a famous person be doing in a grungy place like this? She took in more details of the room: unfinished wood floor, dirty barred window, exposed pipes. What was *she* doing here? Manny swung her legs over the edge of the bed and pushed herself up. "Look, I have to —"

Her knees buckled and her vision blurred. She plopped back down. "What's the matter with me?" Manny closed her eyes and rubbed her temples until she felt a little better. When she looked up again, a man stood in the doorway.

Manny smiled. A familiar face, a kind face. Then her smile faded. A face that didn't belong here.

"Dr. Costello, what's going on? And where's Mycroft?"

The vet turned his back and looked out the only window, a barred opening facing an air shaft. "My wife, Elena, will explain."

"Surely by now you realize who we are, Ms. Manfreda?"

Manny's hands gripped the rough covers of the bed. A man and a woman working together, a person with some medical expertise, born in the late seventies. "You're the Vampire? The two of you?"

Elena smiled.

"Why are you doing this?" Manny continued. "What do you want from me?"

"We want you, and your friend Dr. Rosen, to tell the world about the Desaparecidos," Elena said. "And we have taken measures to make sure the world is finally listening."

This was it. The endgame she and Jake

363

had been predicting the previous night. Manny turned to face the other woman.

"You poisoned my dog to get me here? How?"

Elena laughed. "Mycroft is a creature of habit. He takes a walk in the park every day with his keeper from Little Paws. A woman walking six small dogs is used to getting a lot of attention. While Frederic fussed over the others yesterday, I slipped Mycroft a little treat."

"What did you give him?" Manny demanded. "You killed my dog!"

Dr. Costello looked offended. "Certainly not. It was just a little something to upset his digestion. He didn't get enough to cause serious damage."

"But where is he?" Manny asked again.

Dr. Costello and his wife exchanged a glance. "Don't worry about your dog," Elena said. "Suffice it to say that Mycroft has brought you here in a way that is virtually untraceable. No one knows where you are, Manny. If Jake Rosen wants to save your life, and the life of Travis Heaton, he will have to tell the world about the torture and death our parents suffered."

No longer cool and elegant, Elena paced around the room in rising hysteria, her skin flushed a muddy red beneath her tan. "Jake

Rosen will tell the world how my husband and I and Esteban Sandoval and so many others were ripped from our mothers' wombs and given away to be raised by the very people who had killed our parents. When Lucinda Bettis and the others see how all our parents were tortured, they will finally renounce this lying life they have lived for all these years."

She grabbed Manny by the shoulders. Her eyes were wild; her nostrils flared. "They don't believe what I have told them. It's only words to them, and pictures. They have to see it lived. They have to witness how our parents were tortured. Then they will understand. You and Jake Rosen will make them understand."

CHAPTER
FORTY-FIVE

The first thing Jake noticed when he entered Manny's apartment was a strong, scorched scent of Hawaiian Peabody roast left over-long on the warming plate of the coffee-maker. He looked into the tiny kitchen area. "Pot's full — she left without drinking any," he said to Kenneth and Pasquarelli, who had come with him to search for signs of Manny's whereabouts.

Kenneth looked in the other direction. "And the Murphy bed is still down. Manny always makes the bed before she leaves. Says it tricks her into believing her bedroom and her living room aren't the same room."

"All right, so we know she slept here last night and we know she left in a hurry this morning," Pasquarelli said. "Why? Where'd she go? And how did the dog wind up alone at Little Paws?"

"She never would have left him outside alone," Kenneth said for about the fifteenth time. He chewed on a long pink fingernail as his eyes darted around the tiny apartment.

"I'll get started subpoenaing her phone records," Pasquarelli said. "Get a list of her incoming and outgoing calls this morning."

"That will take hours," Jake said. "There must be some evidence here that will give us a lead sooner."

"Her closet!" Kenneth shouted. "Let's see if we can figure out what she was wearing. Then we'll know where she intended to go."

Pasquarelli raised his eyebrows. "That's one approach."

Kenneth flung open the doors of the walk-in closet, revealing neatly hanging blouses, skirts, pants, and dresses, not to mention towers of shoe boxes spaced between a floor shoe rack.

"It's hopeless," Jake said. "How can you possibly tell what's missing from all that?"

But Kenneth was down on his knees. "Look at how most of the shoes on the shoe rack are thrown around. She was searching for something." His voice grew muffled as he crawled farther into the depths of the closet.

"Eeew!" Kenneth came scuttling out backward, holding his right hand out in front of him. "There's something wet and disgusting on the floor in there."

Jake grabbed Kenneth's wrist, stared at the greenish slime under the manicured nails, then lifted them to his nose to sniff. "Dog vomit," he pronounced. "Mycroft must have been sick in the night. Manny left in a rush to take him to the vet."

Kenneth's eyes lighted up, then immediately dimmed. "But she must never have gotten there. And neither did Mycroft."

"Let's call the vet." Jake snapped his fingers. "What's his name again?"

Kenneth returned from washing his hands. "I have the number here on my phone." He clicked a few buttons and started talking. Jake would have snatched the phone away from him, but Kenneth seemed to be asking all the right questions.

"The vet said she paged him at five-fifteen this morning to say that Mycroft was vomiting," Kenneth reported. "He said he told her it sounded like he'd eaten something toxic to dogs and that she should take him to the Animal Medical Center on Eighty-sixth Street and York. They have an animal poison-control center there that's open twenty-four/seven."

"You call the Animal Medical Center to check if she ever made it there," Jake told Kenneth. "Vito and I will go down and talk to the doorman."

At 10:00 a.m., the morning rush had ended and the doorman in Manny's lobby had settled into signing for deliveries and assisting a few elderly residents and stay-at-home moms.

"Who was on duty at five this morning?" Jake asked.

"I was." The doorman yawned. "We're all working overtime this week to cover for one guy's vacation. I've been here since midnight."

"Did you see Ms. Manfreda leave with her dog?"

"Manny? No, I haven't seen her all day."

Jake stepped closer to the doorman, a good-looking guy of about thirty. He seemed like a heads-up person, but he might have been busy or distracted when Manny passed by. "This is very important," Jake said. "She was probably in a hurry. Maybe you missed her."

The doorman shook his head insistently. "Miss Manny? No way. She always says hello, no matter how fast she's moving. Not like some others in this building."

Vito took over. "Look, we know she came home last night, and she's not in her apartment now, so she had to have gone out. We're trying to trace her steps."

"I didn't say she couldn't have gone out; I just said she didn't pass me. From five to six, no one left but Legere in 12B — he swims laps every morning before work." The doorman shook his head at this insanity. "But lots of people go out the west side service door in the morning. It puts them one block closer to the E train station."

Jake shook his head. "Manny never takes the subway. And she certainly wouldn't take a sick dog on the train. Besides, that subway doesn't take you anywhere close to Eighty-sixth and York. It doesn't make sense."

"Maybe she went out the back door to go to her garage," Vito suggested.

"Her garage is that way." The doorman pointed uptown, proving he knew Manny's routines. "And when she's taking a cab, she always lets me hail it." He dangled the silver whistle around his neck. "She can whistle pretty loud, but this is louder."

Jake looked down, concentrating. Manny was sometimes impulsive, but never irrational. There had to be a good reason why she'd exited through the rear door. What was it?

Kenneth emerged from an elevator and crossed over to them. "The Animal Medical Center has no record of Manny or Mycroft being there today. Something had to have happened to her on the way there."

Jake continued to stare at the tasteful pattern of the lobby carpet. "Illogical." He looked up at Kenneth. "Mycroft should be at Little Paws now?"

"Yes."

"Call them and find out how he's doing," Jake commanded.

Kenneth did not reach for his cell phone. Instead, he put his hands on his hips and glared at Jake. As devoted as he was to Mycroft, he was more devoted to Manny, and he clearly thought they should be focusing their efforts on the owner, not the pet.

"I want to know just how sick the dog is," Jake explained as he walked toward the elevator. "Maybe Manny changed her mind about taking him to the Animal Medical Center."

"Why are you going back up to the apartment?" Vito asked.

"I want a sample of the vomit."

CHAPTER
FORTY-SIX

"Why?" Manny asked.

Dr. Costello had reentered the room and now he carried a gun. Earlier, he'd acted nervous, almost embarrassed, but the weapon seemed to impart confidence.

He pointed the gun at Manny and waved her against the wall. "She's wearing pants. That's not ideal," he said to his wife.

Elena eyed Manny up and down. "She's bigger than I am, but I'll find something that will work."

Bitch. Manny watched her leave the room.

"Why are you doing this?" she repeated to the vet. "You've spent your whole life taking care of sick, helpless animals. How can you hurt people like this?"

"I haven't hurt any *people*," he said. "Amanda Hogaarth and Raymond Fortes were lower than the lowest cockroach that crawls across this floor." He spit in the dust at his feet. "They used their medical training to inflict more pain than the stupid soldiers and police could have dreamed up on their own. For that, they deserved what they got."

Manny wasn't about to argue the negative value of vigilantism with a man holding a gun on her. Still, she couldn't resist probing more. "What about Boo Hravek and Deanie Slade? They have no connection to Argentina."

"Boo Hravek was a thug who sold drugs and beat people up for gangsters. We can't mourn his death." He hesitated. "The girl, Deanie, well . . . I didn't really want to leave her like that. But Elena insisted. Said it was necessary to send a message."

Elena insisted. Costello had taken over the animal hospital when Mycroft's previous vet moved out of state. He had immediately impressed her as a strong, confident man, but she'd known strong men who'd acted against their better judgment to please their wives. Usually, it took the form of buying a bigger house than they knew they could afford, or having another child they really weren't prepared for. But torturing an innocent girl because your wife insisted? Man, that was some screwed-up relationship.

Elena returned at that moment carrying a flowered sundress. She tossed it at Manny.

"Put this on."

"Why? Why do I have to change clothes?"

"You ask too many questions." Dr. Costello pointed the gun at her heart. "Just do as you're told."

Reluctantly, Manny took off her jeans, cashmere T-shirt, and Golden Goose boots and put on the dress. It was sleeveless and well above her knees, made of some thin, slippery fabric. She felt cold, inside and out.

"Turn around," Elena said. She tied Manny's hands behind her back. Then she tied her ankles together. "Go get him," she said to her husband.

Manny noticed that the rope that bound her was quite loose. She knew damn well from what the Costellos had done to Deanie Slade that they were capable of better work. The loose ropes made her uneasy.

A few moments later, the door opened and Dr. Costello returned. He was not alone.

"Travis!" Relief at seeing her client again momentarily buoyed Manny's spirits. At least he was still alive, but he looked terrible. Always thin, his bones now protruded at sharp angles. His sunken eyes peered at her from under matted, greasy hair.

He smiled slightly and shuffled over to her side. What can you say in a situation like this? "Good to see you. How've you been?"

Manny's dread returned as she watched the vet loosely tie Travis. Even if she couldn't save herself, she had to save Travis. She didn't discern an iota of compassion in Elena, but Dr. Costello was different. He had treated Mycroft so tenderly; surely he wouldn't want to hurt a kid. "Travis is just an innocent child," she reminded Costello. "Paco was the person you intended to implicate in that bombing."

"Yes, we wanted his parents to know the pain of having a child imprisoned unjustly," Elena replied before her husband could. "Unfortunately, that part of our plan didn't work out perfectly. Even in this country, the Sandovals are above the law."

"So why punish Travis? Keep me, but let him go."

Dr. Costello turned to his wife. "Please, we could —"

"No!" Elena grabbed her husband's upper arms. She was nearly as tall as he, and she held her face inches from his. Manny could see her chest heaving as she harangued her husband. "You are such a coward. You turn whatever way the wind blows, just like our countrymen who co-operated with the junta. I might have known that when it came to the end, you would be too timid to act."

Impugning his masculinity, the oldest trick in the book. Surely Costello wouldn't fall for it. But no, Manny saw the doctor narrow his eyes, thrust out his chin. That's why it was the oldest trick, because it worked so predictably.

Manny knew she was losing him, but she wouldn't stop trying. "Dr. Costello, stop and think! It's not cowardly to protect the innocent. How can hurting a defenseless teenager ever be justified? Don't sink to the same level as the soldiers who tortured your parents. You're better than that."

Elena whirled around. "Shut up, you pampered American bitch! You know nothing about suffering, nothing. *I* have suffered." Her voice was raw, her breathing like a runner's at the end of a hard-fought race. "*I* will decide what is justified."

Manny watched Costello put his arm around his wife's shoulders and kiss the top of her head. She relaxed into his embrace.

Manny had no ally now.

CHAPTER
FORTY-SEVEN

"Raisins," Jake said, looking up from his lab table. "As few as seven raisins can cause kidney failure and even kill a little dog."

"Must've been that Vietnamese food Mycroft shared with us last night," Sam replied. "The Vampire must've been watching Manny's apartment, just waiting for a good opportunity to grab her. To see her leave alone at five in the morning — I bet he couldn't believe his luck."

Jake shook his head. "The Vampire doesn't rely on luck. This was planned."

"But how could he know Mycroft would get sick from eating Vietnamese food?"

"He didn't. I called the Saigon Sunset. There's no raisins in their spring rolls, just a little scallion. I found four partially digested raisins in Mycroft's vomit; someone must have known he is a food slut. Probably gobbled them in a millisecond. Someone did this on purpose."

Sam looked down at the bundle of red fur reclining on a pallet of morgue sheets next to Jake's desk. "Manny would never let a stranger give Mycroft food. How did the Vampire get close enough to the dog to do this? The only time he's away from her is when he's at —"

"Little Paws," Jake concluded. "I'm speculating the Vampire waylaid the group of dogs and did this to Mycroft during one of his walks in the park."

"So that means the dog walker has seen the Vampire. Can't she describe him?" Sam asked.

"According to Sheila, the owner, the walkers are approached all the time. Even jaded New Yorkers get a kick out of seeing six or eight cute little dogs romping together. And Sheila encourages the dog walkers to talk to people — that's how she brings in new customers. The unemployed actress walking Mycroft yesterday passed out Little Paws business cards to four or five people. None of them made an impression on her."

Sam knelt and stroked Mycroft's head. "I wish you could talk, buddy. Tell us who grabbed Manny and how you made it back to Little Paws."

The dog lifted his head weakly and his tail twitched in what passed for a wag.

"Do you think he's really okay now, Jake?" Sam asked. "He still seems awfully listless. Kenneth took him over to the Animal Medical Center and they gave him the all clear. Kenneth wanted to take him to Dr. Costello, too, but he couldn't get —"

Jake's head snapped up from his microscope. He felt a prickle run across the back of his neck as the piloerector muscles in his skin contracted. "What did you say?"

"I said that Mycroft still doesn't seem himself. Maybe we should take him to Dr. Costello, his regular vet."

"Costello? Costello is the name of Manny's vet?"

"Yeah, the new guy. The one that Kenneth thinks is so hot. Why?"

Jake swung around to face his computer, his fingers wildly tapping the keys. "Nixon's coffee mug. Through a subpoena on the eBay seller, we tracked down the name of the seller. The seller sent me an e-mail with the info. It sounded vaguely familiar, but I hadn't yet tracked it down when Manny disappeared." A final mouse click and Jake leaned forward to squint at the screen. "The buyer is one Elena Costello. The billing address on her credit card is in Manhattan. This can't be a coincidence."

Picking up on his brother's excitement,

Sam asked, "Where in Manhattan — uptown or downtown from Manny's place?"

"The fifties, midtown, near her. That could explain why she went out the back door of her building. Dr. Costello claims he told Manny to take Mycroft to the Animal Medical Center uptown, but he must really have told her to bring the dog to him."

"Is there anything else the eBay seller revealed?" Sam asked.

"It says the mug was shipped to a PO Box in Paterson, New Jersey," Jake continued. "The last known address for Freak, the guy who set the bomb, the guy who has a prior for organizing dog fights, was in Paterson. Pasquarelli tried to locate him, but none of his street friends are talking."

Sam jumped up. "I'll find him."

"I should have seen this earlier," Jake said. "The expertise in drawing blood, the rats, what happened to Mycroft — it all points to a veterinarian."

"No time for recriminations, Jake. You put the police on the Costellos' trail. I'm going to Paterson."

Jake's phone rang. He signaled his brother to wait, but Sam was already out the door.

CHAPTER
FORTY-EIGHT

"All right." Dr. Costello handed a remote-control device to his wife. "Are you ready?"

Elena smiled and nodded. Walking to the far corner of the room, she pressed a few buttons while her husband watched the screen of a laptop. Snapping her fingers to get Manny's and Travis's attention, she pointed above her head to a tiny camera by the ceiling. "Smile, you two. You're on *Candid Camera*. Or candid Web cam, I should say."

Manny looked up at the glass eye focused on her. She'd known military families who used Web cams to let the soldier mom or dad witness their kids' lives in real time. And she'd heard of live porn distributed over the Internet. But what exactly would be gained by showing her and Travis tied up in this otherwise-empty room? Stress, exhaustion, and ether had combined to dull Manny's mental reflexes. She tried to use her imagination to sort things out, but she came up blank.

She looked over at Travis, who stared listlessly up at the camera, then hung his head and coughed hoarsely. He'd been with the Costellos for days now, and he'd lost all his defiance, all his anger. What had they done to replace his youthful passion with this weary passivity? Travis had accepted his status as victim. Would she?

"Is it working?" Elena asked.

Dr. Costello tilted the laptop so his wife could see. A delighted smile spread across her face. Then the vet turned the laptop toward Manny and Travis.

Manny wouldn't have recognized the haggard red-haired woman on the screen except that she was sitting next to Travis, so it had to be her. Instinctively, she lifted her hand to smooth her wild hair. The woman on the screen's hand went up, too. Manny dropped her hand; the screen hand dropped. Creepy.

"What do you think?" Elena asked.

Manny sat stoically. She refused to perform.

"Come now, smile. Soon you'll be a star. Because we've sent an e-mail from the Vampire to every news outlet in the city, so that they can watch what's about to unfold here. And, of course, we'll ask your friend Dr. Rosen to tune in."

"What's about to unfold?" Manny asked.

"You'll see. The whole world will see. Finally."

CHAPTER
FORTY-NINE

"Lookin' for Freak."

Sam had circled Paterson in Jake's car, studying the clusters of young men gathered on certain corners. Although it was the middle of the day during the beginning of a work week, Paterson didn't lack for guys with no time clock to punch. After careful observation, Sam selected the group he would least like to meet in a dark alley, parked, and strolled up to them.

"Lookin' to get me a dog," Sam elaborated after his opening gambit elicited no response. "Friend of mine said Freak's the man to see about that."

The men shifted, dropping their hips and rolling their shoulders. The tallest man stared at Sam. Sam stared back. This lasted a good forty-five seconds. When Sam didn't wet his pants in fear, the big guy broke into a grin, revealing four shiny gold teeth.

"Nice grille," Sam said. "I think you must

be the guy the fellas over on Fifteenth Street told me to look for."

This cracked them up. Sam smiled, too, happy to have brought a little sunshine into their lives.

"Freak ain't been around lately," the big guy finally said through his laughter.

"Well, like I said, it's a dog I want. Who takes care of his dogs when he's gone?"

The big man looked Sam up and down, trying to determine his line of work. Suburban drug dealer? Pimp? Pornographer? "You can't use his dogs for protection, man," he advised. "They fightin' dogs — too mean for much else. Ain't nobody but Freak can handle 'em."

"But Freak's not around. Who's taking care of the dogs?"

"Pauly feeds 'em. But he can't help you." The big guy touched his forehead. "He's not all there, know what'm sayin'?"

"Got it. Okay, then. Be seein' ya."

Sam got back in his car, slipped on his sport coat, and drove two blocks to the Mother of Mercy Soup Kitchen. He entered the crowded dining room, scanned the crowd, and walked purposefully toward a stocky middle-aged woman with a wooden cross on a leather string around her neck.

"Good afternoon, Sister." Sam beamed.

"I'm looking for a young man named Pauly." He dropped his voice. "A little developmentally delayed? But I understand he's a hard worker, and I was hoping I could hire him for a few odd jobs around my warehouse over on Philips Street."

The nun clasped her hands in delight. "Ah, the Lord always provides! Pauly was just here, hoping for a loan to tide him over until his disability check arrives. I'm sure he'd love the opportunity to work, Mr. —"

"Pettengil," Sam said, lying without hesitation. "Where can I find him?"

"Right down the street. He lives above the bodega."

Sam felt a momentary twinge of guilt for having hoodwinked a nun, but it evaporated once he met Pauly. Not only was the young man happy to talk to Sam about his cousin Freak and the dogs, but also he immediately sought Sam's advice.

"Don't know what I'm gonna do. Freak said two days, watch 'em two days. But it's been five — no, six — no, five — five days he's gone." Sam trotted to keep up as the young man walked hyperkinetically along the dingy street. "Runnin' outta food, yes I am. And I ain't got money to buy more. Gotta give 'em meat, that's what Freak says. No dog chow, nope. Only meat."

Sam nodded sympathetically. Pauly didn't require much in the way of dialogue. When he finally got a chance to get a word in, Sam asked, "Where is Freak anyway?"

"Don't know. Bizness, he got bizness." They had reached a dilapidated house, one of only three still standing on the block. A tall board-on-board fence, sturdier than the building it was attached to, enclosed the small backyard. Pulling out a key, Pauly unfastened a thick padlock and pushed the gate as far as he could — about a foot. He slipped through the narrow opening, followed by Sam.

Recoiling from a tremendous volley of ferocious barking, Sam instinctively moved to duck back through the gate. But Pauly shuffled forward and Sam realized the dogs — at least twenty pit bulls — were all caged. They snapped and snarled, their small eyes rolling in fury, their powerful jaws seeking something, anything, to clamp onto. Pauly had been feeding them, but he obviously hadn't been taking care of any of their other needs. The dogs were covered in their own filth and some had bloodied their paws trying to escape their small pens.

The stench, the noise, the rage — it all reminded Sam of a tour he'd once taken of a maximum-security prison in Texas. There, too, the inmates had hurled themselves against the bars, angered beyond reason by the sight of a free man.

Sam looked at these canine prisoners and knew there wasn't much he could do other than call the ASPCA and hope the dogs could be tended to humanely. He gripped the young man's shoulder. "Come on, Pauly — we need to call for some help. You can't keep taking care of these dogs on your own. It's not safe."

Pauly looked uncertain. "Freak said he'd pay me five dollars. If I don't do my job, I won't get paid."

Sam pulled a ten from his wallet. "You did a good job, Pauly. Let's get out of here."

Pauly's eyes lighted up. "Maybe you're right. It sure does stink in here."

Just then, a breeze blew through, stirring the fumes from the uncleaned cages. Sam coughed as he moved toward the gate, then stopped. The powerful smell of dog waste permeated the air, but under that was another smell, much worse, just as distinctive.

"Wait for me outside, Pauly." Sam gave the kid a gentle shove, then crossed the yard to a garden shed in the corner. Covering his face with a handkerchief, he quickly yanked open the door.

What had once been a thin man, wearing a baseball cap with a ponytail extending out the back of the hat, slid out. Sam thought he saw a ghost — his ghost. Instead what he was looking at was the real killer of Boo Hravek.

The dogs began to howl.

CHAPTER FIFTY

The door opened once more and the Costellos returned. Between them, they pushed a large cage on wheels.

They stood aside. Travis screamed.

"He's a little cranky. He hasn't eaten," Elena said.

Manny looked into the eyes of an abused, angry, and restless pit bull. It stared back, its small gray eyes as flat and emotionless as a shark's. Hard to believe that this creature was from the same species as Mycroft. Now Manny understood the plan. She and Travis would be left alone and unprotected to be tortured by this animal while people watched on the Web cam, powerless to help them.

"Wait!" Manny screamed. "You can't leave us here with that, that . . . We've never done anything to hurt you. I would have helped you with your cause if you had just come to me and asked."

"I'm sorry that you and Travis have to suffer," Dr. Costello said. He looked sad. The nervousness had returned. "So often, the innocent do."

Manny sensed his weakness. Elena was ferocious, but Manny felt she could prevail with Dr. Costello. "We can still work this out," Manny pleaded. "I'll help you file a lawsuit against the government."

"The time for that is long past." Elena waved her hand while groaning in disgust. "To get what, lip service — skeleton justice? This is the only way. The right way."

Elena stepped up to the cage and checked what appeared to be a timer attached to the door. The white-and-brown dog lunged at her hand, but she didn't react. "He's not that big. Freak said he wasn't a great fighter. He won't kill Manny and Travis, just as the dogs they used on our parents didn't kill them. These two can survive the bites. This was our plan. To show the world the torture our parents suffered."

Dr. Costello nodded. Manny couldn't be sure if he was agreeing or convincing himself.

"This is *wrong*," Manny said, trying one last time to convince him. "This isn't justice; it's pure cruelty. It's not what your parents would want to avenge them."

"You can't know that." Elena's voice, low and steady now, chilled Manny more than her screaming had. "You don't know our parents. We never knew them. They're nothing more than decaying flesh and bones to us. But we have vowed to keep their souls alive for them, for us, and for all others like us. You preach justice. Can you *guarantee* you could get us true justice, Ms. Manfreda?"

Manny averted her eyes. She had no answer.

"We *will* do this. The others want to forget about the Dirty War, pretend it never happened. We will finally make the world *see*."

CHAPTER
FIFTY-ONE

"The Costellos' apartment and the veterinary office are both empty," Pasquarelli reported by phone. "No one's seen them since yesterday afternoon. We're watching all three airports and the train stations."

Jake nodded without much interest. He knew the Costellos wouldn't try to escape before they carried out their final plan, whatever it was. Finding them mattered to him only if it led to finding Manny . . . alive. "Any information they left behind to indicate where they're holding Manny and Travis?"

"Our computer guys are searching the office computer, but so far it seems to be strictly business. At home, it looks like they used a laptop, which they must've taken with them. There was some ash residue in the kitchen sink, and the smoke alarm was disconnected — they probably burned some papers before they left."

Meticulous. He hadn't expected anything less. Elena Costello's purchase of the Nixon coffee mug using her own name was the only mistake they'd made so far. Any forensic psychiatrist would say it was her way of getting caught — purposely. So that the world would know of her accomplishments, and she would be glorified. The twenty-first-century version of Jack the Ripper. But implicating Travis instead of Paco in the bombing was a more mundane blunder. But they'd made that error work to their advantage, milked it for even more publicity. As his mentor used to say, the hallmark of a professional lay not in never taking a misstep, but in knowing how to recover from it. Jake knew he couldn't count on the Costellos to trip themselves; he would have to trap them.

As soon as he hung up with Vito, the phone rang again. The caller ID indicated it was Sam, who was obviously reporting in from Paterson.

"Hi — what've you got?" Jake said.

"I found Freak."

"Already? Fantastic!"

"Not so fantastic for him. He's dead," Sam said.

Jake's grip on the phone tightened. The Costellos were tying up every loose end, eliminating every person who might intentionally or unintentionally disrupt their plan. Manny seemed to be part of their plan. But when they were done with her, what then? "What happened to him?"

"Shot through the back of the head, apparently while he was getting food for his dogs out of this shed. There's blood and brain matter everywhere."

"Where are you? What's all that noise?" Jake listened as his brother described the house in Paterson and the condition of the dogs. "The local police are here. We're waiting for Animal Control and the morgue meat wagon to arrive," Sam said.

"Don't let them move the body," Jake said, already out of his chair. "I want to see it in situ."

"But the Passaic County ME will be handling this case," Sam said.

"I don't care who has jurisdiction. Just don't let them move the body until I get there." As Jake swiveled his chair to leave, the phone rang again. Caller ID blocked — a Pederson trademark. Damn it — he had to take this call.

CHAPTER
FIFTY-TWO

Elena knelt at Manny's feet and started untying her legs. A surge of hope energized Manny. If they were to be moved, she might have an opportunity to escape. Then Manny realized what was really going on and the hope fizzled out. Elena wanted them to be able to run from the dog — it would make for a better show.

Manny watched Elena work and considered her options. She could wait until Elena was untying Travis, then kick her hard in the head. If she could knock Elena unconscious, she might stand a chance of reasoning with Dr. Costello. It was a long shot, but —

A sensation of being watched made Manny look up. Dr. Costello had his gun trained on her. Amazing how that small black object drained the strength from her legs.

With Travis's feet untied, Elena pulled out

a cell phone and dialed. "Dr. Rosen? Are you sitting in front of your computer?"

Manny could feel her heart rate kick up a notch. To hear Jake's name spoken, to know he was on the other end of that phone. "Jake!" she screamed.

Elena waved at her in annoyance, like a mother hushing her clamoring children. "Never mind who this is," she said into the phone. "You need to go to this Web site: www.the-disappeared-dot-com. You will be interested in what you see there."

Manny looked up at the camera. Could Jake see her now? Hear her?

"Dr. Rosen?" Elena coughed, then continued. "Do you see what I see? Good. Then you also see the list of other people you must get to tune into this Web site, starting with Lucinda Bettis and the others, as well as the Sandovals. And expect your phone to start ringing. Because we've sent an e-mail from the Vampire to every news outlet in the city. And we've given your phone number as the contact person. Only you can explain why this is happening."

Elena paused for a moment as Jake responded to her, careful to stay out of range of the camera. "Well, I think you understand why I can't tell you where they are, Dr. Rosen. But you're a clever man. That's why we chose you. I'm sure you'll rescue them . . . eventually."

Then Elena grabbed her husband by the arm and pulled him out of the room.

The door to safety slammed shut.

They were alone with the pit bull.

CHAPTER
FIFTY-THREE

Jake cradled the phone to his ear, all the while staring at his computer screen. *This must be what it's like to suffer from visual agnosia, that rare condition in which your visual acuity is perfectly good but you can't make sense of what you're seeing.*

He had first thought the voice directing him to this Web site was pulling a hoax, but he had checked it out just to be safe. And now, instead of the blank screen or porn site he had expected, he saw with horrifying clarity the woman he loved and her client, hands tied behind them, in an empty room with a large cage that had some kind of animal in it.

And this was apparently a live feed. When Manny shook her head on the screen, that meant that at the very same moment she was shaking her head in a room where he could see her but not find her. When she had looked up and stared directly into the camera, straight into his eyes, her terror had been as immediate as if she were sitting across the desk from him. His heart felt crushed by it. He slammed down the phone as if that would end Manny's fear.

Jake couldn't bear to look at Manny and couldn't bear to look away. But there were words on the screen, too, running in a column beside the streaming video. He dragged his eyes there to read the text. As he read, the bile rose in the back of his throat. The Vampire was planning on torturing Manny and Travis and broadcasting this live over the Internet for all the world to see. And this monster expected him to participate in the spectacle, provide the color commentary for an act of madness. Well, forget that.

He'd see to it that this live feed was blocked and deprive the Vampire of the publicity he craved. He'd shut down this Web site, and then he'd find Manny. Jake reached for his phone again, but before he could lift the receiver, it rang.

It was the same woman. "Hello, Dr. Rosen. By now you understand what is happening here."

"I understand, and I'm not participating in your madness."

"Don't make that decision until you know

all the ramifications, Doctor."

A knot of dread tightened in Jake's gut. "What do you mean?"

"You have one hour in which to contact each of the Vampire's victims. Tell them to log on to the site. Your friend the detective can help you with all the phone numbers you need. Once there, they must click the 'Contact' button to send an e-mail that verifies their presence. Do the same for the Sandoval family. Once everyone is watching, the show begins."

"And if I don't?"

"Then Ms. Manfreda and Travis Heaton will be executed with a single shot to the head before your eyes. You have sixty minutes from the end of this call."

The phone clicked off.

Chapter Fifty-Four

Manny could see Travis's arms trembling, his eyes wide with fear. He went into another spasm of coughing. Her own throat was raw and she felt like crying, too, but she couldn't. She had to remain calm, make a plan. Hysteria wouldn't help them.

Manny glanced up at the camera. Jake was watching, but so was Elena. Even if she couldn't think her way out of this mess, Manny wouldn't give that woman the satisfaction of seeing her fall apart.

Could Jake see what was in the cage? Did he know what was happening here? Or would he not understand until the timer released the door and the dog charged out? She looked down at her bare legs and arms. Now she understood why Elena had made her wear this ugly dress. She was totally exposed, totally vulnerable.

"What are we going to do?" Travis asked in a soft voice. "Are we just going to stand here and wait for the door to open?"

"Don't panic. That's the most important thing." Manny tried to speak with confidence, but inside she was shaking. Being attacked by an animal, eaten alive. It was as if Dr. Costello had sensed her worst fear. Couldn't he have chosen something else to make his point?

She looked around the room. Surely the door must be locked, and there was only the one window, heavily barred. And absolutely nothing to use as a weapon. Except maybe the cage itself. Could they use it to bludgeon the creature, even if they couldn't force it back inside? Did she have it in her to kill a dog, even one that was trying to kill her? In a way, the dog was a victim, too. Some say pit bulls aren't inherently vicious. But there was no mistaking that this dog had been crossbred to be bigger, and trained to kill. It had been mistreated and punished from birth to turn it into a crazed fighter. She felt sorry for it, but she couldn't undo the damage.

"Why did they untie our legs but not our hands?" Travis asked.

"They want us to be able to run from that thing, even though there's no place to hide, no way to escape. It'll provide more excitement." Manny twisted her hands. The rope was definitely loose. It was as if they had been tied to hold them still just long enough for the Costellos to get away and the cage to open. Everything had been planned for maximum drama.

"If we could get these ropes off quickly, we might be able to use them to tie the cage shut before the timer springs the lock." Manny's voice sounded choked and uneven to her own ears, like it had years ago at her first trial. What she wouldn't give now to have her terror inspired by a two-hundred-pound man in black robes instead of an eighty-pound dog with teeth so big, they jutted out of its mouth.

She'd seen bigger dogs, but she'd never seen an angrier one. Lean and muscular, the dog circled endlessly in the cage. It probably hadn't been out in days. Mycroft went bonkers whenever he was cooped up on a long car trip. Imagine what this much bigger breed, which craved exercise as much as food and water, must be feeling. It wanted out, and when it got out, nothing would stop it from venting its manic energy.

The look on the dog's face drove every rational thought out of Manny's mind.

"Do you think we can gang up on it?" Travis asked.

Manny glanced over at him, and for a terrible, selfish moment she was glad that Dr. Costello hadn't taken her plea seriously and released the boy. A terrified, weakened kid wasn't going to offer much defense, but it was reassuring not to be facing this thing alone.

Manny thought about what Travis had said. "If one of us can distract him, the other might be able to subdue him. But whatever we do, we can't run. Running will just incite his instinct to hunt."

"So if we just stay still, it'll leave us alone?"

Travis sounded pathetically hopeful, the way she used to when she begged her father to promise lightning could never strike their house. Just say it and make it so, Daddy.

Her father used to tell the reassuring lie. Manny couldn't. "Let's work on getting our hands untied."

They backed up to each other and Manny worked by touch to pick open Travis's bindings. As she struggled, they talked.

"Why did you circumvent your electronic bracelet, Travis? Where did you go when you left your apartment?"

"I went to meet Paco. We weren't supposed to talk at school or phone each other, but I knew he had information he needed to tell me. I managed to pass him a note at school and told him where to meet me — a

Laundromat down the block. I never made it there. Elena and Frederic grabbed me."

"Why did they want you?"

"From what I could figure out, they were still working out the details of the Web cam." Travis looked up at the camera lens, which captured their every move. "I didn't understand what they were planning, but I heard the word *camera* over and over again. I think they were afraid that if the police and the FBI kept interrogating me, they'd figure out the bombing was linked to the Vampire too soon. They had to buy time until they got this" — he gestured to the cage — "set up."

"I wish you hadn't been so loyal to Paco, Travis. I could have helped you if you'd told me the whole truth." Travis let out a quiet sob, and Manny regretted her words. This was no time for recriminations. "How many minutes have passed?" she asked as she unraveled another knot.

"About five, I think."

They paused in their conversation. The only sound was the steady tick of the timer.

And the click of the pacing dog's sharpened nails.

CHAPTER
FIFTY-FIVE

With the help of the police and the FBI, Jake met the Vampire's demands. The audience was tuned in. Manny and Travis would not be executed.

Vito had also mobilized a crew of computer geeks to track the transmission and see who owned the Web site, but Jake had little hope that they would be able to work fast enough to do Manny any good. Anyone clever enough to come up with this scheme would know how to cover his electronic tracks. The experts might be able to suss him out eventually, but they didn't have days to rescue Manny and Travis; they had only minutes.

Jake had never felt so helpless, so close to panic. He couldn't let fear get the upper hand, or he would be of no use to Manny whatsoever. He used the only resource available to steady himself: scientific method.

He called Sam and updated him. "I can't

leave my office and go to Paterson now. I need you to be my eyes and hands. That body may contain evidence that will help us find Manny."

"What do you want me to do?" Sam asked.

Jake felt a swell of gratitude for his brother. They could sit around for hours arguing for sport, but in a crisis, Sam followed orders without question. "Look at his clothes and skin. Describe any foreign material you see there."

"Well, he's wearing destruction jeans and a T-shirt, and the jeans have a lot of white dust on them from the knees down. Like he knelt in something, or walked through it."

"Collect some of that and bring it back to me."

"Jake, I don't happen to have sterile specimen-collection envelopes on me."

"Improvise. Scrape it onto a clean sheet of paper and fold it up. It doesn't have to be sterile."

"Okay, I'm using a receipt from my pocket. Got a sample. What else?"

"Take a crisp dollar bill and use the edge to scrape out some of the material from under his nails," Jake directed.

"Done. That it?"

Jake sighed. That body might be a treasure

trove of information, but he could use only what could be analyzed quickly. "Yes. Get back over to my office as fast as possible."

Knowing that the Sandovals and the Vampire's other victims were also watching, Jake sat in front of his computer screen and waited to see what would happen next. He clung to the hope that, having their undivided attention, the Vampire might be satisfied with just delivering a message.

Manny was untying Travis's hands. He wished she would have had the kid untie her first; she would be most useful free. He could hear the low murmur of their voices, but the audio quality was poor. He figured the microphone must not be near them. He wished he could shout encouragement or directions, but of course they could not hear him.

He studied the narrow field of vision displayed by the camera, looking for clues. He could see one large, dirty window, covered with a heavy grille. An old unvarnished wood floor. No furniture.

Manny was still working on freeing Travis's hands. Her work was interrupted when the boy's shoulders hunched, his torso shook, and his face turned red. He was coughing hard, although the sound reached Jake as a distant rustle.

Suddenly, a loud sound filled his office. Harsh, piercing, violent. Jake jumped and saw Manny and Travis do the same. The dog had barked. The microphone was on his collar. So even if the dog and his prey moved out of the camera's range, the witnesses would always be able to hear the barks and growls of his attack. And the screams of his victims.

He watched as Manny's and Travis's heads turned.

Manny looked directly into the camera. Her mouth was open, too. He didn't need the audio to know what she was yelling.

"Jake!"

CHAPTER FIFTY-SIX

"What do you see?"

Jake's head hunched over his microscope. He could hear the impatience in his brother's voice, but he needed to study this sample carefully. He sought certainty, not conjecture.

"There are two types of fibers in the dust you found on Freak's body. One has a very distinctive shape — thin and needlelike." Jake looked up. "It's asbestos, and it's in this sample in a very high concentration."

"And the other fiber?" Sam asked.

"Cotton. Simple cotton."

"I don't see how that helps us," Sam said. "We don't know that Freak picked it up from the place where Travis and Manny are being held."

"True, we can't be certain. But Freak was the dog handler. And a pit bull is there with Manny, so it stands to reason Freak took it there. I'm sure he was once where Manny is now."

"Yes, but he may have picked up the dust elsewhere," Sam argued.

"I would be more willing to accept that if it weren't for the fact that Travis has been coughing steadily since he appeared on camera. Elena Costello also coughed when she spoke to me on the phone. Asbestos is tremendously irritating to the lungs. In these concentrations, the exposure would be enough to provoke coughing in a day or less."

Sam twisted a pencil in his long fingers. The computer terminal had been angled so both men could watch the screen, but neither could bear to keep their eyes on it for long. Manny still struggled with Travis's bindings. The dog had barked twice more.

"Okay, so they're in a place contaminated by asbestos. There must be thousands of locations in metro New York that fill that bill. Asbestos was a commonly used building material — it's in old linoleum, insulation, all kinds of stuff. Seems like every time a building gets remodeled, they have to call in the guys in the white moon suits to clean it up."

"Yes, but these fibers aren't from linoleum or insulation," Jake said. "There are no other building materials mixed in. Just asbestos and cotton."

"What's the significance of that?"

Jake crossed to another computer. "Time for a little research."

"I'll help," Sam offered.

Jake eyed him. Sam had been notorious for completing term papers in a hurry by making up any missing information.

"Don't look at me like that. I want to help. It'll go faster with two."

"Okay, search 'asbestos in clothing.' Let's see what we come up with."

Chapter
Fifty-Seven

Manny finally freed Travis of his ropes.

"Wow, thanks. Now let me untie you."

Manny hesitated. "Maybe it would be better if you used your piece of rope to tie the cage shut before you untie me."

Slowly, Travis bent to pick up the short piece of rope. He took two steps toward the cage, as if he were fighting against a strong gravitational pull from the opposite direction.

The dog barked and flung himself against the metal bars.

Travis leaped back.

"Never mind," Manny said. "Untie me quick and I'll go." As Travis untied her, Manny studied the bars on the cage, wondering if she could sprint across, thread the rope through the bars, and tie it tightly enough to hold that powerful beast in once the lock released.

Hours — days — seemed to have passed

in getting themselves untied. She had no idea how much time she had left until the lock sprang open, or if she could work on the bars while keeping her fingers away from those jagged teeth.

When the rope finally fell off her wrists, Manny grabbed it and ran straight at the cage. She slid to her knees in front of it, inches away from the dog's rolling eyes and snapping jaws. He barked furiously, lunging so hard at her against the bars that the entire cage rocked.

Manny fumbled with the rope. She had acted so quickly, she didn't have time to notice that her arms and fingers were numb from being tied behind her for so long. Clumsily, she threaded the short length of rope through the bars. The dog snapped at her fingers, but she pulled them back in time. The rope dropped and she started again.

"Hurry!" Travis called to her.

Not helpful. Really not helpful at all. The dog continued barking, high, staccato yelps of fury and impatience. Every time he barked, Manny flinched reflexively, and the tying process stalled again. Finally, she got one knot tied, and she set about threading the rope through the cage again to reinforce her work.

Ting.

Such an innocuous sound, like playing the highest note on a piano. The lock clicked and released. The dog lunged against the cage. The door popped open partway. Manny slammed it shut and frantically tried to tie the second knot.

The dog reared back and hurled his broad chest against the front of the cage. The door flew open, and the rope came free in Manny's hand. The dog bounded right over her, heading straight for Travis.

CHAPTER FIFTY-EIGHT

Jake could barely register the words coming into his ear through the phone, because his eyes were mesmerized by the action on the computer screen. The dog had Travis cornered.

The director of the police K-9 unit was on the line, claiming the greatest danger lay in struggling against the dog. Once his teeth clamped down, nothing short of death would get him to release. Struggle would provoke his fighting instinct. He would attack, biting and tearing, until his prey was vanquished. Playing dead might cause him to lose interest.

And then what? Move on to his next victim — Manny.

Normally, Jake found strength in knowledge, but what good did knowing this do? He couldn't get the information to the people who needed it.

Jake slammed the phone down and his

eyes returned to the computer screen. What the hell was Manny doing? She was running toward the dog. Oh God — she was trying to save Travis.

Manny scrambled to get her feet under her, rubbing the long scratch on her leg where the dog's nails had dug into her flesh as it bounded out of the cage. Across the room, Travis pressed himself against the wall, in the vain hope the plaster might open up behind him.

The dog reached the boy in five strides and immediately went up on its hind legs. Instinctively, it sought Travis's throat, but it wasn't tall enough and snapped instead at the elbows Travis had raised to protect himself.

Manny reacted as she always had when a bully terrorized someone small and defenseless. She ran up and kicked the dog's rear hard, just as she had once kicked Johnnie Appleton in the ass when he was pounding little Barry Neufeld on the playground.

The dog swiveled and snapped at her, but Manny was prepared now that she knew how fast the thing could move. She tore across the room toward the one spot that offered a chance of refuge — the window with its metal grille.

She managed to climb up on it just as she used to scale the chain-link fence around the town pool when she was a kid. The dog arrived, enraged that she was just out of his reach. The metal cut into her fingers. She couldn't hang here like Spider-Man for long.

She looked down. The dog lay right beneath her, its eyes riveted on her legs. It exuded some prehistoric evil. But it wasn't evil; it operated on pure Darwinian survival instinct. Kill or be killed.

Not reassuring.

"Travis, get up slowly and get both pieces of rope. Tie them together. Maybe it'll be enough for us to use to subdue him."

But Travis didn't answer. He sat against the far wall, shaking.

Manny was in this alone.

CHAPTER FIFTY-NINE

"What about this?"

Sam had been calling out random bits of asbestos-related information while Jake sat transfixed by Manny's predicament. He was astonished and impressed that she had managed to distract the dog from Travis. Her maneuver, whatever it was, had been out of the camera's range. All he'd heard was screaming, growling, a thump, and a yelp. Then Manny appeared, streaking across the room and climbing up that metal window grille. His joy at seeing her safe didn't last long. The opening in the window grille wasn't big; her toes kept slipping out. Manny was supporting most of her weight with her arms, and he knew her upper-body strength wasn't that great. Inevitably, she would fall off that grille, right onto the waiting dog.

"Jake, does that sound likely?" Sam asked.

"Huh? Say it again."

"I really might be onto something here. Asbestos was used in the manufacture of fire-retardant work clothes up until the 1960s. Then they started to realize that wearing asbestos next to your skin might be more dangerous than getting burned, so they switched to chemical retardants and other materials."

"Uhm . . ." Manny's toes slipped off the grille and she flailed for a moment, then pulled herself back up.

"Jake, seriously, *listen.* There's an old factory in West New York called Fireproof Apparel. Here's a story in the Business section of the *Times:* 'Redevelopment of West New York Waterfront Stalled by Fireproof Apparel.' It turns out the factory is so contaminated, they're afraid to tear it down or remodel it because of the dust it will release. So it's been abandoned for years. According to the article, even homeless people won't squat there because it makes them cough."

For the first time in ten minutes, Jake's eyes turned away from the live streaming video. "West New York is near Hoboken and Club Epoch," he said.

"Exactly. And not far from Paterson. And look at this picture. The building's big enough that no one would hear them, or the dog. And look at the windows."

"All covered with metal grillwork." He grabbed the phone. "Vito can have guys over there in two minutes."

CHAPTER SIXTY

Manny couldn't hang on much longer.

The sharp edges of the grille cut into her fingers. She could have borne that pain if not for the terrible ache in her shoulders and biceps. Somewhere around age thirteen she'd lost her tomboy sinew, and it wasn't coming back. She pumped only enough iron to look good in a strapless dress, not to support her entire body weight for what seemed like hours.

She needed a new strategy, but she had precious little to work with. Somehow, she needed to distract the dog without redirecting its attention to Travis. Then she could get down and . . . what?

Distract and get down. That's all that mattered at the moment, because if she waited one more minute, she'd simply fall into the dog's jaws.

Calling up the last ounce of strength in her right hand, Manny used her left to remove her large turquoise and silver earring. Clinging to the grille with one hand, she tossed the earring low and far. The dog reacted as predictably as Mycroft, chasing down the skittering object.

Manny let go and jumped. The sweet relief chased every other fear from her mind — but only for a moment. She knew the dog would realize the earring held no interest as prey and would turn its attentions back to her. When it did, she had to be ready.

She had already dismissed the rope and the cage as too far away to be useful. In one fluid motion, Manny grabbed the hem of the sundress and pulled it off over her head. Quickly, she twisted it into a long coil.

Attracted by her movement, the dog spun around and charged toward her. Manny stood still, with the window behind her, watching the dog's muscular legs propel it closer. At the last moment, she sidestepped.

The dog reared and hurled itself against the spot where Manny had been standing. Manny used that instant to get behind the creature and loop the dress around its neck.

She twisted and pulled. The synthetic fiber had much less give than cotton would have, and the garrote tightened. She struggled to maintain her balance and keep the fabric taut.

The dog strained and wheezed against the unfamiliar restraint. Certainly he had never been walked on a leash, and for that Manny was grateful. A trained dog might have backed up to ease the pressure, but this dog continued to pull forward, cutting off his own air supply and making her work easier.

The dog staggered and sank to its knees. Manny could sense Jake's presence on the other end of the camera, coaching her. *Don't let go. It's not over yet.* Jake always scoffed at the way strangulation deaths were portrayed in the movies — thirty seconds of airway compression and the victim was dead. In reality, it took several minutes of total oxygen deprivation to bring about a human death. Manny didn't know the canine equivalent, but she wasn't taking any chances. She continued to pull, although her arms ached from the effort.

The dog slumped onto its side and its eyes rolled back in its head. Still, Manny didn't release the noose. She glanced over at Travis, hoping that he might see fit to come and help her now that the dog had weakened. But he sat curled in the corner, glassy-eyed. Shock had rendered him useless.

The dog's legs twitched involuntarily and a puddle of urine appeared from beneath its body. A good sign — it must have lost consciousness. Manny's arms trembled with the effort of keeping the dress pulled tight. If she hadn't spent all that time hanging from the window grille, she would have had more strength for this. She resolved to keep up the pressure for two more minutes. Under her breath, she counted, "One one thousand, two one thousand."

She reached 120 and cautiously loosened her grip. The dog lay immobile. Manny knew she should check for a pulse.

She extended a trembling hand toward the carotid artery in the dog's neck. Its fur was short and coarse, nothing like Mycroft's. Scars from the many fights it had survived crisscrossed its neck and chest. Her fingertips hovered above the dog's body; her eyes swam with tears.

She couldn't do it. She couldn't bring herself to touch this dog. Searching for his pulse would seem too much like petting him, scratching him under the chin the way she did with Mycroft and every other friendly dog who lifted a grinning muzzle to be caressed.

Manny backed away from the dog's body. She was tired, so tired. In a minute, they would look for a way out of here. But first she had to rest.

CHAPTER
SIXTY-ONE

Manny's bravery stunned Jake. But the elation he should have felt at her amazing victory over the dog couldn't take hold. His central nervous system hadn't yet recovered from the shock of seeing the woman he loved go after that brute with her bare hands and a scrap of fabric.

Manny seemed to have shocked herself. She sat a few feet away from the dog, her head in her hands, breathing in deep, shuddering gasps. Not an uncommon reaction to unbearable stress. But Jake had confidence that she would come out of it soon and start looking for an escape route from her prison.

He hoped that Sam was right about the Fireproof Apparel building, although it was a long shot. Manny and Travis might be anywhere. But at least the pressure was off. With the dog out of the equation, it didn't matter if the search dragged on for hours.

Jake shifted uneasily as he watched the static scene on his computer screen. Were the Costellos still tuned in? They would be furious at the failure of their torture display. Furious enough to risk returning to the scene to unleash some other horror?

"Get up, Manny," he urged her through the screen. "Get up and start looking for a way out."

Manny sat crossed-legged on the floor. The only sound she could hear was the unsteady in and out of her own breathing. The current craze for yoga had passed her by — she preferred Pilates or exercising with her Wii fitness program. Nevertheless, she found herself focusing on her breathing, trying with all her will to bring it back to normal. Maybe then she could get up.

Another sound entered her consciousness — a slight whimper from across the room. Travis. She'd nearly forgotten him.

Manny looked up, to see him pointing limply. She let her gaze follow his finger.

The dog was standing up.

Manny scrambled to stand up, too, but her limbs responded as if they were controlled by some other brain.

Time seemed to be moving in slow motion. The dog, never graceful before, floated through the air, coming closer and closer. She could no longer see her foot because her leg was inside a dog's mouth. How odd. She thought she was having an out-of-body thinking experience. *Dr. Suzanne Levine will never get me into my stilettos again.*

The pain she felt was real, not the sharp pain of teeth tearing her flesh but, rather, the shocking blow of a hammer swung at full force. That was odd, too.

And here was another strange thing. Travis was running. Running right toward her, screaming. Running straight at the cage, which he picked up and swung at the dog. It didn't like that. It opened its mouth. She rolled away.

And then there was another crash. The door flew open. The room was full of men. A shot rang out, awfully close to her head.

Manny dragged herself upright and scanned the faces in the room.

"Where's Jake?"

CHAPTER
SIXTY-TWO

"How's your leg? Have another Percocet."

Manny averted her head from the pill. "Those things make me woozy. Just raise the pillow a little. Couldn't I have a glass of Veuve Clicquot Rosé instead?"

Jake scurried to the end of the sofa and fluffed the pillow under Manny's bandaged leg. "How's tha—" Her ear-to-ear grin stopped him. "You're enjoying this, aren't you?"

"It's almost worth being eaten by a pit bull to see you doing this Florence Nightingale routine," Manny said. "And look at this house. You must've had Heloise and Mr. Clean here while I was in the hospital."

"Sam and I did it all," Jake said, looking around the spotless living room. "I thought the bowl of potpourri was a particularly nice touch for your homecoming."

"It would be nicer if the dried lavender

wasn't trickling out the eye sockets of the skull."

Jake took her hand. "I can't begin to tell you how happy I am to have you here."

Manny evaded his gaze. "Well, I appreciate your taking me in. But it's only for a few days. As soon as the doctor says I can walk unassisted, I'll go back to my place."

Jake stroked her hair. "There's no rush."

Sam entered carrying three mugs of coffee on a tray, followed by Mycroft, who bounded into Manny's lap.

"You're serving from a tray now?" Manny asked, glad of the distraction. "What are you, channeling Amy Vanderbilt?"

"Just living up to my surroundings," Sam said. "You should see how nice my manners are when I'm invited to Buckingham Palace."

"Speaking of foreign travel, is it true the Costellos were intercepted at Kennedy Airport, waiting for a flight to Buenos Aires? I thought I heard that on the news when I was lying in my hospital bed, but they had me so doped up, I didn't know if I was dreaming or not."

"You didn't dream it," Jake said. "That's one upside of terrorism. No one can make a hasty escape from the country anymore. Airport security apprehended them as their carry-on bags were being screened. They're in federal custody. Bail has been denied. And the government even added animal abuse charges. The killer pit bull survived both your assault and the police, and now he needs to be a 'kept dog,' courtesy of the Costellos."

"Justice. Travis Heaton and the Costellos trade places. Kind of like your shrimp story." Manny inhaled through her nose, then exhaled though her mouth. "Who's representing them?"

"Why, do you want the job?"

"No thanks, although I do have some free time now that all the charges against Travis have been dropped." Manny sipped her coffee. "What about the Sandovals? Has Señora Sandoval had a complete nervous breakdown since she's learned the truth about her family?"

"Oh, I forgot to tell you," Sam said. "She called while Jake was picking you up at the hospital. She sounded good to me — asked how you were, said she'd call again later."

"And the Vampire's other victims? Were they really all watching Travis and me getting chased by that damn dog?" Manny asked. "Did it have the effect the Costellos were hoping for?"

"They watched," Jake said. "But I think

their reactions are as different as they are as people. Lucinda Bettis is the only one still in denial. The others may have some interest in learning more about their roots, or they may prefer to put it all behind them."

"That's what drove Elena Costello crazy: She couldn't accept that not everyone clung to their anger as she has," Manny said. "She was right that we should never forget the victims of the Dirty War. But she let her anger destroy her."

Jake took her coffee cup from her. "That's enough talking about the investigation. Why don't you relax and watch a little mindless TV?" He handed Manny the remote control. "No CNN, no Fox News, no MSNBC."

"Yes, Doctor." Manny snuggled up with Mycroft and began rolling through the channels. "Sorry, buddy — no Animal Planet, either." They settled on a home-decorating show. Turn an old chest of drawers into a high-tech entertainment center . . . paint an Oriental rug on your wood floor. . . . Manny dozed off just as she was about to learn how to banish the musty smell from an antique armoire.

Her painkiller-induced dreams churned with vivid scenes and choppy transitions, an art-house movie for one. Jungle animals sat on a jury; winding corridors led to rooms full of broken glass; an exam for which she had no answers was interrupted by the ringing of the school bell. The bell rang and rang.

Manny sat up, hot and disoriented. There was no exam; the ringing was real. Looking out through the living room window, she could see daylight fading. Sam and Jake were nowhere around. She stretched to the end table and picked up the phone.

"Hello."

"Hello, is that Ms. Manfreda?"

"Yes. Who's this?"

"Monserrat Sandoval. I hope I am not disturbing you, but I wanted to call and thank you."

"Hi, Señora Sandoval. I was just asking about you earlier. How are *you?* I know Paco has been very worried about you."

"Ay! I have had a long talk with my son and my husband." Her voice sounded strong and confident. "I told them they were very foolish to keep secrets from me all these years. So much pain could have been avoided if my husband had told me the truth when Esteban was a baby."

Manny sat up straighter, fully awake. So, it was true that Ambassador Sandoval had always known Esteban had been taken from an imprisoned woman. "Would you still have adopted him?"

"Ah, that was the problem. You see, at the time, my husband worked part-time for a government ministry while going to school. Jobs were scarce in those days; the economy was terrible. The junta rulers were technically his bosses, but he did not really support their policies. He was just a — a how do you say? — flutie."

"Flunky," Manny said, correcting her.

"Exactly. So when the nurse, who was called Anna Herrmann then, but here she called herself Amanda Hogaarth, offered us this baby, we accepted, believing that he was an orphan whose parents had died in an accident. Six months later, my husband learned the terrible truth.

"By that time, I loved Esteban so much, my husband knew I could never have given him up. He told me he was afraid to protest the death of Esteban's parents, afraid we would have been disappeared ourselves." Señora Sandoval paused for a moment, evidently thinking back on those dark days. "After the regime fell, that is when he should have told me. I would have tried to find Esteban's birth family. His grandparents, aunts, and uncles — they deserved to know that he was okay. But my husband thinks he always knows what is best." She gave a bitter little laugh.

"So that is why I'm calling to thank you. Because of what has happened, Esteban is going to Argentina to meet his birth family. Finally, they will know that he was not raised by killers or torturers. He will tell them he had good parents. He will tell them how sorry we are for hiding the truth. I hope they understand my husband acted out of love for me and for Esteban. I hope they can forgive us."

"I hope so, too, Señora Sandoval. Seems like forgiveness is the only way to move past what happened during the Dirty War. I guess Amanda Hogaarth was looking for a little forgiveness, too. That must be why she left all her money to a legitimate adoption agency."

"You sound strong, Ms. Manfreda. You have not been crushed by what the Costellos did to you," Señora Sandoval said.

"No, my leg's a little smushed, but my spirit is strong," Manny agreed.

"Then I hope you, too, will be able to forgive. You know, the story of the Vampire has been all over the news in Argentina. I have been reading the coverage there online every day."

"Paco told me you didn't follow the news."

"That was true in the past. But I have learned my lesson. It's not good to bury your head in the sand." Señora Sandoval sighed. "The story of Elena Muniz Costello has been in every newspaper in Argentina. It is very sad. She was adopted by a policeman and his wife, a very brutal man who worked for the secret police during the Dirty War. He was cruel to Elena all through her childhood and her adoptive mother was powerless to stop him. Elena never understood why her father hated her so much. Then, as a young woman, she discovered the truth about her birth. But by then, her birth grandparents and aunts were dead. She never got to know them. She couldn't believe that all of Argentina was not up in arms about the terrible injustice she and the other adopted children suffered. After that, Elena made it her mission to make sure every adopted child of the Desaparecidos knew about their birth families."

"Even the ones who didn't want to know," Manny said. "I guess that explains why she did what she did, but it doesn't justify it. And what about Frederic Costello? Was he mistreated as a child, as well?"

"No. It seems he was adopted as a toddler by friends of his birth parents after they disappeared. They never hid the truth about his past — just the opposite. They were activists in the cause. It is through them that Frederic met Elena."

Manny shifted on the sofa. Her leg had begun to throb. "But I don't understand. Why did he allow himself to go along with his wife's cruel and crazy scheme?"

"I suppose we will never truly understand. But me, I think it was a case of the student surpassing the teacher. He got her involved in the cause; then she became more impassioned than he."

"Maybe if they'd never met . . . if they had each married someone else . . ." Manny said.

"None of this would have happened," said Señora Sandoval, completing the thought. "You would not have had to suffer."

"Oh, don't worry about me. I'm not one to carry a grudge. I'll have to testify at Elena's trial, but I'll make sure she has adequate representation. She deserves a fair trial."

"You are a very brave woman," Señora Sandoval said. "You have inspired me to be brave, too. You know that charity, Home Again, that you got me to write the check to? I have become one of their rescue volunteers. Tomorrow, I fly to Gulfport,

Mississippi, to work for a week in the shelter."

"Good for you! I know you'll do a great job."

Manny hung up just as Jake came through the front door. "There you are. I thought maybe you and Sam were upstairs scrubbing tile grout with a toothbrush."

"Ah, you're awake. I just went out to get us some dinner. Your favorite."

Mycroft sprang off the sofa and began to sniff the bags. "None for you, mister. You have dog food in your bowl in the kitchen." Mycroft continued to stare. "Do you know what they do to guys like you in the joint? Can you say rottweiler?" Jake pretended to growl.

Offended, Mycroft jumped back into the protection of Manny's arms. "Ignore his petulance, Mycroft. But I am afraid he's right, Mikey. We can't take any chances with your stomach. Remember, you're currently without a vet," she said.

As Jake arranged the carryout dinner, Manny told him about her conversation with Monserrat Sandoval. She still was troubled by Dr. Costello's involvement, and she came back to that point with Jake. "So, I can understand why Elena was so crazy, but why did Dr. Costello go along? He seemed a genuinely kind vet. How could he have helped Elena torture and kill?"

Jake gave Manny a fork but did not release her hand. "Sometimes, when two people get together, they can assume different personalities. One without the other would have never committed crimes. Put them together and he becomes Jack the Ripper, and she, Elizabeth Báthory. It's a phenomena we have seen in the past."

"Really?"

"Love for a beautiful, passionate woman made the man lose his good judgment and his mind a little. I can relate."

Manny pulled her hand away and tapped Jake's forehead. "Your mind's right where you left it."

"You should have seen me when I was watching you on that Web cam, powerless to help you. It wasn't one of my more scientifically impassive moments."

"But you still managed to help the police figure out who the Vampire was and where we were being held."

"Based on *your* hunch about Nixon's coffee mug being bought on eBay."

Manny grinned and dug into her comfort food. "Forensic pathology, law, shopping, and Mycroft. It's an unbeatable combination!"

ACKNOWLEDGMENTS

We want to continue to thank, from the bottom of our hearts, the many people whose help has allowed Manny, Jake, and Mycroft's relationship to flourish in print. We would be remiss if we did not also thank the best veterinarian in the world, Dr. Lewis Berman of Park East Animal Hospital in New York City, who ensures that Mycroft remains healthy, and Dr. Avra Frucht, who ensures Mycroft's pearly whites stay white. We also thank our dear friends, Judge Haskell Pitluck (ret.) and his wonderful wife, Kay, who read and reread every draft of this novel.

Bar none, the best assistant in the world, Patricia Hulbert, and her family, Todd, TJ, Amanda, and Christina, who support us in all our endeavors, deserve a special mention apart from all others.

Obviously, our agent, Leigh Feldman, along with our publisher, Knopf, and the entire team assigned to ensure the success of Manny and Jake, especially Jordan Pavlin, our editor; Erinn Hartman, our publicist; Leslie Levine, our contact extraordinaire; and our remarkable copy editor, Carol Edwards, and production editor, Maria Massey — whose skills make us look good.

As usual, we could not function without the support and encouragement of our many author friends — Ann Rule, Linda Fairstein, Kathy Reichs — just to name a few. To our handlers Maria Lago, Sondra Elkins, Colin Lively, Pilar and Paul Conceicao, and Michael Greenfield, we thank you again for your unending loyalty and support.

We want to thank Marco Pipolo and his staff at Scalinatella for their never-ending hospitality in providing the backdrop for the Italian food and heritage that has made it into our novels.

Finally, we thank our families, including our children, Christopher, Trissa, Lindsey, Sara, Sarah, and our grandchildren; along with the many forgotten families in the world, for both the inspiration and story line embodied in *Skeleton Justice*.

ABOUT THE AUTHORS

Michael Baden, M.D., is one of America's leading forensic experts. He is the host of *Autopsy*, the HBO hit documentary series. He has investigated the deaths of many, ranging from President John F. Kennedy, Rev. Martin Luther King, and Tsar Nicholas II and the Romanov family to John Belushi and Billy Martin. He has served as an expert witness in countless criminal cases, including the trials of Claus von Bulow and O. J. Simpson. He has been a consulting forensic pathologist to the U.S. Department of Justice, the U.S. Department of Veterans Affairs, the FBI, and the Russian government, as well as a visiting professor at John Jay College of Criminal Justice, Albert Einstein College of Medicine, Albany Medical College, and New York Law School.

Linda Kenney Baden is a trial attorney who has won dozens of civil rights lawsuits, participated in many high-profile criminal cases, and has appeared as a guest legal commentator on numerous television networks.

They are married and live in New York City with their dog, Mycroft.